The Eliminated

Laurel Solorzano

Published by Laurel Solorzano, 2023.

The Eliminated

Book 2

ISBN: 978-1-7373974-9-6

Cover Design by: Christine Savoie

To my dad, who has always encouraged me when I want to chase my
dreams

Chapter 1

Eden's eyes fluttered open, and she immediately sat up, adrenaline coursing through her veins. Where was she? How had she gotten there?

Trying to take deep breaths, Eden evaluated the situation. The room was made up of four shiny, silver walls, so clean that she could clearly see a shadow of her reflection in them. As her eyes darted from one wall to the next, a distinct feeling of claustrophobia set in.

Eden stretched her arms out to either side, but she couldn't quite touch the walls. Her fingertips brushed the air only a few inches away on either side.

Eden rose from the floor and stepped over to one of the walls, pressing her hand against the metal. To her surprise, the metal's warmth singed her hand, and Eden pulled it back quickly. Why was it so warm?

As Eden assessed the space once more, she realized something she had overlooked on her first scan- there didn't seem to be a door.

"Hello?" Eden said cautiously. In two short strides, she was across the room. She didn't dare touch the wall again, but there had to be someone on the other side of *one* of these walls. Right?

"Hello? Can anyone hear me?"

Eden held her breath, nearly touching her cheek to the wall as she listened.

Nothing.

Nothing other than the distant whir of some sort of machinery.

"Okay, think this through," Eden coached herself. She looked at the ground where a pallet lay, the pallet where she had been lying a few moments before. Eden ran her hands over its foam surface. It didn't reveal any secrets to her, but it reminded her of the pallets she had used for taking naps when she was in first grade. In the corner of the room sat a large bottle of water. It looked like it was unopened.

Eden's eyes roamed the space again, but there was nothing she could do, literally nothing. She wasn't going to try banging on the wall when it was hot unless...

Eden picked up the pallet and folded it in half. She went around to each wall and banged on it a good thirty seconds before moving on to the next. When she had beaten on all four walls, she took a deep breath.

Still ... nothing.

There was lots of breathing from her though, as she struggled to contain the panic rising within her.

She had to *think*. What did she remember?

She had been eliminated...or at least, she was supposed to have been eliminated. She hadn't won a medal fairly, and Xander had surrendered his. Xander! Eden looked around the room with renewed strength, but her looking didn't make Xander appear. Where had he gone?

They had both been taken to a little boat, a boat that would take them somewhere. Eden pressed a hand against her forehead as she *tried* to remember, but the remembering stung. They had been given something to eat, and she recalled how difficult it had been to eat while the boat was moving underneath them.

Then ... then ...

Eden couldn't remember what had happened after that. Clearly, they had been drugged. But why? Why drug them if they were going to be eliminated anyway? Unless elimination meant something other than death.

Suddenly, the floor beneath her lurched, and Eden stumbled backward into the wall. Its heat instantly pushed her away, and Eden pressed one of her hands against her arm as she massaged away the slight burn.

She was moving. Or... the whole room was moving. That meant she had to be on some sort of vehicle, but she didn't feel the vibrations and bumps of the road. Was she in the air ... or in a boat?

Eden scanned the walls of the room for probably the thirtieth time.

Was this like the logic test? She had to find a way out of the room? If she didn't, what would happen to her?

This time, Eden thought she saw a crack in the wall, and she approached it with caution. Yes, there was definitely a small place between the squares of metal. That meant there was a door, and just knowing it was there calmed Eden. It had to open eventually.

She appraised herself. Even though there was a faint red mark on her arm, she hadn't really burned it. Her stomach felt full which meant that she had eaten the food on the boat not too long ago. She also didn't need to urgently use the bathroom.

Things would be okay. Someone would come soon. At least, that was what Eden assured herself as she paced in a tight circle.

Chapter 2

Xander stared at the space in the wall that he knew contained the door, daring it to stay closed. Unfortunately, the door took his dare and didn't move. He had already tried everything he could think of to get out of this room, and he was out of ideas *and* hope.

He couldn't stay still, especially knowing why he was being held in this tiny room. Xander was pretty sure he knew what the purpose was, though. Why else would they put him in this tiny room except to prepare him for a bloody death?

If they planned to keep him alive, then they would have at least given him a container where he could relieve himself. Instead, he was waiting here like an animal, hoping that he might have a chance to attack his captor whenever he or she chose to make an appearance. Even though Xander had volunteered for this, that didn't mean that he was going to give up easily.

Xander wondered if Eden was in a room like his or if it was already...too late for her.

The floor shifted under Xander's feet again, and his stomach indicated that the whole room was moving. Was he in a room under the ship? Why didn't they just shoot him already instead of putting him through this torture?

The floor moved again, and this time, the movement was so violent that Xander stumbled, smacking his hand on the floor as he tried to catch himself. Then, the whirring noise in the background died out, and the wall slid aside.

Xander stared at the open space for a moment as he processed what was happening. The door had opened, and this was his chance to leave. Xander dashed out of the open doorway and almost collided with someone else.

He didn't know the boy's name, but he recognized him. This boy had competed in the wrestling competition, though the two of them hadn't fought each other. Xander stared at him for a minute, but he didn't have time to stay for long. He had to get moving and find Eden. Even though he had no idea what he was doing, he knew that he couldn't stay there.

To the left, Xander heard more movement, and as he turned his head to take everything in, he saw that these two weren't the only doors open. It appeared that a row of doors had all opened along the hallway. Boys were peering out in different stages of confusion as they tried to figure out what was happening. Some of them dashed out of their doorways while others looked scared.

The problem was that they were all boys. Eden wasn't among them.

Xander turned to the right, but he saw that the hallway ended after two more sets of doors.

"Where are we?" one of the boys finally asked.

Xander didn't stay around to talk. He began jogging toward the end of the hallway, hoping that there was something promising that way. He couldn't actually see the end of the hall, but he had to hope there was one and that it had stairs or some way to get to the top of the boat.

Then, just as Xander determined that there was indeed a set of stairs at the end, the hallway exploded with noise. Footsteps, running footsteps, echoed down the stairs, and something told Xander that he should stand aside.

Just as he pressed himself against the wall, a steady flow of people came down the stairs. Xander studied each face that passed him briefly. Men and women alike, but these weren't eighteen-year-olds, or anyone else that seemed like they were slated for elimination. They seemed to have a purpose, and one of them had a retreating hairline that indicated he was older than everyone else.

"Where are we?" Xander asked one of the passing adults, but none of them acknowledged him.

They rushed down the hallway, turning into room after room and pushing aside the occupants as they stood dumbly in the doorways. Xander wasn't sure what they were doing. If this was some sort of rescue mission, then they were failing miserably.

He didn't waste time on any more questions. Instead, he took the stairs two at a time. The stairs doubled back on themselves, and Xander wondered as he climbed how the ship had so much space on it. When he and Eden had boarded, he didn't know how long ago, it had barely seemed big enough for everyone to have a place to sit, let alone have their own room.

There had to be another set of stairs that led to the rooms for girls. Xander didn't know why the doors had just flown open, or if the same had happened wherever Eden was, but he was past thinking rationally.

When Xander reached the top of the stairs, he stopped, shocked to see what lay before him. He wasn't standing on the deck of the ship, the waves making the whole thing move. He was on a kind of ship, but not the kind he had thought.

Pulling his feet forward heavily, Xander approached one of the windows that lined the left side of the hall. The whole wall was made of windows, but Xander wasn't admiring the glass. What was *beyond* the glass had caught his attention.

There was no ocean or fish or even hazy horizons that hid the country he had known his whole life. Instead, all he saw were pinpoints of light in the distance. It looked like someone had thrown a black blanket over the windows, but punched in a few air holes for the safety of its occupants.

One slow step at a time, despite the frenzied activity behind him, Xander approached the window and pressed his hand against the glass. Unlike the walls of his room, the glass was cool to the touch. The frigidness of it grabbed his hand and held it in place, freezing everything but his eyes as he tried to understand.

Was that big round thing down there ... Earth?

There was no way. The technology for a place like this- it was just being developed.

And even if scientists had found a way to make life in space viable, then why would they have sent Xander and the other failed competitors who were slated for elimination? Was this ... their elimination?

Since Xander had led the way, boy after boy emerged from the staircase behind him, wild looks in their eyes as they searched for some sort of escape. Some of them stopped and stared alongside Xander while others continued down the hallway.

"Where are we?"

"What? How did we get here?"

"Do you think we're not going to die after all?"

"I'm not going to die."

Xander didn't participate in the conversation, but seeing the looks on the other boys' faces indicated that his brain wasn't fabricating something elaborate. They really had left the Earth, and everything he knew on Greenland, behind. The question was- why?

Xander finally pulled his hand off the glass and looked around for someone who could answer his questions. A couple of adults hurried by, toward the stairs, but neither of them responded as Xander tried to get their attention. A minute later, the adults from below emerged carrying the water bottles and mats that had been in each of the rooms. Some of them carried large sheets of metal- had those been the walls?

"Hello?" Xander tried. But again none of them responded. One of them pointed further down the hall, but barely looked at him. Xander wasn't sure if the instruction was meant for him or not. Either way, he wasn't going to stand around waiting for someone to pay attention to him. They were clearly too busy.

Xander set off at a quick pace down the hallway which seemed to curve ever so slightly to the right. He saw a door to his right and immediately tried the handle. It wiggled in his hand but wouldn't open.

A few steps later, he found another locked door. The group of boys seemed to dwindle out the further he got from their ... cells. Finally, Xander reached the end of the hallway. There was an open doorway, and a man that Xander didn't recognize welcomed him with a smile.

"Come in, come in," he said, motioning for Xander to pass through the doorway.

Xander tried to see past the man's broad shoulders and light brown beard, but the room beyond didn't reveal any of its secrets.

"Where are we?" Xander asked, stopping and crossing his arms.

"Everything will be explained in just a few minutes. Please go through here and proceed to your right."

The man's tranquil demeanor instantly had a calming effect on Xander. Even though he wasn't sure who to trust at the moment, just knowing that there was no immediate threat made him feel a little better.

"Where are the girls?" Xander asked, unwilling to wait for everything to be explained. He pointed over his shoulder. "There are just boys in that hall."

"The girls are coming from that direction, but you can come right through here. They'll join us in a minute."

Xander shook his head and started back down the hallway. Maybe the girls were behind one of the locked doors?

"Hey! Come back here!" the man called after him.

Xander ignored the man's call and continued back down the hallway from where he had just come. A couple of the boys he didn't recognize were walking slowly down the hallway, differing emotions on their faces. Some of them looked absolutely terrified, while a couple of others looked confident that something good was happening.

Xander tried the locked doors again, but nothing had changed.

Adults rushed past him carrying more sheets of metal in gloved hands. Others had the mats and water bottles. Xander frowned as the stream of adults slowed to nothing.

"Xander!" Connor exclaimed, running forward and hugging Xander. "We're still alive!"

Xander nodded as he pulled away from his friend. His eyes darted down the hallway. "They keep pointing that way," Connor told him as Xander continued to walk against the flow of movement. "Maybe we should go that way."

"I already went that way," Xander responded, dismissing his friend's concern for him. "I need to find Eden."

Connor glanced back and forth between the way he was supposed to take and his friend, but Xander hadn't asked for company. He continued down the long hall until he reached the doorway through which he had come. He tried the handle, but it was locked. Someone appeared behind him and smacked his hand.

Xander jumped into a defensive position, but it was a woman. His dad had always taught him not to hit women, but he was ready in case she tried anything else.

"Go that way with everyone else," she directed, pointing over her shoulder.

Xander crossed his arms. "I'm not just going to go that way if no one will explain why."

The woman rolled her eyes as several more adults appeared behind her. They stared at the door impatiently, and Xander watched the door as well, wondering what would happen. Suddenly, there was a click, and the woman pulled the door open. It clanged against the wall behind her, and everyone rushed in after her.

Xander stayed by the doorway, peering down the stairs. Something was happening down below, but he wasn't sure if he should go check it out or turn around and follow Connor to the big room.

Chapter 3

Eden slowly stepped through the open doorway. She thought she must be hallucinating or something. She had stared at the crack in the wall for so long that she had imagined it opening. That must be it.

But no, she was really outside of the closet-like room. Eden glanced over her shoulder, and risking entrapment again, darted back inside and grabbed the large bottle of water. She had no idea where she was or where she might go, but water was always a good thing to have.

The floor shifted slightly under her feet, and Eden wondered if they had docked. She had to still be on the boat, right? She stepped back outside the room and saw other girls looking just as confused as she was.

Clutching the bottle of water, Eden looked to the others, hoping they had answers for her. She recognized faces from the boat- faces that had been long and drawn as they headed toward their elimination. But now, everyone looked confused.

"What happened?" one girl asked, clearing her throat with a nasty-sounding cough. "Why aren't we dead yet?"

"Maybe they're going to do experiments on us," someone else piped up.

Eden shivered at the thought. That was one of the theories back home-that elimination really meant that your body was given over to science so that scientists could figure out the cure for cancer or something. Eden didn't feel any different though, just disoriented.

"Let's go that way," one of the girls suggested. A couple of girls followed her to the left, but Eden stayed put for a moment. She thought she heard footsteps, but then the sound of the girls tramping down the hallway covered any sound she had thought she heard.

"Dead end!" one of the girls called from around the corner.

"The other way!" another girl shouted, and the group came pounding back down the hall. Eden reluctantly followed them at a slower pace.

"Adults!"

"People!"

"Get ready to fight!"

Eden heard from ahead of her.

However, when she saw the adults pushing through the group of girls, they didn't look like they were trying to fight. Their faces showed grim determination as they stepped inside each room. One of them saw Eden carrying her water bottle and reached for it.

"This is mine," Eden responded, clutching it tightly. She didn't have anything else she could call hers at the moment, and the water seemed to represent life itself.

The adult motioned for it again, not speaking, which somehow frightened Eden more than if she had just yelled. Eden was distracted by a few adults coming out of the rooms around her. Some were wearing gloves and carrying parts of the wall with them. Others were carrying the tiny pallets and water bottles. A feeling of panic overtook Eden. They were dismantling the rooms which probably meant that Eden wasn't going to live much longer.

A couple of other girls who had failed to win medals trailed after the bigger group. The adult finally stopped trying to get the water bottle from Eden and pointed down the hallway in the direction that everyone else had gone. Eden trudged forward, nervous to see what might be waiting at the end.

The set of stairs didn't look so foreboding, and Eden climbed them slowly, even as adults rushed past her with supplies.

"Hurry!" one of them shouted at her as he ran by.

Eden looked behind her and realized that she was one of the last trailing up the stairs. A sudden fear of being left behind spurred her forward, and she took the last few steps at a run, almost stumbling.

At the top of the stairs, she saw a long hallway that stretched out before her. The pattern in the carpet was the same as the hotel's at the Olympics, but this carpet looked faded, like it had been there a long time and was in serious need of an update.

"Eden!" a familiar voice shouted, and Eden jerked her head up.

It was ... Xander. Relief flooded her body, and she ran toward him. He wrapped his arms around her, and she hugged him back, pressing the water bottle into him.

Xander winced and touched his back. "Still a bit sore," he said, and Eden remembered that there had been a life before she had woken up in the tiny room.

"Let me see it," she suggested hesitantly, wondering if she could tell how much time had passed by the healing of Xander's wound.

Xander lifted the back of his shirt, and Eden studied his skin. The wound had a patch covering it, so Eden couldn't see much other than a tiny copper-colored stain of blood that had leaked through the patch. It seemed to be dried now, though.

"How does it look?" Xander asked.

"Not too bad," Eden replied.

As Xander dropped the edge of his shirt, Eden wanted to hug him again, close her eyes and be able to forget where they were and what was happening to them. "Do you think it's going to happen now?" she asked in a quiet voice. "The ...elimination."

Xander shook his head, his green eyes studying her with concern. "Did you look out there?" He pointed to a bank of windows that Eden hadn't noticed once she had heard Xander's voice.

"Oh," was all she could say as she studied what looked like the night sky outside. "Are we... in the air?"

Xander nodded. He motioned for her to follow him, and he walked directly over to the windows. "We're in space. I've been trying to figure out what we're doing here and why they drugged us. I'm thinking that they're trying to settle some other planet or something, and we're the experiment."

Eden's eyebrows rose as she trailed after Xander. The emptiness around them appeared interminable. Xander's idea made sense, but she didn't want to think about herself as an experiment.

"So ... you think they're going to drug us again and hurt us or something?"

"No, I think they're going to see if we can survive here."

"But you know what we learned in school. Venus is too hot and Mars is too cold. They tried before to send astronauts to those planets to set up viable living situations despite the circumstances, but it never worked." As Eden realized what she was saying, her voice drooped. It had never worked, which meant that if they were doing the same thing to Xander and Eden, then it wouldn't work again.

"Do you think we might be able to survive?" she asked, looking for hope.

"I don't know." Xander shook his head. "There are a lot of adults here, but I guess they're just officials who are supposed to guide us to the station or whatever it is they have set up. Then, before starvation or dehydration or anything else sets in, they'll jet off back to the safety of Earth. They aren't dressed like officials though..."

It all seemed a bit far-fetched, but Eden couldn't believe she was still alive enough to worry about what seemed likely or unlikely. She had thought they would be executed minutes after the ceremony, but here they were, still breathing.

A group of adults rushed past them carrying more of the parts of their rooms. A couple of them paused long enough to indicate that Xander and Eden should move down the hallway too. Eden looked around and realized that the hallway was mostly empty now.

"I think we need to go that way," she said, shifting the water bottle to her other hand.

"Or maybe we should just stay here," Xander suggested. "I don't know if I want to find out what they're going to do to us. Even if we only have a few more minutes, or a few more hours, I'd rather spend it here than pushing through all the other eighteen-year-olds."

Eden looked at the worn carpet just under the edge of the window. It *did* look comfortable, and she liked the idea of staying with Xander and just ... talking. But at the same time, she couldn't ignore what they were supposed to do, even if it meant they were marching to their deaths.

"Have you seen anyone from Group 2 here?" she asked suddenly, her stomach flipping over.

Xander looked confused. "What group?"

"You know ... in the dining hall, before they marched us to the boat, they asked us to separate into two groups. We were in Group 1, and they took us outside. But Group 2 was left behind. Have you seen anyone who was in that group?"

As she asked the question, Eden tried to remember the faces that she had passed quickly in the hallway, but she honestly hadn't paid much attention to them. She remembered a blonde girl who looked like she had been underfed her whole life. Eden knew that the girl had been in their group, but she hadn't been paying much attention to who else.

"I don't know," Xander responded. "Why?"

"I just wondered where they are."

The idea that they might have chosen their own fate, even if they had no idea what they were choosing, nagged at Eden.

A muscled woman emerged from the doorway to the stairs and turned around, pressing some buttons on the keypad next to it. She seemed completely absorbed in her work, but when she turned around, her eyes drilled into Xander and Eden.

"What are you still doing here? Go down the hall!" she commanded.

"Is someone going to tell us why you want everyone down there?" Xander asked.

"You'll know everything once you attend orientation." The woman made a shooing motion.

Eden took a few steps down the hall, and it took Xander a moment to catch up with her. She could hear the woman following directly behind them. The hall was long with multiple doors off the right of it, but Eden couldn't keep her eyes away from the windows on the left. Space. The thing that had been above her for her whole life was now around her. It felt... wrong...weird.

"There you are," a bearded man said from an open doorway. "Right through here."

Eden glanced back at Xander, and he nodded to her. She walked through the doorway and saw that whatever they were on was bigger than she had first thought. A large room, similar to the room that had been used to hand out medals at the hotel, spread before them.

People were sitting on the carpeted floor, all faces she recognized from this year's Olympics, and Eden didn't see any chairs. Then, she saw a face though that made her stop in her tracks- Derry. He looked up at her from the floor, and Eden's stomach clenched. She might not remember all the details of that night, but she knew that she had been kidnapped. Derry was the reason that Xander had the knife wound in his back.

"Come over here," Xander suggested, plucking at her arm. Eden tore her eyes away from Derry and followed Xander to an open spot on the floor. Once they were settled, she could no longer see the boy, but it didn't mean she could switch off her thoughts about him. Why was he here? He had been taken to a cell or a room or something once he proved dangerous to other competitors. Now, he was sitting around with everyone else like he wasn't a danger to society.

"I would like to have everyone's attention," a man said from the other side of the room. Eden peered curiously in his direction after taking a long sip from her water bottle. He looked young but confident in what he was doing. How old was he?

"I know that you must be feeling confused, maybe worried as well. This transition is always difficult."

Always?

"You have been eliminated," the man said.

People started whispering around the room, and Eden frowned at Xander. "Eliminated? I thought they were going to eliminate us now."

Xander just shrugged. "I guess we're about to find out what elimination really means."

"The government is no longer responsible for your well-being. We are, which means that I want you to pay close attention to the rules here. We don't have space for rule-breakers or trouble-makers. The resources on this station are limited enough as it is."

Eden's stomach seized up in concern. Limited resources? Trouble-makers? "So ...we're not going to die?" Eden whispered, leaning a little closer to Xander.

Xander grinned at her and put a hand on her shoulder. He squeezed it excitedly, and for the first time since the Olympics started, Eden felt joy bubble up inside her. She had a chance? It seemed too good to be true.

"Please listen," the man said slowly. He didn't seem amused by everyone's excited chatter, more like overly tired. "Everyone will be assigned a room and duties around the station. As I said, resources are limited, though we're working on helping the greenhouse produce more. Theft is punishable by death, instant death, and there are no excuses."

The anxiety returned just a little, but Eden knew she wouldn't steal anything. Unless ...what if they weren't given anything to eat? Left to starve slowly to death? Her mind started spiraling into different possibilities, but Xander squeezed her shoulder and brought her back into the moment.

"There are some areas of the station that are off-limits to the recently eliminated. Respect those boundaries. To receive your individual duties and dormitory assignment, come up to the front now."

That was it. That was his speech. Eden bit her bottom lip, considering everything the man had just said. They were going to be given another chance, a chance at life, even if it wasn't the life she had always imagined. She didn't know what quality of life she might have in space, but she couldn't contain her excitement. She turned around and wrapped her arms around Xander, squeezing him tightly and remembering how close they had become.

He had asked her to be his girlfriend once they had both had medals. Would he want the same thing now? But Xander's hug back to her seemed reluctant. Eden pulled back and looked at his face to see that he was deep in thought.

"If the eliminated are brought here ..." Xander said slowly, "then I have to find Matt!"

Chapter 4

Xander hurried to the front of the room where a few adults were talking with the recently eliminated. He scanned each of their faces, wondering how Matt's might have changed over time. But no, none of them looked familiar. Besides, Matt was only a few years older than Xander. He wouldn't look ... so old.

Eden had caught up with Xander, and he felt her right behind him. He didn't say anything to her, though. He needed to speak with one of the people in charge of this place and figure out where Matt was.

Suddenly, a loud sound rocketed through the room, and many of the occupants covered their ears. Xander turned around slowly, afraid he would see a gaping wall or something like that. It had sounded serious, like the place was being torn in half, but none of the adults who lived here seemed concerned.

"What was that?" Xander asked, loudly enough to get someone's attention.

A tired-looking man sighed. "That was us discharging the ship that was used to bring you here. The government doesn't want to give us any more resources than we already have, so they set the ship to explode five hours after it arrives."

Xander's eyebrows rose. That explained the frantic scrambling to gather as many supplies from the rooms as they could. While he had the man's attention, he asked about his brother. "Is there someone named Matt who lives here? He's kind of tall, lanky, brown hair, mark on his cheek?"

The man studied Xander for a minute before he nodded. "Yes, Matt lives here. He was eliminated a few years ago."

Xander's heart leaped up, and he wanted to jump up and down. "Where? Where is he?" He knew this was ridiculous. It had been years since he had seen Matt. A few more minutes wouldn't matter either way, but he felt like he had to see his brother right then.

The tired-looking man sighed and checked his timepiece. "He's probably on bridge duty."

"Where's that?"

"Go out the hall that way and go to the left. The doors are labeled."

Xander started to jog in the direction the man had pointed, but the man called him back. "You can't go anywhere until you've received your duties and dormitory assignment."

Xander reluctantly turned back. He didn't want to make trouble on his first day, but just knowing that Matt was so close made it hard to contain himself. He had never pictured any sort of reunion, because everyone knew that there was nothing after you were eliminated. But now, that nothing had become a something.

"Matt's really here?" Eden asked, touching his arm.

Xander nodded, a smile spreading unconsciously over his face. "I don't even know what I'm going to say to him, but... wow. I thought he was gone forever. Everyone did." He ran a hand through his light brown hair and glanced at the two people giving out duties. If only they would hurry up!

"I wish my parents could be here too," Xander said, the sadness filling him once again. He wondered how his mother was doing. What had she done when she realized he wasn't coming back with the other medal winners? She was the only regret he had, not getting the chance to say a real goodbye, especially since she was so sick.

"I wonder what Matt will say when he sees you," Eden commented. "I bet he won't believe you're here."

"What? Because I was supposed to win a medal?" Xander felt a little of the injustice rising up in him again, the same injustice he had felt when Matt didn't win a medal. His brother had trained so hard. Just like Xander, he had concentrated daily on fine-tuning his body.

"Name?" someone said, and Xander realized that the adults were ready to assign his duties now.

"Xander Coxon," Xander said, waiting as the woman scrolled through a list of names on a screen that looked very similar to the one the officials had held back at the hotel.

"How do you spell that?" she asked.

Xander painstakingly spelled his name, even though he didn't think there were other ways of spelling it.

"I ... don't see you here." The woman looked panicked. "Wait a moment." She hurried over to another adult, and they started whispering.

Xander rolled his eyes at how long this was taking. He should just explain that he had given up his medal and chosen to be eliminated, but the woman seemed determined to find his name.

Eden gripped his arm. "What do you think they'll do if they can't find your name?"

Eden worried too much, but Xander knew she couldn't help it. "I guess I won't have any duties," he said to set her at ease.

"*Or* a place to sleep. Unlucky you."

"I guess I'll just have to find where you're sleeping and come visit you."

Eden giggled, and a sudden burst of excitement filled Xander. This was nothing like the future he had imagined for himself, but was it really so bad? He had Eden, and the stress of the impending Olympics had been lifted. He would have Matt, who had been such a good brother to him despite their differences.

"I have a question for you," the woman said, looking at Xander sideways as she came back with her companion. "Are you sure ... you were eliminated?"

"I gave up my medal," Xander explained with a sigh. "Maybe they didn't have time to finish updating the computers or something after the adulting ceremony."

"You gave it up?" Both of the adults looked intrigued, but Xander didn't want to talk about it.

"Can you just give me some chores to do?"

"It helps to know your strength back home for us to be able to assign duties."

"Wrestling."

"Maybe you can be assigned as a builder once you've had some training. Until then, you can have morning kitchen duty. You have to start an hour before the other shifts. No one ever wants that."

Xander nodded and didn't wait to ask where the kitchen was or what he would have to do. "Eden, I'm going to find Matt. I'll catch up with you later, okay?"

"Wait," the woman said, not letting him go yet. "Your room." She looked at her companion, and they spent minutes scrolling through the screens again. Xander crossed his arms and waited impatiently. "You can have Room 161," the woman finally said, clicking something. Xander started to take another step backward, but the woman stopped him one more time.

"You'll have your surgery in one week in the medical center. That's on the first floor."

"Okay," Xander responded, without really processing the information. He nodded to Eden then rushed out of the room, following the directions he had been given earlier.

Straight.

Left.

He scanned the doors on his right and left, having to slow down so he could read the tiny names. Finally, he saw the word "Bridge" and reached for the handle. It was locked.

Xander jiggled the handle again, but it wasn't going to open. He knocked instead.

Some voices inside rumbled through the door.

The door opened, and Xander stared at his brother's face. He knew it was his brother, but so much had changed. The familiar mark on his jaw under his eyes remained, but his jaw was covered by a scruffy beard, the kind of beard that is embarrassing when someone tries to grow it out because he doesn't have enough hair to really grow one.

But his eyes ... his eyes were so familiar that despite his initial hesitation, Xander knew it was Matt.

"Matt!" he exclaimed, wrapping his arms around his brother.

Matt took a moment longer to react. "Xander?" he questioned, his voice shaky, not like the confident brother that Xander had known. Then, Matt wrapped his arms around Xander and squeezed him in the same way he had always done. This time, though, his hug pulled at the wound on Xander's back, and he winced at the reminder of the fight he had been in.

"Xander, you're not supposed to be here," Matt said once he pulled back.

Xander felt his older brother studying his face. "I know. I'm not," Xander agreed. "But I'm here now. And it's good to know that this is what the eliminated life looks like."

Matt shook his head and glanced over his shoulder at someone else in the room. "I'm going to step outside for a few minutes."

"You're on duty until 14:00," the person reminded him.

"I know. I'll be right back. I know one of the newly eliminated." Matt frowned at the person, then closed the door behind him. He and Xander stood in the hallway, and Xander couldn't stop studying his brother's face.

"It's weird that you're alive, and ... you're older."

Matt smiled for the first time, and it was so familiar that Xander felt a sudden pull of homesickness. "I didn't just freeze in time, but what are you doing here? You were always so focused on training, and you were *good*."

Xander took a deep breath. He knew that Matt wouldn't understand his explanation, but now that they had discovered there was life after elimination, he was glad that he hadn't made Eden go through with it alone. Xander briefly imagined the lonely life he had been set to lead back in Greenland. With the exception of his mother, there weren't many people he would miss. Even Connor had been eliminated.

"Well?" Matt prompted.

"I won a medal," Xander confessed, "in wrestling, even though the competition didn't turn out how I wanted. I was injured pretty badly, and I still have a few bruises from it. The guy I was competing against got angry and started attacking me after the round was over."

"You won by default?" Matt didn't sound impressed.

Xander shrugged. "I had a medal with my name on it."

"And that's all that matters there." Matt crossed his arms, pinching his face together in that way he always did when he was thinking.

"Yeah, but my best friend, she didn't win a medal."

"You're still close with that girl. What's her name?"

"Eden."

"Yeah, Eden, she didn't win a medal, so you gave up yours to be eliminated?"

"That's about right."

"Man, you're dumb."

Xander frowned. "What did I have waiting for me at home? Mom, she's ..." Xander hated the lump of emotion in his throat. He took a deep breath and passed the news along to Matt. In Matt's mind, maybe their parents had ceased to exist long ago when he was sent away from Greenland, but Xander thought he deserved to know.

"Mom got really sick after you were eliminated. She found out she had cancer. She tried to hide it for a long time, but she called me after I won my medal to tell me that the doctors found out how serious it is. They don't give her long once she isn't able to work anymore."

Matt nodded, then let his head hang down so that he was staring at the worn carpet. Xander searched his brother's face for comfort, but Matt didn't give him any.

"Man, even if she's not there, you could have had a life ... freedom ... food."

"What do you mean? You have all of that here. I mean, maybe not the same freedom, but I didn't think that elimination would be a chance to live, even if that looks different."

"It's not. I may still be alive, but I'm not living." Matt's head snapped up, and he stared directly at Xander. "This kind of life isn't worth it. There aren't enough resources for everyone here, let alone for everyone new coming in. We had to..." Matt stopped talking for a minute as Xander realized how unhappy his brother was with life here.

"But ... I mean, maybe it's not as great as Greenland, but I couldn't let Eden face it alone. I thought they were going to shoot us, or ... I don't know. Eden's my best friend, and if I couldn't be with her and I was going to lose Mom too, then what was the point?"

"You're still stupid," Matt told him.

Xander wasn't sure if he should believe his brother's dour outlook or still have hope. Maybe the difference was that Matt hadn't stared death in the face in the last day.

"I don't know why they sent the eliminated here. We don't have any more room, but I think they feel guilty. Like ... at least if they send you guys here, then you have a chance. They don't just have to shoot you. But it's wrong. This is all wrong."

Xander swallowed. Matt knew more about the place than he did, so he should probably trust Matt's opinion. But he still couldn't accept that the only life he had available to him was no kind of life at all.

"I should get back to work," Matt said, pointing over his shoulder.

"Yeah, I wouldn't want to keep you from it," Xander responded. Still, he didn't move. He hadn't seen his brother in years. He wanted to hug him again, but being emotional wasn't really Matt's thing.

"See you later, man," Matt said, thumping on the door so someone would let him back in. Xander stood in the hallway, ignoring the occasional passer-by as he contemplated everything his brother had just told him.

Chapter 5

Eden watched as Xander left the room in a hurry so that he could find his brother. She knew that they had been close growing up, and Matt's failure to win a medal had disappointed Xander's whole family. Hopefully, the reunion would meet Xander's expectations.

"Name?" the woman with the screen prompted, and Eden focused on the woman in front of her.

"Eden Pearce."

The woman quickly found her information. "It says that your best competition was science, so you've been assigned to the medical team. You'll work every day from 7:00 to 12:00, starting tomorrow. Your room is Room 182. There is a map of the station on the wall there." The woman pointed, and Eden squinted across the room. She had so many questions to ask, and this woman seemed to know as much as anyone else.

"Are the people who are eliminated sent here every year?" she asked. She wanted to ask the woman when she had been eliminated, but that seemed a little too personal.

"Some of them."

"What am I supposed to do when I'm not helping the medical team?" Even the idea of working in medicine scared Eden. She might have been better in science, but that didn't mean she was equipped to stitch people up. In fact, if everyone here had been eliminated, that meant the whole place was run by sub-par individuals.

"Whatever you want," the woman said, then, "I need to finish assigning everyone."

Eden didn't like being pushed aside, but she didn't want to cause waves either. She wandered over to the map, studying the faces of the others who had been eliminated. She recognized a few from school, no one she had really been friends with, but then again, she hadn't been friends with a lot of people.

The map laid out the station in three levels. Apparently, they were on the lowest level. There were two more floors above them, and it looked like all of the dorm rooms were on the middle floor. With nothing else to do, Eden decided to find her room and get settled in. It couldn't be any less comfortable than the one she had woken up in a few hours ago.

Eden found the stairs which bent back and forth on themselves a couple of times so that they didn't take up very much space. On the second floor, it was easy to find her room number, though the spacing between the doors indicated that she shouldn't be expecting a luxurious suite.

Eden stared at the door with the number 182 on it. Shouldn't she have a key or something? She shrugged. Maybe there was a key inside. Or maybe there wasn't anything worth stealing. It wasn't like she had brought her suitcase with her.

Turning the knob quickly, Eden pushed open the door, bracing herself for whatever her new quarters might look like.

She did *not* expect to see two people sitting inside the room.

"Hello," Eden said, starting to back out as she twisted her water bottle in her hands. She must have gotten the room number wrong. No, the door said 182. Maybe she had misheard the woman. This room was clearly occupied already.

"You must be one of the newly eliminated," the girl on the left said. She was sitting on the top mattress of the bunk bed, her legs dangling over the bed below. "I'll share with you, Avery," the girl said, swinging onto the bed below.

"Yeah, I am," Eden responded. Her eyes slowly counted the beds, only two, and the realization hit her that maybe this was the right room after all. She would be expected to share the tiny space with two other girls? Maybe ... three.

"My name is Nicole," the girl said. "I was eliminated two years ago."

Eden couldn't believe how casually she was talking about something so serious. Her eyes flicked to the girl with straight, blonde hair.

"Avery," the blonde responded. She studied Eden carefully, and Eden suddenly felt self-conscious. She had been traveling for who knew how long, and her face was probably still streaked from crying about her elimination. She hadn't seen herself in a mirror for a long time.

"I'm Eden," Eden said. "So ... we all share this room."

"Jazzy is in here too," Nicole explained. "But she's on shift right now. She works mornings, and Avery and I work afternoons."

Eden nodded, accepting the information. The beds looked normal-sized, but apparently, she would be expected to share a bed with someone she hadn't even met yet. There was no room for her to have any sort of luggage. Speaking of which, where were their ... things?

"So ... were you really close to getting a medal or were you like no chance in hell?"

"Honestly, I kind of expected to be eliminated." Eden thought about admitting that she had actually won a medal, but she didn't want to explain about the cheating. "I didn't think this was what elimination would look like."

"Not for everyone," Nicole replied. "Some people choose Group 2."

"What happens to Group 2?" Eden asked, remembering how they had been forced to choose a group in the dining hall right before they were eliminated.

"I don't know," Nicole shrugged. "Maybe they're just shot. There's not room for them on here anyway. There's not even room for you guys."

Eden frowned. It *did* look like they were crowded for space. "How many people are on this ship?"

Nicole and Avery traded looks, and Eden didn't know them well enough to understand what that meant. "Too many," Nicole responded.

"So, why did they send us here if there isn't enough room?"

Eden finally stepped fully into the room and closed the door behind her, making the space feel even more cramped. There must be a bathroom somewhere else on the floor, because she didn't see any other doors in this room. The only light was a single bulb that hung from the ceiling flickering intermittently.

"Because everyone on Earth doesn't care about us. We've been eliminated. If we survive, then great. If not, then that's cool too. It's not *their* lives on the line."

Eden thought about that.

"You can have that bed." Avery pointed to the upper bunk. "Jazzy won't mind sharing." Eden thought sitting down might make this conversation easier than just hovering in the doorway, so she nodded her thanks to Avery and sat on the edge of the thin mattress.

"So how long has this thing been here?"

"Seven years," Nicole answered. She seemed all too happy to talk to someone. "Seven years. The first group that was sent here was more of an experiment, just to see if they could survive. They've survived, obviously, so more and more people just kept getting sent here."

"What happens if there's not enough room?" Eden had to know. She had heard what the man said about robbery being punishable by death, but it seemed unlikely that people would go around robbing other people and get thrown out just to reduce the population.

"That's why ..." Nicole slid her eyes in Avery's direction. "Look, I don't know if you want to hear all this. I'm sure you're excited about not being dead and all, but we should be honest. People have started disappearing."

"Disappearing?" Eden repeated the word. The comfort she had found in the last hour when she realized that things weren't as bad as she had first thought slowly seeped out of her, a cold fear replacing it.

"Yes, disappearing. We don't know what's happening to them."

"You never see them again? Are they... troublemakers or just regular people?"

"Some of both," Nicole responded.

"My sister disappeared," Avery piped up.

"Your sister?"

"Yes, my twin-Maya. One day, we went off to our jobs in the afternoon. I came back, but she never did."

Eden swallowed. Something sinister was happening here, and she wondered if she would ever be able to recapture the excitement she had felt upon entering the orientation room.

A single chime sounded out in the hallway, and Avery and Nicole hopped up. "What does that mean?" Eden asked.

"It means it's time for us to eat," Nicole explained. "After we eat, then Avery and I will go to our shifts. I guess you'll start working tomorrow?"

"Yeah, that's what I was told." Eden left her water bottle on her bed and trailed after Nicole and Avery.

The hallway, which had been deserted before, was now filled with people all walking in the same direction. Well, at least it wouldn't be hard to find the food. Eden was so nervous about what she had just learned, though, that she wasn't sure if she would be able to eat very much.

Eden stayed silent, listening as some people chatted amiably on their way to the meal. Despite Nicole's pessimistic outlook, some of them seemed very happy. Maybe Eden shouldn't give up hope so easily after all.

When Eden reached the dining hall, which she realized was the room she had been given instructions in earlier, she looked around for Xander. There were too many faces to be able to see each one clearly, but Eden searched those with dark hair, looking for him. Nothing.

"Does everyone eat at the same time?" she asked as she got in line.

Nicole explained, "Almost everyone. Some people have shifts during mealtimes, because it's not like the station can just be left on its own for an hour. But they eat afterward."

Eden tried to remember what job Xander had been given, hoping that he was okay and not lost. Maybe she should save some food for him just in case he didn't know it was mealtime.

However, when she got to the front of the line, she realized that saving food for someone else wouldn't be an option. She was given a bowl with a gross-looking, soupy mixture that looked like watered-down oatmeal.

Eden blinked at it for a moment before the person behind her bumped into her and almost caused her to spill it.

Nicole and Avery had pulled ahead. There weren't any tables and chairs. Everyone was settling into groups on the floor, eating the mixture quickly before getting up and making room for others. Eden hurried after the two girls. She wasn't sure if she would classify them as her friends, but at least she knew them. It was better than eating by herself.

A couple of other girls sat down with them, and they started asking Eden questions as soon as she joined them.

"Has there been any progress on reducing global warming on the Earth?" one of them asked.

"It doesn't matter even if there has been. They'll never let us back down there."

"I just want to know if there's a chance."

Both girls peered at Eden, waiting for an answer. "I don't think so," Eden responded. The truth was that she had never really kept up with the news. It wasn't her thing, but now, she realized that these people were stuck out here with no idea what was happening on Earth.

"What do you mean, you don't think so? Either they have or they haven't."

Eden didn't like the girl's pushy attitude, so she focused on her food instead.

"At least tell me if a girl named Willow Preston won a medal," another girl said.

Eden shrugged. She hadn't memorized the names of every winner. "I'm not sure. What was she competing in?"

"It would have been logic for her," the girl said.

Eden thought for a moment, but the name didn't ring any bells. "Sorry, I don't remember."

The other girl stood and moved to another group. Eden could hear her asking after Willow again. Eden wondered who Willow was in relation to her- a sister, a cousin, a friend?

The meal was just as tasteless as Eden had first assumed. However, she was able to force it down, knowing she would regret it later if she didn't have anything in her stomach. She remembered the pancakes her mother had made on the morning of her eighteenth birthday, and her mouth watered.

"What's your name?" a girl asked, and Eden's head snapped up. She stopped smiling at her bowl of food and focused on the dark-skinned girl in front of her. She had long braids all over her head.

"Eden," she answered the girl's question. "What's yours?"

"Helena," the girl responded. "You're going to be my assistant, I guess, in the medical center. I wanted to come say hi, so 'hi.'"

Eden waved her hand in an awkward circle before the girl turned away and marched back over to her group of friends. Well, at least she knew someone else on the space station now. Eden was eager to learn whatever she could to help life on the station run more smoothly, and she hoped that those working with her would help her know what she needed to do.

Once again, Eden looked around the room for Xander, but she didn't see his brown hair that was usually gelled straight up in front. Most of the people here had long hair, even the guys, and Eden wondered if a pair of scissors was scarce.

After she finished, her stomach felt a little unsettled, like maybe she shouldn't have trusted in the cook's expertise after all. Eden stood and took her bowl to the washing station like she saw so many other people doing. There were two trays with tall sides. One had lukewarm, dirty water with crumbs floating around in it. The other pan of water seemed a little cleaner. Eden rinsed her bowl, using her hand to scrub the sides since there didn't seem to be a sponge or anything. Then, she dried it on the towel beside the pans of water. The towel didn't seem much drier than the bowl, but she at least made an effort before stacking her bowl with the others.

Now, what was she going to do with the rest of her day? Eden felt exhausted, but she didn't think she would be able to fall asleep in a room with so many other people in and out. She hadn't met her third roommate yet either, and the idea of the girl coming in while Eden was sleeping bothered her.

Maybe she would just wander around and get to know the place a little better. If she was lucky, she might run into Xander.

Eden headed out the doorway she had used to enter the big room. Instead of heading to the stairway, though, she began moving to the doors along the hall of Level 1 and examining the plaques along the doors. Most of them had boring names like "Storage Room." Those were, of course, locked, and Eden moved forward. Then, she started finding some unmarked doorways.

Eden tried those doors as well, but the handles wouldn't turn. A lot of the doorways were locked by key, nothing hi-tech, though Eden remembered the one door they had come through to enter the station having a keypad.

How hard would it be to pick the lock? Not that Eden knew how to do that sort of thing, but for someone who did, it might not be that hard.

"Hey!" someone shouted from the other end of the hallway.

Eden jumped.

"What are you doing?" the man asked, hurrying toward her. His beard made him look at least fifteen years older than Eden, and clearly well into adulthood.

"I was just ... exploring," Eden said, shrinking back as the man stopped too close to her.

"Well, stop. There's nothing for you to see here. Stick to the places you're supposed to be."

The man continued to stare at Eden, his eyes boring into her, and Eden looked around for an escape. It wasn't like there were designated "areas" for her to be or a sign that told her where not to go. Still, the last thing Eden needed was to get in trouble in a place where punishments were so serious.

"Sorry," she mumbled and hurried back down the hallway toward the dining hall.

Chapter 6

Xander waited around outside the bridge, his mind churning. He knew that Matt was working another few hours, but he had nothing else to do except let the thoughts turn over and over in his head.

Matt was his one link back home, and as Xander paced the space outside the bridge waiting for Matt to finish his shift, he couldn't stop thinking about his mother.

Xander finally sank down, his back sliding against the wall, and curled his face into his knees. This ... this was it. He would never see his mother again. She could be dying right now, maybe all by herself. He had turned his back on her for ... Eden. How could he have done that? His mother needed him.

Silently, Xander let out the tears he had been holding in, his throat slowly unclogging as they fell down his face and onto his knees. After a few minutes, he just felt empty. No more tears or emotions, it seemed, remained. Strange, mourning his mother's death before it had happened, but he wouldn't be alerted when it did happen. This was his time to let the emotions move through him.

"Xander?" Matt's voice asked.

Xander looked up, taking a deep breath. He wondered if Matt could tell that he had been crying or if his face had hidden all signs of his emotions.

"What are you still doing here? It's been, like, two hours since we talked."

"I was just ... figuring out my life."

"Good luck with that." Matt sounded flippant, but the familiarity of the phrase he hadn't heard in so long made that same ball of emotions reappear in Xander's throat.

"Thanks, appreciate the support, man." Xander stood and resisted the urge to scrub at his face.

"Did you get something to eat?" Matt asked.

Xander shook his head. "You know, I haven't really felt hungry since I woke up in an isolated room in space."

"They pump you with fluids before they put you in there, so you might be good. But just so you know, skipping a meal isn't something you want to do. You can't just go in the kitchen and get food any time you want."

"Thanks," Xander said. He studied his brother's changed face, the ways it had grown in three years. If he weren't wearing such a ridiculous beard, then he would look the exact same, but the facial hair really changed his appearance.

Matt stared at Xander for a few minutes, and Xander met his eyes. Then, something he hadn't felt in years nudged him. He knew that Matt had to tell him something, but he couldn't right then. Before, it had usually been because their parents were listening or a teacher was nearby. Even though this was a completely different place, Xander hoped that his brotherly senses hadn't faded so much that he didn't recognize the meaning behind Matt's face.

"Do you want to show me around the place?" Xander suggested.

"Yeah, there's actually a pretty good gym here," Matt responded. "We have to stay fit somehow without running up and down the halls."

Xander's eyes lit up at the idea of a gym. Even though he didn't feel like working out right then, he wanted to see the place. "What floor?" he asked, trying to add on to the mental map he already had of the place.

"Third," Matt responded, pointing upward. He led the way in silence, striding quickly through the halls and leaving Xander to match his pace. For the first time since he had seen his brother, Xander wondered where Eden was and if she was okay. He should probably try to find her, but right now, he needed to find out what his brother couldn't tell him outside the bridge.

"Here," Matt said, pointing to an open doorway on the right. Xander stepped inside and paused, taking in the machines. There was nothing hi-tech with screens or anything, but the machines did the job. The weights in the corner would help him not lose the muscle mass he had spent years building up, and the treadmills would help him get in a good run every day.

There was no place to practice wrestling, but ... he had to remember that the wrestling was done for now. It wasn't the one motivation that gave him life, because he had already chosen elimination.

"Nice," Xander said. His eyes scanned the room once again, and he realized how small it was for the size of the whole station. "Not a lot of people come here?" There was only one person on one of the treadmills, and he stared directly ahead at the wall in front of him as he ran.

Matt shook his head. "I think a lot of people here have given up."

"Given up on taking care of themselves? Why?"

Matt shrugged. "Different reasons for everyone. Some people here are like zombies. You know? Once the excitement over not being killed goes away, I think people realize how hopeless it is. This place has been around for seven years. That's a long time in a tiny space."

Xander marched over to one of the treadmills and began messing with the buttons to see how it worked. There was no on/off switch or power cord. This thing ran completely on the energy of the person on top of it. Eager to experiment, Xander hopped on and began moving at a steady walk.

"What's the difference between here and Earth, you know? I mean, down there, we work, we eat, we play. Here, seems like it will be the same."

"But on Earth, you earn money, and you can spend that money however you want. You can get married and have a life. Have children, a family, you know."

"Then send them off to the Olympics when it's their time," Xander muttered angrily.

The one person in the exercise room hopped off his treadmill and wiped at his brow before squeezing between the two brothers and leaving. As soon as he did, Matt leaned closer to where Xander was striding in place.

"That's how some people feel, but the others who know what's really happening have given up altogether. They don't even come in for their shifts anymore."

Xander's eyes darted to the doorway. "What do you mean by 'what's really happening'?"

"I mean that we've detected an asteroid headed our way."

Xander hadn't excelled in science class, or really any academic classes, but he knew enough to know that a large rock moving toward them wasn't good.

"So... can we just move out of its trajectory?"

"We can't control where we move. We have no motor on this thing. It's not a spaceship," Matt explained. "It's meant to be stationary, though it actually slowly orbits the Earth all the time.

"Based on the predictions of our orbit and the asteroid's path, it's going to hit us in eleven days more or less. Most likely, we will all die. They are trying to build a few smaller ships, big enough to hold maybe ten people each, but not everyone will survive, even if they figure out a way to build these ships. And...even if some people get out in those ships, where will they go? Hopeless."

Xander stared at his brother, but Matt wasn't joking. "So ... is anything being done to stop it?"

"The scientific minds are at work, but keep in mind that everyone here didn't win a medal. We're not working with the brightest people."

Xander thought about Eden. She was smart, better at science than she had ever let on. Still, he knew what his brother meant. The people with a chance of coming up with a viable solution to save the population before global warming took over Greenland, Russia, and Alaska had all been kept on the Earth.

"So why doesn't everyone know that?"

"Because if everyone knew, then they would just stop working. They would give up. If everyone gives up, then we might die even sooner than when the asteroid reaches us."

Xander nodded, his feet slowing as his brain sped up. Maybe everyone didn't need to know, but Eden did. Xander had to tell her, and Matt would understand.

"So, there's no hope?"

"I'm not giving up yet," Matt told him, crossing his arms. "But you should know. The problem is that we don't have many tools, not enough materials to do anything." Matt closed his eyes and shook his head. "Sorry, man."

Xander hopped off the treadmill and smacked his brother on the back. "Guess I should make the most of these next few days then." Setting off with more confidence than he felt, Xander hurried along the station's hallway on a quest to find Eden.

His search required him to walk through most of the structure, but Xander didn't mind. The thoughts coursing through his mind kept his feet moving.

Finally! Xander rushed toward Eden when he spotted her familiar, brown hair. She deserved to know about this as much as anyone on this space station did, though he couldn't exactly go telling everyone without betraying Matt's confidence.

"Xander!" Eden squealed in surprise when he snuck up behind her and poked her in the ribs.

She whirled around and studied him, her brown eyes wide in her freckled face. "What's...wrong?" she asked. "Something's wrong. I can tell."

Xander tried to rearrange his facial features so that he didn't look as concerned or whatever it was she had detected on his face. "I was just looking for you," he said. "After I went off to find Matt, it was hard to find you."

"This place is pretty big, right?" Eden asked, looking down the hallway lined with doors behind her.

"Yeah," Xander agreed, blinking as he focused on the facts. "Why don't we go to that hall where we first entered this place? You know, the one with all the windows?"

Eden shrugged. "Sure, I don't have anything to do until my shift tomorrow. I'm going to be working in the mornings. You are too, right?"

Xander nodded, trying to remember the way *to* the hallway he had just mentioned. "I think we need to go that way," he said, pointing to the left. He was pretty sure there was a set of stairs down there.

"I think you're right, but...I'm not sure." Eden smiled.

She seemed so carefree, so alive for the first time in months. Xander realized that she finally had *hope*. She hadn't survived the Olympics, but she was still alive, even if that life was far away from everything she knew.

Xander trailed after her, trying to match his pace to her bouncy one. "I started getting to know the place," Eden said, lowering her voice as they entered the stairway. "And there are a lot of areas that are 'off limits.' Did you notice that?"

"Kind of," he said, just to respond. But really, he was thinking about what Matt had said.

"Yeah, it seems like they're hiding something. I mean, why have some-thing off limits unless you don't want everyone to know what it is, right?"

Xander nodded. "You have a good point there."

As they reached the bottom of the stairs, Eden frowned. "Which way?"

"That way." Xander pointed to the right.

As they walked side by side down the hallway, Xander felt something brush against his fingertips. His first instinct was to pull away, but then, as he jerked his arm toward his body, he realized that it had been Eden's hand. Was she trying to hold his hand? Great, now he had just rejected her.

Xander kept striding forward like he hadn't noticed anything. How was he supposed to manage their impending deaths and Eden's feelings at the same time? Both tasks felt equally large.

"Oh wait, I think I remember this hall," Eden said, pointing. "That's the door to the big room where we ate lunch. I didn't see you there."

"Yeah, I was talking to my brother," Xander replied.

"Wait. How was that?"

"It was ... fine," Xander responded. "But he's changed a lot."

"It's been ... three years, right?"

"Yeah, three years."

"I bet he thinks you've changed too. You used to be all awkward and now you're ..." Eden didn't finish her thought.

"I'm what?"

"You're ... less awkward."

Xander raised an eyebrow at Eden. "Well, glad to know I'm becoming less awkward."

Eden smiled shyly and looked away. Xander didn't think of her as a shy person, so the movement surprised him. They passed through the large room where Eden said everyone had eaten. Xander could still smell the wisps of some sort of food, though his nose wasn't keen enough to tell him what he had missed out on exactly.

Together, they walked to the doorway at the far end of the room. Xander reached for the handle first and held it open for Eden. Once she had passed through, Xander was relieved to see that the hallway was empty. To him, it seemed like a miracle to have so many windows and be able to peer outside and take in the world around them. But for everyone who lived here, the wonder of it must have already worn off.

"Want to sit here?" Eden suggested a space of wall that didn't have any doorways interrupting it.

Xander shrugged and sat in the place she had suggested. He settled his back against the slightly curved wall and gazed out the large windows. The sky looked exactly as it had when they arrived, and it made Xander question if there was a night and day in this place. Supposedly, it was just after lunchtime on the ship, but there was no sunlight streaming through the windows.

"You're really quiet," Eden commented.

"I just have a lot on my mind. Matt-" Xander stopped abruptly as he tried to gather his thoughts. Eden seemed so happy. He didn't want to be the one to burst that bubble. But didn't she deserve to know?

"What about him?" Eden asked, looking at Xander closely.

He hedged around the truth. "He's just different. Apparently, he works in the bridge, so he must be somebody pretty important. I never thought I would see him again, so I didn't have time to think up expectations, but...I don't know."

"Do you feel disappointed he's changed or something?"

Xander shrugged. He touched his chin. "How do you think I would look with a beard? Apparently, getting regular haircuts isn't a thing here."

Eden reached out and touched Xander's chin. "I think you would look like an old man." She smiled before fingering the ends of her own hair. "I don't think my hair will grow much longer. I've been trying to grow it out for years, and it's just stuck at this length."

"Well, for the record, I think you would look great with a beard, so if we're not able to cut our hair or shave, then just know that."

Eden rolled her eyes, and Xander grinned back at her, a little of the stress on his shoulders lifting. "You're ridiculous. But seriously, are you going to grow a beard? I mean, some guys don't have to shave that much, right?"

"Yeah, I'm one of them," Xander admitted, rubbing at his chin. There were a couple of firm hairs there, but nothing that really stood out against his skin. "I think I'm safe for a few years." Just saying that out loud, recognizing that they would be on this space station for...years, was crazy to him.

"So, I guess we just live here forever then? Did you find out how long this place has been around?"

"Seven years," Xander responded. "No one knows why it was started back then or how long they'll keep sending the losers here, but ... I do know seven years."

Eden gazed out the windows, and Xander noticed the sadness in the corners of her eyes. She bit her lower lip, and he could tell that she was fighting with something.

"What's going on?" he asked her, putting his arm around her shoulders and giving her permission to let out her thoughts.

"I mean, I wonder what my parents are thinking right now. They probably think I'm dead, and...it's not *that* bad, even if I have to share my room with a bunch of people. I mean, I have a chance to have a life and...be with you."

Xander was still stuck on the "sharing a room" bit. He and Matt had shared a room for most of their lives, but that was his brother. It would be weird to share with strangers.

He needed to speak comforting words now. "Maybe they'll just know," Xander tried to say. "I mean, you're not with them, but they have each other, so it's not so bad. You know? They don't have to deal with it alone."

Xander thought about how his father might feel when the inevitable happened to his mother.

"Yeah, I guess that's true. They're not alone. Me neither." Eden smiled up at Xander, and his heart quickened just a little. She was opening up the conversation, the one that had last ended with them being officially together before she lost her medal.

Xander studied her eyes. They were so close. He could see flecks of lighter brown in Eden's eyes and the sincerity behind them too. All Xander wanted to do right then was distract himself, not think about how little time they might actually have. So, he did it. He kissed her.

He leaned down and pressed his lips to hers, pulling her closer to him with his hand around her shoulders. She kissed him right back, and a warmth seemed to fill Xander as he felt her body against his.

Xander placed his other hand on her leg, squeezing her thigh gently. He had no idea what he was doing, but he knew that he liked it. He leaned further into the kiss until he felt the flick of Eden's tongue against his lip.

Pulling back for breath, Xander smiled at Eden, not sure exactly what to say after that. "Well," he finally said.

Eden just grinned at him and snuggled her head back into the crevice where his shoulder met his arm. "So, I guess we're still together and everything even though we don't have medals anymore."

"Yeah, together," Xander echoed. He wanted to squeeze her to him tightly, close his eyes, and make all of the bad news disappear, but he couldn't. He *had* to tell her. She deserved to know.

Chapter 7

Eden closed her eyes as she leaned against Xander. For the first time since she had arrived in this place, no, since she had lost her medal, she felt happy. She never wanted to move from Xander's shoulder as her mind skipped ahead to what was to come. Did people get married here? They had to...right? But she hadn't seen any babies or little children running around.

The place had been around for seven years, Xander had said. That was enough time for a few children to make an appearance. Eden wasn't sure why she was even thinking about all of this, but she had to wonder.

"We're probably going to die," Xander said, right by her ear.

"Wh-what did you just say?" Eden asked, sure that she had misheard something. She pulled her head back from his shoulder and studied his clear face. Xander's eyes displayed sadness, and Eden's heart sank. He must know something she didn't. Had her sneaking around earlier caught up with her? It hadn't been *that* serious.

"My brother, Matt...he knows more than some other people here. You can't tell anyone what I'm telling you."

"Who would I tell? I don't have any friends here," Eden responded, eager to know what he had learned from Matt.

"There's an asteroid coming toward us." Xander's voice remained low, but Eden could detect the urgency in it.

She didn't react at first, because it seemed so absurd. The kinds of things that had bothered her up until that point had been the upcoming Olympics, her mother's occasional nagging, and if Xander really liked her or not. Asteroids or lack thereof had never been something in her mind.

"So...what are we going to do about it?" she asked, looking around to see if anyone could hear them even though the hallway was obviously empty.

"Matt said that there's not much we can do. He said no one has the materials to even think about building anything."

"So...what do *we* do?" Eden asked. Xander was usually the one coming up with the solutions when she was freaking out.

"I don't know. I know nothing about this place." Xander was staring out the windows across from them instead of looking at her.

Eden stared out the windows too. She couldn't see anything. There was no large rock zooming toward them, so it seemed like the whole thing was a weird problem that someone else was facing.

"If we found out more about it, do you think we would be able to fix the problem? I mean, living here is better than not living at all."

Xander fixed his green eyes on her, and Eden waited for him to break into a smile, to tell her that it wasn't actually *that* serious. Everything would really be okay. He didn't do any of those things. Instead, he reached up and brushed a loose strand of hair behind her ear. His touch made her tingle, and she remembered their kiss from a few moments before. Maybe *that* was their solution, she thought mischievously. Just distract themselves with each other so they didn't have to think about the impending problem.

Eden swallowed, but she didn't have the nerve to try to kiss him again.

"Well, thanks for telling me," she finally said, breaking eye contact. She looked down at Xander's knees, a safe place to look, and settled her head against his shoulder again. After only a few hours here, just as the hope of a new, though strange life had grown within her, she had learned that this life wouldn't last very long after all.

"What room are you in?" Eden finally asked. She just wanted to keep talking, something to distract her from her thoughts. It wasn't until the words were out of her mouth that she realized how much they sounded like an inappropriate innuendo.

"I should remember that, but I was too busy trying to find Matt. I forgot the number." Xander touched the end of Eden's hair again. "I should probably find someone to ask."

"I have *three* roommates," Eden told him. "I've only met two, and they seemed pretty nice. One was really chatty. But she said..." Eden frowned, trying to remember Avery's exact words. "One of them said that her twin sister had disappeared."

"Disappeared?" Xander echoed.

"Yeah, like she should have come back from her shift, but she never did." Eden pulled away from Xander's shoulder so that she could try to read his eyes.

Xander stared ahead, not seeing her. Eden watched as Xander thought. "You're right. Something is going on here. Do we know who's in charge?"

Eden frowned and thought about his question. There was the guy who had given their orientation, but he seemed too young to really be in charge. Someone who was in charge of the whole place would have to be more experienced and more excited about the new people arriving. At least, that would be how Eden imagined him, though it could be a woman.

"We need to figure that out," she said, getting to her feet. Xander didn't rise immediately, so Eden went to the window and pressed her hands against the cool glass. If she closed her eyes and felt the window underneath her fingertips, she could almost imagine that she was back home, standing at the window of her bedroom.

If she opened her eyes, she would see the other gray apartment building behind hers, the messy porch on the floor just below theirs, and the apartment that had at least four children squeezed into it.

At least, that was what she hoped to see. But as Eden slowly cracked her eyes open, just tiny little slits, disappointment filled her at the star-speckled sky beyond.

Xander stood and approached the window, standing next to her. "I'll ask around. Matt should know," he said.

Eden dragged herself back to their current conversation, her eyes resting sadly on Xander's face. This was too much. She kind of just wanted the chance to be alone and cry. She wanted the chance to say goodbye to her parents and to the life she and Xander had thought they had for one night before she had had to deal with this one.

"Yeah, I'm sure. Actually, I'm feeling kind of tired. I don't know. Maybe I should go sleep for a little while," she said, hoping that the third roommate wouldn't decide that naptime was the time to bang into the room and introduce herself.

"I'll walk you to your room," Xander offered.

Eden didn't mind a few extra moments with Xander, so she agreed. She wondered if he would hold her hand, but he didn't. They walked silently side by side until they reached her room.

Then, she stood there for a minute, not quite ready to leave him.

"I guess I'll catch up with you at the next meal," Xander said, touching his stomach. "What did you have? I could really go for a hamburger right now."

Eden's eyebrows rose, her face giving away the truth about how the meal had tasted before she had a chance to tell him tactfully.

"That bad, huh? Well, I have kitchen duty, so maybe I'll be able to teach them a few tricks."

"Good luck with that," Eden told him. "I'll see you later then."

Eden entered her room, her eyes blinking a few times to adjust to the darkness as her hand searched for a light switch. The third girl wasn't in their room. She must be out enjoying her free time. Eden noted the location of the bed, then snapped the light off again. Not having outside windows really made the space feel smaller.

She climbed into the bed, which wasn't too uncomfortable, and lay there, thinking through everything that had happened since she had awakened in the tiny room. Panic had passed through her first, then excitement and hope, and now, a feeling of dread had settled into her stomach.

Eden forced her eyes closed, wanting to escape from the difficulties, but sleep tried to evade her as the previous events played out in her head. Finally, she drifted off to sleep.

EDEN'S MOM PEEKED INTO the doorway of her room, and Eden slowly opened her eyes. She wanted to keep sleeping, but her mom was telling her it was time for classes. Why? Hadn't she already finished school?

"Morning, Mom," Eden said.

Her mom frowned and came over to the bedside. "Eden? Stop playing like you're sleeping. You're going to be late if you don't get up, and I know how much you hate being late."

A surge of panic ran through Eden, and she flipped the covers off. Stretching, she stood and yawned. "Sorry, I don't know why I'm so tired," she said.

Her mom didn't smile, though, or leave the room. She continued to stare at the empty bed with concern. When Eden whirled around to look toward the bed, she saw that it wasn't empty after all. She was still lying on the bed. She could see herself there, not moving at all.

Eden's mouth dropped open, and she stepped forward to touch this ghostly projection of herself. Her mother reached her first. "Eden," her mother said in a concerned voice, pressing her hand against the other Eden's forehead.

"Eden?!" Now, her mother's voice had changed from concerned to panicked. "Eden, wake up!" Her mother shook the other Eden viciously, back and forth, back and forth. But Eden could tell that there was no life in the doll's body.

"Mom, I'm right here. I'm okay," Eden explained, reaching forward and touching her mom's shoulder. She could feel her mom right there, but her mom didn't react to her touch.

Instead, her mom started crying, burying her face in her hands as Eden looked on helplessly. She continued to shout, hoping that her mother would look up and realize that she was right there. "Mom! Mom! Can't you see me? I'm right here! Mom!"

But no, her mom didn't turn around. Eden stomped her foot with the agitation of it all, and sharp pain ran through her heel.

She blinked her eyes open and found herself in a dark room. Eden sat up quickly and clutched her heel, her breath coming quickly. She was...in her new room in the space station. Her mom wasn't there.

Eden's heel really was throbbing though, and Eden slowly massaged out the pain as she realized it had just been a dream. Still, she couldn't shake the discomfort she had felt at knowing that she was responsible for her mother's pain. Surely, her mother was mourning the loss of her only child. If Eden had just refrained from cheating, then maybe she could have won a medal and gone home fair and square. The old guilt swept through her. She was a disappointment to her parents, and that would never change.

She had been in the dark room for too long, and she didn't want to be there anymore. Eden rose from her bed and decided to find the nearest bathroom.

Wandering outside the room, she found that the hall was busier than it had been earlier. A few people were walking up and down it, and Eden hoped she hadn't missed the bell for dinner. Despite how disgusting the last meal had been, she still had hope for future meals.

There. The bathroom.

Eden went inside and spent some time splashing water on herself to shake the remaining feeling of sadness that her dream had left behind. The water smelled slightly metallic, and she didn't feel much cleaner after wiping her face. Once she emerged from the bathroom, she saw a familiar and unwelcome sight.

"Heyyyy," Derry greeted her like they were friends.

The night where he had been responsible for keeping her locked in a room with other drugged competitors ran through her mind. Eden shuddered, even as she tried to control her reaction to him.

She stared at him with barely restrained anger to show that she hadn't forgotten about the night. She might have been drugged, but her memory hadn't been affected.

"Look, I hope there's no hard feelings between us," Derry said, actually turning so that he was walking the same way as she was.

Eden glanced around, comforted by the fact that there were plenty of others in the hallway. If Derry tried anything, then she would have witnesses. Eden was definitely not capable of physically fighting him.

"I don't have anything to say to you," Eden finally said when he wouldn't stop waiting for an answer.

"I'm sorry. I did what I had to do. We all know that not everyone competed in the Olympics by following *all* the rules." He gave her a significant look there, and Eden's conscience pricked as she remembered all of the rules she had broken.

"What you did affected a *lot* of people. I'm sure the drugs were still affecting me the next day," she said. "That's not fair."

"You think little cheats along the way don't affect everyone else too?" Derry asked.

Eden glanced around. It was like Derry *knew* what she had done. But how could he know? Only Xander knew what she had done, and he wasn't going to share that with anyone. "I know that the Olympics aren't fair," she finally responded. "But what you did made them even more unfair."

"Look, I did it for my girl," Derry explained. "Carly wasn't going to make it, and we both knew that. I know it was extreme, and it got out of hand, and yeah...but can't we put that behind us?"

He was acting like a genuine person, but Eden had no reason to trust him. "I understand being desperate, but you *stabbed* Xander. That goes beyond desperate. I can't believe they even let you come here."

"What? I deserve to die or something? Is that what you're saying? That I should be dead right now?"

"I'm not..." Eden let out a long breath as she narrowed her eyes. "Look, I don't think anyone deserves to die, and I'm glad there's this option," she waved her hands at the place around them, "but that doesn't mean that we have to be friends."

"I just don't want you hating me. I mean, I'm a cool dude."

Eden rolled her eyes. She couldn't stop herself. Anyone who called themselves cool wasn't, at least in her mind. "Well, just because you think that doesn't mean I have to. I would appreciate being able to walk on my own now."

Derry didn't say anything, but he continued to walk beside her. Eden had forgotten where she was going while talking to him, and she struggled to find direction. She actually had no idea where she was or where she could even go to get rid of Derry, but she kept walking anyway.

Finally, Derry must have taken the hint. He stopped walking beside her and ducked into a room along the hall. Eden didn't take the time to note which room it was. She was just glad to be free of him. Just wait until *Xander* heard about Derry being here and trying to be her friend.

Chapter 8

Eden hadn't been lying when she told him about the size of the rooms. Xander had never needed a lot of space, but he would feel claustrophobic if he spent a lot of time in this tiny place. The room came with one redeeming factor, however. Connor appeared to be one of his roommates.

"Man, you're here!" Connor said, slapping hands with Xander.

Xander smacked Connor on the back and settled onto one of the beds. "Yup, I'm here."

"Like an idiot," Connor said, shaking his head. "I mean, I know you like Eden and all, but come on. You couldn't find someone else, back in the real world?"

Xander shrugged. He didn't really like to talk about what he felt or didn't feel for Eden. It was something he didn't really understand himself. Trying to explain it to someone else was like trying to do the chicken dance while speaking a foreign language. Not his thing.

"You look all depressed. You're not excited to be alive? I thought I was going to wake up dead."

"If you were dead, then you wouldn't wake up," Xander pointed out.

Connor tried to smack him, but Xander ducked, grinning again. "Hey, you're the one to blame for this," Connor joked back. "You're the one who trained me."

"I can't be blamed if you don't have any natural talent."

"Gee, thanks a lot. Not even a little natural talent?" Connor held up his fingers and pinched them together. At least he was in a good mood, but it was probably because he had no idea that an asteroid was headed toward them at a rapid pace. Xander opened his mouth to tell him, but he had already betrayed his brother's confidence once. He couldn't start telling everyone he cared about. Besides, Connor wasn't well-known for keeping his mouth shut.

"Not even a little," Xander confirmed.

Once their joking died down, Xander stared at the small patch of ground beside the bunk bed.

"So, what happens now?" Connor asked.

"I guess I learn how to cook. I'm on kitchen duty."

Connor had a good laugh at that. "I don't know who thought you would be good at that, but I guess I should watch my meals. Who knows what you'll put in them?" His face sobered. "Seems like the food here is going to suck though. Can you believe what they gave us for lunch?"

Xander hadn't been there, but he nodded in agreement. He didn't want to explain about his brother. Connor had met Matt a few times, back when they were younger, but Connor didn't seem to remember him. And Xander wasn't sure his brother was up for meet and greets.

"Maybe if I'm in charge, it will be better," Xander said, trying to stay positive.

"Not likely, but eh, whatever. If it doesn't get any better, then I guess I'll have to cut off my taste buds."

Xander made a face at Connor's disgusting threat. "I don't think that's the solution. Hey, did you see the workout room?" he asked.

Connor's eyes lit up, and Xander offered to show it to him. He needed something to keep himself busy so Connor wouldn't pry too hard into Xander's thoughts. When they reached the workout room, they both took a machine and got to work.

Pretty soon, the sweat was pooling around Xander, and he felt much better. He had pushed all of his worries into the machine, and as he toweled off his face, a little hope rose within him. Things couldn't be so bad. He and Matt would find a way to fix them, the way they always had before.

THE NEXT MORNING, XANDER woke up to a shrill alarm. He sat up quickly, dizziness filling his head as he tried to orient himself. Realizing that he was on a top bunk, he grabbed the end of the bed carefully to lower himself to the floor as he looked around for some sort of lightswitch, trying not to step on the one guy who was sleeping on the ground.

"Turn it off!" one of his new roommates shouted as though Xander were sleeping through it.

"Where is it?" he asked back through a clenched jaw.

"Wall," the guy responded helpfully. There happened to be four walls in their room, all of them equally capable of holding a blaring alarm.

Xander squinted at the wall under the bunk bed, but he didn't see anything there.

The guy swore when Xander didn't find it fast enough, and he hopped out of bed, slapping his hand at a dark wall. The alarm silenced, but Xander could hear the faint echo of it coming from other rooms up and down the hall.

"I guess it's time for my shift," Xander muttered. He didn't see a time anywhere, though that would be a helpful invention in his mind. How was he supposed to know when he needed to go anywhere without a clock?

Connor mumbled something and rolled out of the bottom bunk he was sharing with another guy. "Morning shift," he grumbled.

Xander looked around for some clean clothes, but it wasn't like he had been able to bring a suitcase with him when he was eliminated.

Well, even if he didn't have clean clothes, he could get a good shower. Sweat was still crusted onto his skin from his workout yesterday.

Xander left Connor to his grumbling as he shuffled down the hallway. By the time he found the bathroom, the sound of the alarms had shut off down the hallway. Life here would take some getting used to, for sure.

The showers were all being used, so Xander leaned against the bathroom wall to wait for one to open up.

"You won a medal!" someone behind Xander shouted.

Xander whirled around, because what was he supposed to do when someone shouted right in his ear? The guy was looking *right* at him, so Xander knew he wasn't addressing anyone else. Xander didn't recognize the boy, but there had been a lot of people at the Olympics this year.

"I did," Xander finally admitted when the boy wouldn't stop staring at him.

"What are you doing here?" the boy asked.

Xander took a deep breath. Maybe he shouldn't have admitted to the truth. People weren't going to understand him no matter how he explained it.

"I'm...here for my friend," Xander finally explained.

The guy's eyebrows shot up, the sounds of shower water hitting the ground in the background. "Some friend. What's the point of dying for somebody when they can't even live? Unless...did you give up your medal to your friend?"

Xander wished he could have given his medal to Eden, but the officials had said that wasn't possible. She had cheated, tried to hijack the competition. He couldn't just *choose* to give her life or they would have a population of cheaters. It was the same for that guy who had attacked him. Supposedly, nothing would save him from elimination. Yet, here he was. Xander had seen the guy's annoying, smiling face in the halls.

"No, not like that," Xander explained. He remembered the moment when he had talked to the officials. They had tried to talk him out of it once they had pulled up his stats, letting him know that he wouldn't be able to change his mind once he had done it.

"So...we've got time. What was it like?"

Xander turned to check on the showers, but none of them had emptied. He was stuck talking to this guy. He didn't want to make enemies on his first day here, so he should probably keep the conversation friendly, even if this guy was pushing him to talk about something he didn't want to talk about.

"What's your name first?" Xander asked.

"Raymon," the guy responded.

"Xander."

"I know," Raymon responded, shaking Xander's hand. "So?"

He was worse than a girl pushing for gossip. "So, the girl I'm with..." Xander didn't know how else to phrase it. "She won a medal, but she did it by cheating. They took her medal away after she won it. I couldn't let her be eliminated on her own, and I don't really have a home to go back to. I figured, why not?"

Raymon stared at Xander for a few seconds before shaking his head. "Now, you're here and thinking that whatever terrible life you had to go back to is better than this. They're going to wring every ounce of labor they can out of us. Can't you tell? They'll feed us just enough to give us energy to work. We're going to die here."

"That's one way to look at it," Xander responded. Raymon was complaining about life on this station, but he didn't even know half of it. "Maybe it won't take as long as you think."

"What? To die?"

"Yeah, who knows? Maybe it'll be quick and easy." That was all Xander was going to say. He hadn't exactly died by asteroid before, but he assumed that it would be a quick death.

A guy stepped out of the shower, and Xander slid past him to take the free stall. Enough bathroom talk. He needed to get to the kitchen and find out what sort of daily duties he would have.

After Xander had cleaned up, someone pointed him to a shelf that held clean clothes. It felt strange putting on what felt like someone else's clothes, but his only other option was his wrinkled and stinky ones. Once dressed, Xander headed toward the dining hall. He knew where that was thanks to dinner the night before.

When he reached the place, it was empty. He finally spotted a clock on the wall and saw that it was one minute past seven.

"Hello?" Xander called.

No one answered.

There was a door on the far end of the space, so Xander strode toward that. When he reached the far end, he flung it open and saw a bunch of activity. Everyone was wearing a cloth on their heads, and one of them looked at Xander angrily. "You're late."

"It was one minute." Xander held up his hands. It was like Eden scolding him all over again. "It would also help if there was a clock somewhere other than the dining room so I could see what time it was."

"Start mixing," someone called to him.

"Cover your hair," someone else called.

There didn't seem to really be anyone in charge, so Xander figured things out for himself. There was a stack of clean cloths on the counter, and he carefully tied one around his head like some sort of maid. He was glad there weren't any mirrors around...or Eden. She would probably have a good laugh at his new look.

Then, Xander tried to figure out what he was supposed to be mixing. He walked behind a row of three people, all of them with big pots in front of them, arms tirelessly moving wooden spoons around and around the pot. There was no fourth pot.

Two other people were cutting something on the counter. It smelled like something with at least a little taste, unlike whatever was in the pots.

"So ..." Xander finally said. "What am I supposed to be mixing?"

"This one," one of the mixers said, stepping back from the pot and rubbing her arm. "I'm tired."

Xander stepped forward and began moving the spoon rhythmically through the sludge. Dinner last night had been recognizable, tiny carrots that looked like they hadn't been able to finish growing and a substance that looked like cat food but tasted like meat. Xander hadn't asked any questions about where it had been obtained. He just knew that it had helped soothe his hungry stomach. This stuff, though, looked disgusting.

"Take the first pot out to the dining room," one of the others commanded.

Xander looked around, trying to figure out if that meant him. However, the person next to him started struggling to move the pot. "I've got it," Xander said, dropping his spoon into the mixture and picking up the large pot. It had to weigh at least fifty pounds. "Just out there?"

No one answered him, so Xander pushed his way through the door to the main room and was surprised to see at least thirty people milling around. They must have shown up after he had. "Food," Xander announced cheerfully, setting the pot on the only table in the room.

"Where are the bowls?" someone asked.

Xander looked at the table, then the food, then the people. "I'll find them," Xander offered.

As he pushed back into the kitchen, he ran into one of the others coming out. "Oops, sorry there," Xander said.

The person just glared at him as he carried bowls and a large serving spoon to the pot. Xander shook his head. Apparently, he was going to be working with a bunch of people who hated him. Awesome.

Once inside the kitchen again, Xander approached the pot he had been stirring and got to work with the wooden spoon again.

"Why are you still stirring that?" someone asked him after he had given it two good whirls.

"I thought you wanted it stirred. I'm stirring it." His patience was beginning to run thin. If they were going to criticize him, then they at least needed to give him instructions first so that he would know what was expected.

"No, it's been stirred enough. It needs to go out to feed everyone."

Xander mumbled something rude and carried the second pot out. He started to go back into the kitchen when the person standing at the first pot stopped him. "Where are you going?"

"To … ." Xander pointed at the kitchen. "You know, since that's where I'm assigned." He couldn't keep the sarcasm out of his voice now.

"You're supposed to serve people," the person explained.

"Where is another serving spoon?" Xander asked.

"With all of the serving utensils." The person didn't even look at him as he ladled sludge into bowl after bowl.

Xander marched back into the kitchen and began banging open drawer after drawer, scanning the things hanging on the wall as well.

"Why are you doing that?" someone else asked him. "Just take a serving spoon and get back out there."

Xander closed his eyes and searched for patience deep within himself. "Where are the serving spoons?" he asked.

The girl at the third big pot came to his rescue and opened the drawer right in front of her. "Here," she said, handing him a spoon.

Xander nodded his head once to her in thanks and returned to his big pot of sludge.

People began lining up in front of him, and he tried to scoop even portions into each bowl. Even though it looked disgusting to him, everyone else seemed excited to have it.

Xander glanced up at each person's face as he served them, but he didn't see Eden. Where was she?

The person who had the third pot never came out to help serve the crowd, and Xander wondered in the back of his mind what had happened to that large amount of sludge.

"Kitchen duty," someone said, and Xander's head snapped up.

Xander smiled at his brother. "Yes, it's wonderful. No one tells you anything, but they expect you to know everything."

"That's life in this place." Matt smacked Xander's shoulder as he rinsed out his bowl in the dirty water. "I'm about to go to my shift. Good luck on yours."

Xander tried to think of a question to ask his brother, something that would get him information without letting those around him know what Matt wasn't supposed to have told him. But Matt left quickly, and Xander didn't have a chance to speak with him.

Once everyone had eaten, the somewhat clean bowls had been stacked up next to the pans for washing. Xander studied them, knowing that something should be done with them, but not sure what. If he tried to take them into the kitchen, he would probably get sent back out for not bringing the pans of water first.

Xander decided to go for the dirty water. He carried it carefully into the kitchen so that it wouldn't spill over the sides. Once inside the kitchen, he set it down on the counter to shake out his hands and figure out where he could pour the dirty water.

"Don't just leave it there," someone complained. "You need to dump it into the sink."

"On my way," Xander responded as cheerfully as he could manage. He picked the pan up again, took it to the sink, and dumped it down the drain. Everyone seemed to have their jobs, and it felt like they didn't really need him. Still, he looked around for things to do to keep himself busy. There was nothing left in the two big pots, and they would need to be washed, so he brought them into the kitchen and set them next to the sink. Then, he turned on the water.

"Stop!" someone else said. "You're supposed to use the water from the washing pans to clean those. You don't want to use clean water on something that big."

Xander frowned. The water from the pans had had fragments of sludge floating around in it. He wasn't sure it was the best thing to use to *clean* something. "I already poured it down the sink like you said," he told the man.

The man came over to the sink and looked into it like he thought Xander might be lying. "You just *wasted* all of that water?" he asked like he couldn't believe Xander would be so reckless.

"I wouldn't say I wasted it. I would say it's served its purpose already."

The guy shook his head and walked away like he couldn't deal with such an asinine individual. Xander had never had a short temper, but he was starting to lose it now. "If you want me to do something a certain way, then you need to *tell* me how to do it," he said loudly to everyone in the kitchen. "You can't expect me to just *know*."

He turned around, and everyone was staring at him. Xander stared back at them. Finally, the one who had helped him earlier broke away from everyone. "You need to dump the water into the sink, but you use this stopper so that it stays at the bottom of the sink. Then, you can wash the bigger pots."

Thankful that someone was finally giving him instructions, Xander asked a question. "Why can't we use new water? I mean, the water I dumped in here wasn't clean anymore."

"The water passes through a filtration system, and if we just run spigots all the time, then the filtration system won't be able to keep up. This is one of the ways we've slowed down our water use."

Xander gave a quick nod. It might not be the most hygienic, but the idea of not having enough water scared him. "What about the showers?" he asked. "Those seem to use water pretty quickly."

The girl had started to move away. She glanced at the others like she was worried about upsetting them. Then, she answered his question. "They recycle water too, but they don't always clean it before recycling."

Xander went out to retrieve the other pot as he thought about her answer. Basically, she was saying that if someone peed in the shower, it would be reused on their own head. Good to know, but there should probably be some sort of warning posted about that.

Xander worked on scrubbing the pots clean without using very much water while everyone else cleaned up. There were a few bowls of sludge left on the counter, and each person took one before sitting down to eat. Xander collected the last one and reluctantly put the stuff in his mouth.

His first thought was to get it out of his mouth as quickly as he could, but his stomach was begging him for food. Xander forced himself to swallow, the sludge rolling down his throat. It hadn't tasted like anything, though it kind of had the consistency of oatmeal.

"So, is this the typical meal around here?" Xander asked, motioning to the bowl.

Once again, no one really answered him. Two people were talking quietly between themselves, but everyone else was scooping the mess into their mouths quietly. Xander looked down and thought about his co-workers. Either these people were depressed because of the life they lived *or* they had decided they hated him for some reason.

As Xander finished up, the girl who had helped him stood up to clean her bowl. Xander followed her to the sink where the last of the dirty pot water was sitting at the bottom. He waited his turn to wash his bowl.

"How long have you been here?" Xander asked.

"A year," the girl responded.

Xander wanted to ask about her Olympics, but he thought that might be insensitive. "Thanks for helping me out. Everyone else seems determined to make me fail."

"I think," the girl sighed, "they're tired of it here. Life here isn't...well, I think sometimes we think it would have been easier to just have gotten shot in the head. I don't want to speak for everyone, but that's what I get a sense of."

Xander considered that. Life was so bad that they would rather die?

"But you only have to work a few hours a day, even if it is *way* too early in the morning. The rest of the time, you can do what you want."

The girl shrugged. "I don't know. I thought everyone was crazy at first. I mean, I hadn't been killed, that's great!" A smile flashed across her face as she exaggerated her words. "But then...time passes, and life up here is so monotonous. I don't know. Maybe if there was more to live for. But me, I always wanted a family. I dreamed about getting married, having two perfect kids, you know, the basic girl dream."

"And? Can't you get married here?" Xander asked.

The girl frowned. "I guess you could call yourself married if you wanted to, not that there is any sort of priest or pastor to officiate a wedding. But there will never be any kids."

Xander thought about that for a second. No kids. He hadn't seen any, but he hadn't really thought about it. Of course there wouldn't be kids. No one was sent here until they were eighteen years old. But some people had been sent here years ago. Surely, some of them had fallen in love and had kids.

"Why not?"

"There's not enough space for them." The girl placed her clean bowl next to some others, and Xander stepped forward to wash his, assuming that they would continue their conversation. However, when he turned to ask something else, the girl was drifting to another part of the kitchen. So much for that!

Chapter 9

Eden studied the map on the wall. Funny how they gave her a work as-signment but didn't think it was important to tell her where it was. It looked like the clinic was on the first floor, so Eden looked around. There was a set of stairs down the hall and to the right, but maybe it would be faster to go left. She didn't want to be late for her very first day at work.

A couple of people rushed past Eden to the stairs, and she stood aside so that she wouldn't be in their way. Most others, however, moved at one slow, steady pace.

Eden couldn't believe that she was going to her first job. She had never wanted to work in the medical field, but a job was a job. It made her feel like such an adult, even though she had no idea what she would be doing.

When Eden arrived at the medical center, her stomach grumbled. Din-ner last night had been tolerable, but Eden feared what might be served for breakfast. The clock above the door read five minutes before seven, and Eden knew she didn't have time to get breakfast then come all the way back to the clinic.

With only a little hesitation, she pushed the door open and stepped in-side. She took in as much as she could, her eyes bouncing from person to per-son. There were three people wearing clean, white coats and masks over their faces. She could only see their eyes, and it was hard to distinguish them.

"Hello," Eden said, stepping forward. That was when she noticed a male lying on a bed across from the doorway. He blinked his eyes sleepily at her, and she forced her lips into a smile.

"I'm Eden Pearce. What would you like me to do?"

"Get dressed," one of the medics said, pointing to a cupboard by the door. Eden opened the cupboard and saw a matching uniform to what the others were wearing. She carefully pulled on the white coat and mask, wrinkling her nose at how it affected her breathing.

"What should I do now?"

"Did you wash your hands?"

Eden glanced at the sink and gave her hands a good washing. "We've got a busy couple of weeks ahead of us," one of the medics said. As she pulled down her mask, Eden recognized her from the day before as the girl who had greeted her while she was eating.

"Hi, Helena," Eden said, glad she remembered the girl's name.

"I've been working here two years," Helena responded, "and last year was the same."

"Why is it going to be busy?" Eden asked.

"Because there are a bunch of new arrivals." Helena signaled to the man on the bed. "We have to give all of the men vasectomies."

Eden frowned. She recognized that word, but she couldn't remember exactly what it meant. What *was* a vasectomy? Still, she had been assigned to this unit, and she didn't want the person about to receive the procedure to hear her asking what kind of procedure it was.

"What would you like me to do?" Eden asked, glancing at the other two. They were snapping on rubber gloves. None of them seemed very old, and Eden was glad that she wasn't having to undergo a procedure performed by someone who hadn't even been able to win a medal in science. She *had* won a medal, but she still didn't know very much. Hopefully, they had some very informative books laying around here.

"You can just watch this time. We may ask you to get something, but we don't expect you to perform a surgery without practice."

Eden smiled gratefully, turning when there was a knock at the door. Helena nodded to the door, and Eden went to answer it. Letting people in was something she was comfortable doing. Cutting them up was not.

She recognized the boy's face from the Olympics. It was someone she had seen around the hotel, though she couldn't put a name to his face.

"I'm here for the, uh, surgery," he said nervously.

Eden pointed him to Helena and closed the door soundly behind him. She watched as Helena got him settled onto another bed and drew a curtain between the two boys. "Go ahead and drink this. We'll give you some sedation specifically for the area, but this will help you stay calm while the vasectomy is taking place."

The guy looked at the cup that only had a couple splashes of liquid in the bottom. "How do you get drugs up here?" Eden asked curiously. Based on everything she had learned so far, she didn't think that the scientists down on Earth were sending monthly supply rations. It seemed like they pretty much shipped everyone up here and hoped they didn't die.

Helena watched as the guy took the drink, one big swallow that downed it all. Then, she accepted the cup and motioned for Eden to follow her to the far side of the room. She placed the cup next to a collection of things that needed washing and lowered her voice. "There was nothing special about that mixture, no drugs involved. Have you ever heard of a placebo?"

Eden *did* know what that meant, and she felt proud of herself for knowing it. "Yes, it's basically like a fake drug."

"Exactly, we don't have anything to give them. But if they think that we're giving them something, then they tend to not feel as much pain when we do the procedure."

Eden blinked at Helena in surprise. "You're joking, right?"

Helena shook her head. "There were some drugs originally, back at the beginning, at least that's what I've been told. But, those ran out pretty quickly. And the people on Earth don't think we're worth wasting resources on."

Eden nodded slowly as she followed Helena back over to the two men. "So, now, you just wait for him to feel sleepy?" she asked.

Helena shrugged and nodded. "Pretty much it. I don't do the actual procedure, but I do know how to do it."

"How?" Eden asked. She tried to peer around the three other medics who were surrounding the first man. She couldn't tell exactly what they were doing, but it seemed like from the man's face that he might have figured out the drug was fake. He looked like he was in pain.

Helena began explaining the surgery step by step, Eden's jaw falling open with each step. So *that* was why there were no little children running around on the ship.

Eden felt a little weak-kneed, and she leaned on the counter behind her. Helena smiled sympathetically. "It sounds disgusting, but it's really not that hard. I mean, we barely have enough resources to keep ourselves alive. We can't afford to be having babies."

Eden understood the logic behind it, but that didn't mean that she could just accept it like that. "So that's going to happen to everybody?"

"Well, just the guys. It's easier to do on them. No one here could figure out how to do it on a female, and none of the females wanted to volunteer their bodies to be an experiment."

Eden's eyebrows rose. "You mean there were experiments on the guys?"

"They volunteered for it. Some of them didn't want kids...like ever. And once these guys figured out the surgery, then it seemed a given that everyone should have it done."

"But what if someone *does* want to have kids?"

The guy on the other bed yelped, and the second guy started to look worried.

"It's more a matter of survival than what we want right now. We have to make unselfish decisions. Why would we bring a baby into this world if we can barely take care of ourselves?" Helena led the way back to their patient, and Eden trailed behind her.

She wondered if Xander knew about this surgery and when he would get one done. As the guy on the other bed made more noise, Helena stepped up to the most recent entry to soothe him. He was starting to get a wild look in his eyes.

"Are you sure the numbing medicine is working?" he asked.

Eden watched as Helena lied straight to his face. "The drug you just drank is designed to help you feel calm, but it won't work if you let yourself get worried. We'll apply the numbing medicine right before the surgery starts."

Eden wondered if the numbing medicine was a fabrication as well. She sincerely hoped that she never hurt herself living here because she wasn't sure she would be able to go through with any surgery.

Eden couldn't watch while the surgery took place. The steps Helena had told her just kept running through her mind. She didn't think it was fair that they were taking away people's choice to have babies, but at the same time, she was supposed to be dead. Did she really have the right to complain?

During the second surgery, the guy groaned and complained just as much as the first one had. Eden kept herself busy on the far side of the only spacious room on the station by washing the dirty implements and cups.

The first guy was still lying on the bed, but he didn't look so sleepy now. His eyes were glossed over in pain, and he wasn't moving.

Eden slowly approached him. "How are you feeling?" she asked, trying to keep her voice friendly. She couldn't let him figure out how much the whole thing had freaked her out.

"That *hurt*," the guy said.

Eden nodded. "Sorry about that," she said, apologizing the same way she would if she accidentally stepped on the back of someone's foot.

The guy grunted in response just as the second guy groaned. "I can't believe I volunteered to be one of the firsts."

Eden grimaced along with him. "Well, it's done now."

"At least I don't have to work the next few days," he said.

"Can I get you anything?" Eden asked.

"Nah, I'm through the worst of it. Not like your pain medication works anyway," he muttered.

Eden drifted away to walk past the second surgery, just to see how close they were to being done. She didn't want a view of what was happening, but she got it anyway. She turned away quickly, her face reddening with embarrassment. She had never thought of herself as an overly private person, but there was something about the lack of shame that she couldn't quite grasp as quickly as the others in the room seemed to have.

Finally, it was over, and Eden was relieved to see the guys fully dressed again.

"What should I do now?" she asked Helena.

"Now, I'm going to teach you how to take care of the wound. Sometimes, the guys will get infections if they don't follow the instructions. Let me show you here." Wishing she hadn't asked the question, Eden settled in for the instructions, grimacing as Helena opened a cabinet.

Instead of an array of drugs, though, she saw bowls of steaming food. Breakfast had arrived. Her stomach rumbled and reminded her that she hadn't eaten yet.

"It's here," Helena said. "Time to take a break and eat." Eating a mud-like substance had never been so exciting before.

Chapter 10

Lunch was the same thing- more pots of gross sludge to be made. "What *is* this?" Xander asked as he glanced at the girl who had been friendly toward him. He still hadn't gotten her name.

"It's a mixture of nutrients we need in order to survive," she said. Even *she* seemed to be getting tired of his questions, so Xander didn't follow up even though her explanation wasn't very clear.

It was more complicated to cook than Xander had thought, and it took them at least an hour to properly mix the ingredients, then stir them in the big pots that he had just washed. Xander didn't complain, even though his arm muscles were wondering what sort of strange new exercise he had signed them up to do.

Meanwhile, the other cooks, if that was what he could call them, kept themselves busy working on the real food for dinner.

"There," one of them said, finally stepping back from the counter. "That's done."

Xander glanced over his shoulder to see that the cook had cut five cucumbers into such evenly shaped pieces that no one would be able to pick out one over the other as being bigger. He rolled his eyes. At least his shift was almost done. If the clock was anything to go by, then he only had fifteen more minutes.

Xander watched one of the other cooks struggle to take the big pot out to the serving area. "I can do it," Xander offered, taking the pot. His arms strained, but he could carry it. The person gave him a dirty look like he had insulted him. Xander rolled his eyes, took the pot out to the table, then returned to the kitchen.

However, when he got there, everyone was taking the cloths off their heads and laying them in a neat pile by the door. "Is it...time to go?" Xander asked, motioning to the pots of sludge that hadn't been touched yet. "What about serving lunch?"

No one answered him as they filed out of the kitchen.

Xander glanced up at the clock. There were still five minutes left. He looked around the kitchen. The cucumber cubes were just sitting there, and even though he had never thought of cucumbers as appetizing before (he was more of a broccoli guy), his mouth watered for real food.

Xander sneaked over to the counter, grabbed five tiny cubes, and popped them into his mouth. He was contemplating grabbing more when he heard the door creak open behind him. He couldn't turn around, or whoever was coming inside would see him chewing. So, Xander pretended to be organizing the utensils while he quickly swallowed the pieces, some of them not chewed fully.

"Hello," Xander said, turning around, even though everyone was always rude to him.

However, the person donning the cloth didn't look familiar at all. Xander began to take off his cloth and follow the process everyone else had. "Is it time to change shifts now?" he asked.

The person nodded. "We'll serve lunch and clean up."

"Cool. Thanks." Xander nodded at the person in a friendly manner, and the person nodded back. Then, Xander escaped from the kitchen as quickly as he could.

The large room was full of people, and Xander looked around for Eden. His stomach felt unsettled from the cucumber he had quickly swallowed. He felt like it might come back up, but he got in line for his portion of sludge anyway.

"Xander!" Eden exclaimed.

Xander turned and saw Eden coming toward him. Something about her eyes looked wild. "Eden from Sweden!" Xander greeted her.

She threw him that unimpressed look she always used when he called her that.

Xander laughed. "What? If your name was easier to rhyme, then I wouldn't have to call you that."

"How about you stop trying to be a poet?" she suggested. She got in line behind Xander, but he turned around so that he was facing her, his back to the rest of the line.

"How was your first shift?" he asked.

Eden took a slow, deep breath. "It happened," she finally answered. She glanced toward the ground, then back up at him. "You're, uh, getting a surgery soon?"

"Is that a question?"

"Are you?"

"Yeah, when I got my room assignment, they said something about a medical procedure. I'm not sure what it is though. I'll ask some questions before I get there."

"I know what it is," Eden told him. "I'm pretty sure it's not optional either."

Xander frowned. He had gone to the doctor regularly as a kid, but now, even though he hadn't officially gone through the adulting ceremony, he wasn't a kid anymore. He didn't like the idea of a surgery that wasn't optional when there was nothing wrong with him.

"Some sort of tracking device?" he asked. That was the first thing that popped into his mind.

"No. Where could people even go once they get here? It's like...I can't remember the name of it right now, but it basically makes it so you can't have kids."

Xander thought about that for a second, glancing over his shoulder so he could keep up with the rest of the line. "So everyone here has been sterilized basically?"

"No, that wasn't the word she used." Eden wrinkled her nose as she tried to remember it, and Xander smiled at her.

"It means that no one here can produce any offspring," Xander defined.

"Oh," Eden's eyebrows went wide. "Yeah, well, they just do it to the boys, I think. But, you know, that takes care of the problem essentially."

"Essentially," Xander agreed. "Okay, wow. Huh, so do they tell them what they're doing before they start this procedure?" Xander had never really thought about having kids other than if he did he would make sure that they would be able to win a medal easily.

Someone from the line right beside them was watching their conversation, and Xander had a feeling that the news was something else that was kept secretive here. Xander didn't like it. He didn't like that this place was run by people who had all failed to win medals. The people in charge, whoever they were, had no specific medical training, and they were performing procedures without consent or without divulging all of the information.

The annoyance of each of these things, unfair as they were, began to build up inside him, and Xander nodded to the guy watching them. "Apparently, that surgery they've scheduled us for is to sterilize us," he said, wanting to see what said "leaders" would do if a bunch of guys just refused to have the surgery.

"To make us clean?" the guy looked confused.

"Sure, yeah, clean out everything that would make us able to have kids," Xander shrugged. "I can go into more details if you want."

The guy nodded slowly. "I wondered about that surgery. Why do they want to do that?"

Xander shrugged. The reasoning didn't matter. The justice behind it did. "I don't know, but I don't want them doing that to me, so I'm not going to my procedure."

The guy continued his bobbing head motion. "Yeah, that doesn't seem right. I don't want to go either."

A couple of people around them started paying more attention. "What? They're snipping us? No way, man!"

Eden leaned forward, her lips right next to Xander's ear. "You can't tell anyone, please, but they don't have any numbing drugs either."

Xander pulled back from Eden to check her brown eyes for truth. She was being completely honest. Even though everything in him wanted to spread that news as well, he held back for Eden's sake. He didn't want to put her position in jeopardy.

"I'm not getting clipped," someone else said. "I mean, I don't like kids, but come on. That might change in the future."

"You didn't have a future until we arrived here," someone else commented.

Xander could hear the guys spreading the information, and he smiled in satisfaction as a plop of sludge was placed in his bowl. He wasn't sure why he wanted to upset the delicate balance on this space station, but the idea that everyone just followed a faceless leader without asking questions bothered him.

"Where should we sit?" Xander asked once Eden had her bowl.

Eden shrugged. He saw her eyes flick to a group of girls in the corner, but the girls didn't look back at Eden.

"There," she finally decided, pointing to a tiny patch of empty wall. Xander followed her to the wall, leaning against it as he started to force down his lunch. "You're on kitchen duty, right?" Eden asked.

Xander took a deep breath. "Yeah, that's me. It's not a fun job, so don't envy me."

"No, I was just wondering how you could be such a terrible cook." Eden motioned to her bowl with her spoon. "I mean, I didn't think it could get any worse, but I think yesterday's was at least warm. This one is cold."

Xander shrugged his shoulders. "To be honest, I've never had a job before, you know that. But working here is like following an unseen set of rules. They don't tell you what to do until you step out of line. Then they're all like 'Why did you just do that?' like I purposely messed things up."

Eden frowned at him sympathetically. "That sounds terrible. I wonder why they were so rude. I mean, only one of the girls on my shift talked to me, but she was pretty nice. Everyone else was busy doing the surgery and stuff, so...they weren't really able to talk."

"Do you think you'll have to help with those surgeries?" Xander knew it was her job, but he didn't like the idea of her performing that surgery on other guys.

Eden shrugged. "I hope not. I'll keep my position of washing everything as long as I can."

"Good plan." Xander took another bite, and Eden was right. The sludge was even more disgusting than earlier. He hadn't thought that was possible.

Xander heard a conversation happening in a group next to him about the vasectomy that they were performing on people. He smiled secretly to himself.

"What are you going to do this afternoon?" Eden asked.

"I don't know. No plans really, though I *would* like to work out at some point."

Eden touched his arm lightly. "Have to keep up your Hulk muscles, huh?"

Xander flexed his muscles and saw her blush as he showed off. "Of course! I may not be getting any nutrients, but I *do* want to stay in shape." His back had hardly bothered him when he exercised yesterday, and he hoped that meant it was healing quickly.

"I guess I could come with you," Eden said. "I mean...it's not like I have anything else to do, and maybe a walk would be good for me."

"It's settled then," Xander decided. "We'll go work out after lunch, then find a quiet place."

"Why a quiet place?" Eden asked.

Xander shrugged. He wasn't even sure why he had said that, but he liked the idea of going somewhere to be alone with Eden. It wasn't like either of their rooms provided that sanctuary.

"I mean, it makes it easier to talk without people listening in." Xander's stomach turned over. It also made it easier to kiss Eden without people watching, but he wasn't going to admit that out loud.

Once they finished and had rinsed their bowls in the dingy water, Xander showed Eden where the workout room was. She surveyed it from the doorway.

"Not as big as the one at the hotel."

"But there also aren't many people here trying to stay in shape," Xander pointed out as he approached the weights in the corner. "I'm honestly surprised this is even here. Have you wondered how this whole place started?"

"People wanted to stay in shape?" Eden ventured a guess.

"No, not the workout room, this whole place." Xander waved his hand in a wide circle to indicate the space station in general.

Eden thought for a second. "I haven't thought about it, but I guess it was because they didn't want the guilt of everyone dying on their souls. I know that sounds dramatic, but I want to think that someone somewhere has a conscience."

"That's the difference between the two of us. You see the good in people. I-"

"See the bad in people?" Eden finished.

"No, I see them for how they really are."

"And how are they really?"

"Most of them are inherently selfish."

"I don't think-" Eden started to protest.

This time, Xander cut her off. "Think about it. They'll do anything to save their own butts."

Eden listened quietly as Xander explained between lifts, his breath coming out in angry grunts. "Colt, the guy who got my medal...he told me that he researched the...people who started the Olympics."

"Okay," Eden nodded. Xander didn't think she had met Colt, and he wished she had. He would have been better at explaining it.

"He said that out of the twelve people who started the Olympics...none of their children or grandchildren lost."

Eden stared at him for a minute, and Xander did several lifts without saying anything as he waited for it to sink in. He finally set the barbell on the ground and wiped at his face. Then, he touched the bandage on his back gently. Maybe he wouldn't push himself too hard today.

"So you're saying that the Olympics are rigged," Eden verified.

"Oh yes, just not for us."

Eden wandered over to one of the treadmills and hopped on it. "Well, it doesn't really matter anymore. We're here now, and the Olympics are behind us. I mean, even if we had proof of some sort of cheating, and that's a big *if*, what would we do with it? It's not like we can just call people and spread the information."

Xander disliked the acceptance in her voice, like she was just giving up. "Okay, sure, there's nothing we can do about it now, but what about here? We can do something to change this place, right?" That was, if the asteroid didn't destroy it in a few days.

"I don't know. We just got here. We barely know anything about what's going on."

"Here's what I think. I think that the people down on Earth, the scientists or whoever is running the show, built this thing as a solution to the global warming problem. They thought that if they could provide an alternative solution, then they wouldn't have to conduct the Olympics, and everyone could live in space happily ever after."

"So we're an experiment?"

"Maybe? I'm not sure they didn't try it out themselves first, you know, send people who weren't eliminated. But then, when things didn't work out, maybe they realized that life wasn't sustainable here, then they just gave up and went back to Earth where at least they have good food."

Eden made a face at the mention of food. "Look, I don't want to hurt your feelings or anything, but what does it matter? We're here now, so what?"

"Because it affects the future. Knowing the purpose behind this place-"

"Xander!" a voice said loudly above him. Matt sounded angry, and Xander stood up, facing his older brother in the doorway. He studied Matt's face, trying to figure out what was wrong.

Eden looked back and forth between the two of them, clearly not recognizing Matt right away.

"Matt, do you remember Eden?" Xander asked, trying to be polite and not make Eden feel any more awkward than she might already.

Matt nodded at Eden before striding over. "You've been causing trouble. Seriously?"

"Trouble?" Xander thought about the pieces of cucumber he had sneaked. How could Matt know about that and who had told him? He didn't need to explain anything to his brother.

"You're talking about the procedure and convincing guys not to get it."

Xander waved his hands. "No, no, it's not like that. I just told them what the surgery was."

"And how do you know?"

Xander didn't want to drag Eden into the conversation, but his eyes shifted to her before he could think about his body language. Matt turned on Eden. "How do *you* know?"

Eden took a step back, clearly intimidated by his tone. "I just started working in the medical center, and I thought Xander should know what the procedure was."

Xander stepped forward so that he was even with Matt. His brother wasn't usually the angry type, and he had never thrown a punch. Still, there was a first time for everything.

"Why do you *not* want people to know?"

Matt rolled his eyes. "It's not about them not knowing. We tell them when they arrive. But when you get people hyped up about something, they freak out. When there's mass panic, it just causes more trouble."

"I wasn't trying to cause mass panic, but I think that everyone should have the right to choose if they want that done or not. I mean, we're young. We've got years ahead of us. That's a big thing to get done right now."

"We might have years or we might have days," Matt said, and Xander knew he was referring to the asteroid coming in their direction. "We have to be prepared for both situations. And if we *do* have years, then we can't have miniature people running around everywhere."

Xander rubbed his face. "You had space for us when we came. If someone wasn't responsible and had a kid, then I'm sure we would find space for them too. I don't remember you being this uptight when you lived at home."

Matt made another face that showed just how uptight he was. "Look, you can't go around making trouble like this. If you understood what was happening..." Now Matt was the one rubbing his eyes.

"Okay," Matt said, coming to a decision. "I'm going to show you something." He glanced over at Eden. "She can come too, since you'll tell her whatever anyway."

Matt strode toward the door of the workout room, and Xander made eye contact with Eden. He motioned for her to follow them, and he jogged to catch up to his brother's long strides.

Chapter 11

Eden followed the two boys down the hallway. Matt clearly knew where he was heading- none of the staring at maps that Eden had spent the last twenty-four hours doing. She took a few hurried steps so that she was even with Xander, and he grabbed her hand.

Warmth grew in Eden's stomach, and she glanced at the back of Matt's head, wondering if he knew that they were together. He had always been the silent, mysterious type when she had spent any time at Xander's apartment back home in Greenland.

Now, he was anything but silent.

Matt veered to the left and took another hallway. Eden wondered how big this place was. It seemed to have lots of unexplored places that she hadn't found yet. But she was sure that in a month or two, it would start to feel small. There would be no riding her bicycle until her calves burned, then realizing she had a two-hour bike ride back home.

"Do you know where we're going?" Eden asked Xander quietly.

He shook his head and just continued to tug her forward after Matt. Finally, Matt stopped in front of a door. This one had a keypad beside it and was clearly fortified to prevent just anyone from going inside.

Matt blocked their view as he punched in a code. If the beeps were anything to go by, the code was ten digits long. That was a long code to remember.

Matt stepped inside and motioned for them to follow. Then, he secured the door behind them. Eden stopped just beyond where she was, because she couldn't believe what she was seeing.

Everywhere in front of her, stacked so closely that there were just passages small enough to squeeze in between, were tanks of water- the water that Helena had cautioned her was so precious in this place.

But when she realized what was inside the water, her whole body went cold. Bodies. Stacks upon stacks of bodies in water.

Eden's knees felt weak as she craned her neck to see further up. Who *were* these people? She took a few deep breaths, then looked to Matt for an explanation. He was staring at their faces almost like he was drinking in their surprise.

"This is how we made room for more people," Matt explained.

"Are they...dead?" Eden asked. If they *were* dead, then why were they keeping the bodies around? But if they weren't, why were they in water tanks? Wouldn't they drown? She saw a tube running from each person's face to the edge of their tank. The tubes intertwined, and the rope of tubes became thicker the further down it went until they plunged into a circular machine beside the tanks.

"No, they're in stasis. Honestly, though, I thought they were volunteering to die by doing this. I can't believe it worked."

For the first time since Eden had seen him, Matt smiled.

"So...they volunteered to do this?" she asked.

"Most of them."

"And the others?"

"The others were picked randomly," Matt replied.

"Hold on, so you're just keeping them alive, giving them nutrients and oxygen, right?" Xander confirmed as he let go of Eden's hand and approached a tank for a better view. He pressed his hand against the glass which made Eden shudder. She didn't want to get any closer than she already was. She felt like they could open their eyes and come after her at any second.

"Yeah, that's the basics."

"Why?"

"There's not enough room for everyone. If we do this, and we can find some sort of solution to the space problem, then they can come back out."

"But where are you going to 'find' a solution to the space problem? It's not like this place is just going to grow another floor."

Matt shrugged. "I don't know. I think it's impossible. If the scientists on Earth, the smartest minds according to the Olympics, can't find a solution, then what are we, the dumb ones, supposed to do?"

"Don't call us that," Xander said, annoyed.

Eden ignored their conversation as she got up the courage to take a few steps closer. If she believed Matt, then these people had been volunteers. She wondered if Avery's sister was here. Her eyes flicked to the faces, but they looked distorted in the water. And if they really *had* been volunteers, then why didn't Avery know what had happened to her sister?

There would be no easy way of telling who was who, even if Avery's sister resembled her.

"So, what happens next year when there are more people sent?" Eden asked, turning around.

Matt crossed his arms and shrugged. "I don't think you want to know what the discussed options are. One of them is just to not open the door to the stairway. The ship lands there. In all past years, we've opened the doors, gathered what little supplies are sent with the eliminated, then shoved the ship away from us before it explodes." He shrugged like it was no big deal. "Maybe next year, we just shove it away."

Eden remembered what it was like waking up in that tiny room and freaking out. She imagined the door remaining firmly closed, then the whole place lurching away and being absorbed in flames.

"What if you could stop it from exploding?" she asked.

"We've tried. No one on Earth wants us to make a reappearance. The two years between when I came and when you did, at least twenty people lost their lives trying to stop the ship from exploding. We couldn't risk them trying to stop the system's automatic self-destruct feature while it was right next to the station, so we had to shove them away. Once they figured out they couldn't stop it, there was nothing that could be done to bring them back here."

Eden swallowed hard. "So, we're doomed?" she summed it up.

Matt's mouth twerked upward. "I guess you could say it like that."

Xander looked at Eden, and she pressed her lips together to keep from freaking out. She couldn't do that right now. She couldn't let herself freak out. She had to stay in the moment. No one was going to die right now. She could figure out the rest later... hopefully.

"Why are you showing us this?" Xander asked.

"Because you want to populate the place with little Eden and Xander babies, and there is *not* space for that. If you get her pregnant, then you're subjecting someone else to one of these things." Matt pounded on the glass.

"I'm not...that's not going to happen," Xander responded, and Eden felt her face flush. She and Xander had never gone beyond kissing, and even though it had been something on her mind occasionally, she also wasn't into throwing herself into passionate relationships when she was in life or death situations.

"You may say that, but the only way to make sure it doesn't happen is the procedure. That's why we started doing it. I've had it done, and everyone else has too. Nothing makes you above the rest of us."

"Whoa. I'm *not* saying that. I just think that we should have choices, or at least give people the right information. Why are you being so secretive? Why aren't you or everyone else talking about these people?" Xander motioned to the bodies. "Why aren't you talking about the asteroid?"

Matt glanced at Eden, and she shrank back. Xander probably wasn't supposed to tell her about that, but Matt should understand by now that there were no secrets between the two of them.

"Are you just going to spread that around the ship? Man, I thought I could trust you." Matt closed his eyes and rubbed his forehead the same way Xander did when he was upset.

"You can trust me," Xander responded. "I'm not telling everyone about that, even though they should know. Do they know about the asteroid back on Earth? Did they send us up here knowing that?"

"Well, let me just check my emails," Matt responded sarcastically. "*No*, they don't know, unless they've found out on their own. They have things set up so that they can send us information, like about the newly eliminated, but we can't send them anything back. The information just appears in our system overnight. They don't care about us, whether we live or die. Stop thinking that there's going to be some sort of rescue."

Eden felt tears brimming under the surface, but she wasn't going to cry here, not in front of Matt. "If you're done showing us," Eden said, "I'd like to leave now."

Matt shrugged, and Eden took that as a yes. She pushed back through the door into the empty hallway. For a place that was supposedly so full of people, there seemed to be a lot of empty hallways. Just as she was turning the corner and realizing that she didn't know exactly where she was, Xander came out of the door and lost no time in catching up with her.

"Are you okay?" he asked.

Eden bit her bottom lip and fought the annoying tears. She didn't want to be a crier. If Xander always felt like he had to comfort her, then he would get annoyed. So, she swallowed back her tears and nodded. "Fine, just thinking."

"I had no idea that had happened."

"I don't think they were volunteers," Eden finally admitted. She could hear the door behind them and knew that Matt was emerging. She sped up so that he wouldn't be able to catch up with them.

"Why not?"

"Because Avery said that her sister disappeared. If they had just asked for volunteers, then Avery would know, right? I mean, she would have been asked too?" Goosebumps rose on Eden's arms, and she shuddered involuntarily.

"Good point."

Xander grabbed her elbow and pulled her down another hallway. Eden wasn't sure where they were headed, but she trusted Xander enough to follow him. Neither of them spoke as they strode forward. They reached the end of the hallway and found a set of stairs. Xander pulled her into the stairway, and they sat on the bottom step, leaving enough room to the left that someone could pass by.

Eden glanced up at the ceiling and walls, looking for a camera. She realized for the first time since she had arrived that they weren't constantly being filmed. It felt like a relief to know that not every one of her silly conversations was being replayed for someone else to watch.

"What are we supposed to do?" Xander asked.

Eden brought her eyes back down to his. "About everything? Nothing. I mean, what can we do?"

"We can tell everyone what's going on."

"But your brother was right. That would just cause mass panic."

"Maybe, but it also might help solve the problem. I mean, if there are ten people thinking about how to solve a problem, there are a limited number of options or solutions. But if you have a couple hundred or more thinking about it, maybe someone would have a good solution. If they don't know there's a problem, then they'll never be able to help."

Xander had an excellent point, but Eden's stomach felt sick. Nothing was going like it was supposed to go, and she felt like it was her fault. But she couldn't focus on her regrets, because in the end, she couldn't do anything to change their situation.

"I don't know. Your brother would probably hate you forever if you did that. I mean, he wouldn't trust you with anything anymore."

"Forever might only be a few days."

There he went with those excellent points again. Eden hung her head, the weight of their decision, if they could really think of the decision as in their hands, weighing on her. "We don't have to decide tonight, right?" she asked. "I mean, we can take some time to think about it."

"Not too much time. Come on. Let's go to that hallway with the windows again."

Eden followed Xander to the familiar hallway. It felt like their safe space, and Eden was grateful when they reached it, even though they took a wrong turn along the way. Once again, they sat with their backs against the wall and stared out the sheet of glass. Everything looked exactly the same.

Eden burrowed her head into Xander's shoulder. "Let's say we aren't killed by an asteroid. They find a way to destroy it, and we all live."

"Okay..."

"What then?" Eden asked, her thoughts pulling her in.

"Then, we do our duties, help the place run, and ..." Was Xander coming to the same conclusion she was? "I eventually hope to be moved to a job where not everyone hates me."

Maybe not.

Eden laughed. "That's a good plan. I don't know how you worked this morning with that going on."

"It was worse than what I described," Xander responded. "I mean, I'm not an angry guy, but I felt myself getting to the boiling point."

Eden patted his arm reassuringly. "I'm glad that you managed not to boil over. Maybe we can switch spots, and you can perform operations for me." She made a face and wondered what other sorts of duties she might have in the place once the new round of surgeries had been performed. She didn't know how many guys were in their group, but if they did two or three surgeries a day, it would take them a long time to finish. Then again, if Xander had his way, not everyone would be attending theirs.

"I'd gladly do that. Maybe I could learn a little something. That is...if they're doing it right."

"It must be working." Eden motioned to the station behind them. "I don't see any babies."

"You're right," Xander responded.

Eden closed her eyes and listened to the hum of the whole machine. It was giant, considering that it was just suspended in the air, slowly orbiting her old home. There were so many questions she had, but she wasn't sure who would have the answers. Matt pretty much hated her already based on the fact that Xander had told her things he shouldn't have.

"What are you thinking?" Xander asked.

"About your brother."

"What? My brother? Why?" Xander sounded worried, and Eden sat up so that she could see his face.

"He seems to be a pretty important person around here. He knows a lot of things and has access to an off-limits spot. How do you think that happened?"

"Matt has always been good at getting people on his side," Xander responded. "He's a very personable guy most of the time. This angry, stern guy isn't who he really is."

"I guess we would all be like that if everyone knew what was coming."

"Maybe, the point is that he probably came on board, and everyone liked him and trusted him."

Eden rolled her head back and looked at the ceiling. "So if they liked and trusted one of us, then they would tell us more information."

"Who is this ambiguous 'they' you talk about?" Xander asked.

"I don't know. Whoever is in charge."

"That's something I've been thinking about. Who *is* in charge?"

"It-" Eden stopped abruptly as she thought about his question. It was a good one. No one had introduced themselves as the leader, and when she was working, everyone seemed to be on equal footing. "Do you think...there has to be a leader, right?"

"Some sort of leader, even if it's more than one person, like a board of directors. There has to be *somebody* who makes decisions. *Somebody* decided not to let everyone know that they only have a few more days to live."

Eden pressed her hands into her head. This was too much serious talk. She just wanted to forget about it and be able to enjoy herself. "Is there a room around here that people go for fun? A screening room or game room or something?"

"There *should* be," Xander responded. "Let's go look at the map over there."

They studied the map for a few minutes. Not every room was labeled, and some parts of the map just showed white blocks without even separating them into individual rooms. "Maybe there." Xander pointed to an area. "We can go check it out anyway."

He reached for Eden's hand, and she smiled. The world might be about to end for them, but at least she knew where she stood with Xander. They walked hand in hand to this potential place for fun and discovered that they were right.

Eden could hear a video game before they even went through the door. Her eyes widened. "Video games?" she asked, shrugging her shoulders. Neither she nor Xander had ever been big gamers, but if it provided something fun to do, she might be willing to try it.

Once inside, the room was bigger than the workout room- showing the intentions behind the people who had built this place. Clearly, they were focused more on enjoyment than physical maintenance. Inside the room, there was a small TV with some controllers attached to it. Another game in the corner was more immersive with a whole seat for the player to sit in.

Other than those two areas, which were already occupied, there were a few tables and chairs with some basic board and card games stacked beside them.

"Not bad," Xander said, looking around.

Eden approached the pair of players in front of the TV. They were driving little cars, racing them across a track. She put her hands on her hips and watched the cars' progress. Because of the split screen, it took her a minute to figure out who was leading and who was losing. When she did, she looked down at the players' faces to see if they were people she knew. Her whole body froze as she realized one was Derry.

What was he doing there?

Eden took an involuntary step backward and put her hands out for balance. The other player zoomed across the finish line just then, and Derry slapped the controller down. "I know the buttons now, so I'll be better next time. I just needed a chance to figure them out."

He turned and saw Eden watching him, staring at him like she had seen a ghost, and he waved at her, a tiny, excited wave like she was a good friend he hadn't seen in a while. "Hey," he said.

Eden took another step backward without looking and stepped on Xander's toes. He reached out to steady her, putting an arm on her elbow. "Watch where you're going," he told her not unkindly.

"He..." Eden tried to say, not taking her eyes off Derry. She had to snap out of this. She couldn't freeze up every time he came around.

"Hey, I'm Derry," Derry said, abandoning the controller on the floor completely. He stood up and offered his hand to Xander. "I know things between us at the Olympics weren't the best...but I hope you're not going to hold that against me."

Eden watched as Xander touched his back where the knife had gone in.

Xander stared at Derry without taking his hand. "What are you doing here?" he asked.

"Well, turns out when they eliminate someone, it doesn't mean death after all. Who knew?" Derry shrugged playfully and pointed toward the game. "There are two more controllers if you want to give it a try. We're about to start another race."

"No," Xander responded.

Eden clenched her teeth. There was something about this guy that set her on edge. The fact that he had been responsible for drugging and kidnapping her was probably only part of it. There was something else about him that was very...snake-like.

Derry shrugged. "Your loss. You would have had an easy win, because I'm not very good at this game." He turned away from them and bent to pick up the controller.

Eden noticed Xander's hands curling into fists, and her heart raced. She didn't know what the rules were here, but she didn't need Xander starting a fight to find them out.

"Let's just go," Eden suggested, touching Xander's arm lightly. He continued to stare at the back of Derry's head like he was in some sort of trance.

Eden became more insistent. "Let's get out of here," she suggested.

Xander blinked and looked over at her for a moment, before looking back at Derry. "I can't believe him," he muttered. "Why would they put him here?"

"It doesn't matter," Eden told him, aware that Derry was probably listening to every word of their conversation despite his pretended focus on readying himself for the next race.

Not willing to be a part of a fight, even if it was for a just cause, Eden walked toward the door and yanked it open. Xander followed after her, just like she had been hoping. Once they were outside, Eden took a deep breath. It was over. They were away from him.

But the realization hit her that they would never really be away from him. He would always be around the next corner, in the other room, smiling that grin that said he had gotten away with near murder.

"I can't deal with him," Xander muttered. They were walking, though Eden didn't really know where they were headed.

"I know. The first time I ran into him, it really bothered me too."

"You *knew* he was here already?"

"Saw him in the hallway on my way to get food. He...it rattled me. But what can we do about it?" Eden shrugged her shoulders.

"Look, I know that cheating isn't okay. We both know that, but there are two kinds of cheating. There is the kind that only helps yourself, and there is the kind that hurts others. What he did could have ended with several deaths. He's the reason I have *this*." Xander tugged up his shirt to emphasize his point.

Eden's eyes flitted across his naturally-tan skin, which was so different from the ghostly pale color of other people on the space station, to the mark. It hadn't gotten any better, and she thought she could see some pus oozing out of it. "Oh," she said involuntarily.

"Does it look bad?" Xander asked, stopping in the middle of the hallway and twisting to see himself a little better.

"I don't know, but maybe you should have the doctors look at it just to make sure. At least they can change the bandage."

"I don't trust them," Xander said darkly.

Eden sighed. She knew this was because of the information she had given him, and for a moment, she wished she could take it back. She just wanted to have a nice life, even if it was here in this place. But it seemed like the universe was determined to stop her from that.

"Well, *I* could change the bandage. I can at least do that, even if I don't know anything about medicine."

"Where are you going to get a new bandage?"

"From the medical center, but if I change it, will that make you feel better?"

Xander thought about her suggestion and finally nodded. "Fine, you can do the changing. It probably should just be looked at and cleaned."

Eden pressed her lips together, determined to do it for Xander even though she very much disliked any sort of injury. "Let's go this way then."

She led him toward a set of stairs and toward the medical center, wondering who would be on duty when they arrived. No one would recognize her as the new person, so she would have to be very convincing.

The repetition of what Xander had said kept pounding through her head. Her cheating had definitely hurt other people. She remembered the seizure one of the runners had had. All for nothing. Were any of those girls here? Someone who was supposed to have won a medal relegated to this life as a result of her cheating? Eden determined not to look at anyone else too closely, because she didn't want to know the truth.

When they arrived at the medical center, Eden pushed through the door cautiously. Another procedure was taking place, and one of the medics broke away from the group to greet them. The girl's face was tight, and as she removed her mask, Eden's stomach seized up. This was one of the ones who had been affected by the powder she had put in the oatmeal the morning of the races. Of course, just as she was thinking about them, one of them had appeared, proving to her that she had changed someone else's life and not for the better.

"Um, I just need a bandage for him," Eden said, pointing at Xander.

The girl clearly didn't recognize them. "I'm new here. All of the real medics are busy, so maybe we should wait for them."

"I actually work here in the mornings," Eden explained. "So, I know where they are. I can just grab one."

The girl looked uncertain, and even though Eden wasn't normally a pushy sort of person, she knew that she had to be today. "They're just right there," she said, pointing in the general direction of some drawers. She *had* seen some bandages that morning, even if she couldn't remember exactly where they had been.

The girl finally stepped aside, and Eden hurried forward to the group of drawers, glancing at the medics as she went.

The first drawer she looked in contained a few different sizes of needles, and they made Eden shiver as she looked at them. What could those possibly be used for?

The second drawer held a variety of bandages and cloths. Some of them looked stained, like they had been used, then washed. Eden wrinkled her nose, but reduce, reuse, recycle seemed to be this place's motto. Selecting a bandage that looked relatively clean of live bacteria, she approached Xander.

"You can sit here," she said. "I'll clean up your wound and put this one on." Realizing that she hadn't grabbed anything for the cleaning part of that promise, she returned to the drawers and did a little more searching until she had everything she might need.

Xander peeled off his shirt and leaned forward so that she could see his lower back clearly. Eden took a deep breath, hoped that nothing monumental was wrong, and peeled off the bandage.

Wrinkling her nose to keep the nauseous feeling at bay, Eden placed the dirty bandage on the counter and wished she had grabbed a pair of gloves. The new girl at the clinic watched curiously.

"What happened to you?" she said, not taking her eyes off Xander's bare back.

"Knife," Xander responded, not moving his head.

Eden dabbed at the wound with water, she hadn't been able to find any antiseptic, and wondered if recycled water was actually a good thing to put on a wound that hadn't quite closed yet.

"Does that hurt?" she asked as she wiped off a not-quite-transparent liquid that was clearly pus. Did that mean it was infected?

"Yeah, it's sore, but it's always sore. You're not injuring me any further."

Taking a deep breath, Eden carefully folded the new bandage so that it would properly cover the wound. "Okay, it's done," she said, securing it with some medical tape. "You should change the bandage every day, though, or it will get worse."

Xander reached back and touched the new bandage delicately. "Thanks," he said. He turned around and smiled at her, but Eden thought she detected pain in his voice. She glanced at the medics who seemed to be close to finishing.

"We should probably get out of here," Eden suggested as Xander put on his shirt.

"Where did you learn how to do that?" the new girl asked.

Eden could hear a little awe in her voice. "From falling off my bike so many times," Eden answered truthfully. If changing a bandage was considered medically advanced, then no wonder she had been placed in this position.

Once they were outside the medical center, Xander touched his back again, then looked at Eden with concern. "Do you think it's actually healing?"

"I don't know," Eden answered. "I mean, the stitches look good, and I'm glad you got real medical attention before we came up here. But it...could be infected."

Xander nodded. "Thanks for the honest answer."

Eden stared at the hallway in front of them. They were walking at a quick pace as though they actually had somewhere to be. "Where are we going?" she asked.

Xander stopped, then looked behind him. "Away from those guys." He pointed at the medical center. "I don't want them to pull me in and force me to do something."

"It's not like they could sedate you," Eden pointed out. "They might have a lot of needles, but they don't have anything to put in them."

Xander wrapped his arm around her shoulders and kissed the side of her head. "Good thinking. I always knew you were smart."

They still didn't have a destination, but it felt good to just walk. Eden tried to keep the conversation flowing, so that she wouldn't think about what was really going on around them- the end of everything.

Chapter 12

The next day, Xander entered the kitchen with irritation already just below the surface. He just knew that things would be the same way today as they had been the day before, but at least he knew somewhat what he would be expected to do.

"Good morning," he greeted cheerfully as he glanced at the clock. He was actually five minutes early for once in his life.

One of the kitchen workers growled at him. "Our shift starts one hour before the others. You're supposed to come directly in here when you hear the alarm."

Xander made a face when she had turned her back. It would have been nice if someone had told him that. Trying to be useful, he approached a large pot and saw that there was nothing in it. He looked around for the ingredients, his mouth already opening to ask a question. Then, he snapped it shut and began poking around. He would find the ingredients to make his own container of sludge since that seemed to be the meal of choice.

Finally, though, after poking in every cabinet and annoying people as he accidentally hit them with cabinet doors, he had to ask the question. There was no way he was going to figure it out on his own.

"So...is anyone going to tell me where the ingredients are for the..." he realized he didn't know the actual name for what the food supposedly was.

"We're not making another pot. Two are in enough," someone said.

Xander glanced at where the two pots were being made. The tireless stirring almost hypnotized him.

"Is there a reason for that?" They had made three yesterday. Wouldn't they need the same amount of food today?

"Same reason for everything," someone muttered.

"Care to share what the reason is?" Xander wasn't usually so rude, but there was something about this group of people that he just couldn't stand.

"Rationing," someone said.

Xander knew what the word meant, but he had to take a few minutes to absorb it. "So you're saying that there's not enough food for everyone."

"No," someone else responded.

"So who's going to go without?"

"You, if you don't shut your mouth."

Xander's eyes flashed, and he gritted his teeth. The tightness seemed to spread to his back, and he forced himself to take a deep breath. His stomach had barely felt full for an hour after last night's meal before it had started grumbling for more.

He couldn't miss out on a meal, but he had to bet that everyone else here felt the same way. Xander offered to take over the stirring, so he at least had something to do as he thought. What were the people in stasis being fed? What would happen if they put more people in stasis? Did it even matter if an asteroid was going to hit them anyway?

If they only had a few days left to live, around a week if Xander was counting correctly and his brother's estimate was right, then why shouldn't they eat up the rest of the stores? Live like kings?

Even though something within Xander told him that he was making the wrong decision, that he should keep it a secret, he couldn't help it. People deserved to know what was going on, even if all of the people currently around him disliked him.

"I didn't know there wasn't enough room for all of us," he said, stirring the sludge at a constant pace.

No one responded, but he could feel eyes on his back. He turned and saw the nicer girl watching him. "How could you have known?" she finally asked. "You had no idea we even existed. We are a well-kept secret."

Xander thought back to his Olimpics, his chance to prove himself worthy of adulthood. He had been worried about ceasing to exist, but he hadn't known that a shortened life on some sort of vessel in space was even an option he needed to worry about.

"People have disappeared because of *you*," one of the others finally spoke. "You think we don't know what happened? Roman decided that we had to make room for the newbies, so he started picking out people one by one, real elimination now. People don't just disappear in a place this small."

Xander thought back to the room. Matt had lied to him. Even though he had suspected it before, rather Eden had pointed it out to him, he now realized that he couldn't get around it. Matt had lied, really lied. Nobody in that room of bodies had volunteered. They had been selected by someone else and hidden there until room could be found for them again.

"They're not dead," Xander said, volunteering the information even as the floating bodies came back to him. He had trusted Matt when Matt said they weren't dead, but it wasn't as though Xander had checked their pulses. What if they were dead?

"What do you mean?" the nicer girl asked. She looked intently at Xander, and he took a deep breath. He couldn't hold back now.

"They're...sleeping," he tried to explain. "There wasn't enough space for them so they were put into stasis."

The kitchen grew quiet as the stirring, chopping, and opening and closing of cabinets ceased. Xander glanced around to see everyone watching him. "You really don't know?" he asked, even though it was obvious.

"How would you know that?" someone asked.

"Because..." Xander had already shared the information, but he didn't have to give out Matt's name. "Because I got lost and found a room. And I saw them all there."

"They were still breathing?" someone asked.

Xander nodded.

The nicer girl covered her face with her hands, and Xander could see that she was crying. He laid a hand on her shoulder. "Are you okay?" he asked.

"It's just that my best friend disappeared, and two days before that, she was caught sneaking an extra mouthful of food while we were cooking. I know how serious they say stealing is, but I just couldn't turn her in, and..." she sniffed.

Xander patted her shoulder. "Well, I'm sure she's just one of those in stasis," he said, even though he had no way of being sure of that.

"Can you take me there?" the girl asked, rubbing at her eyes again.

Xander glanced at the others in the kitchen. "I don't know if we're really supposed to go there."

"But we can just look through the window, like you did," the girl suggested. "We don't have to break into the room or anything."

Xander was getting wrapped up in his lie. He didn't think there had even been a window in the door, but he couldn't be sure. Every time he thought of the room, he just remembered the rows and rows of floating bodies.

"I didn't say there was a window," Xander said. "Besides, I don't want to get in trouble."

"What floor is it on? We can figure out a way to see what's going on."

"Third floor," Xander answered reluctantly.

"Okay, I'll find it myself then." The girl's eyes slid to the clock. "As soon as our shift is over."

Xander had four and a half hours to think about how he was going to keep this girl from going to the room that held something she wasn't supposed to see. If she discovered that the room didn't have windows, then she would either think he made the thing up or know that he had gone inside. And if she knew that he had gone inside, then she would deduce that someone had let him, which could get Matt in serious trouble.

Someone else motioned for him to take the pot of sludge out to the main eating area, and Xander did so, remembering that the main problem here was cut rations. He hungrily remembered the few pieces of cucumber he had stolen the day before.

A line of people stretched in front of him, and Xander returned to the kitchen for a spoon. "Half portions!" someone commanded him as they prepared bowls to send out to the serving line.

Apparently, Xander was going to be the face of the cut rations. Great. He was sure everyone would be pleased with him. The first person grabbed a bowl and shoved it toward him. Xander carefully measured the spoon so that it wasn't quite full and slopped the mixture into the bowl.

"New guy," the large second person in line said. "You're supposed to fill it up."

Xander looked at the bigger guy in line. He could take him if it came to wrestling, but he didn't want to risk spilling the hot mixture and burning people. The last thing anyone needed was Eden treating a burn. Xander smiled a little at the thought.

"What are you smiling for?" someone else asked him.

The first person still hadn't moved as she looked at her bowl forlornly. "They're right," she said, speaking up in a mousy voice. "Everyone gets the same amount."

Xander glanced at the big pot, then at the line of people. No way was this one pot going to feed everyone if he gave them full bowls, and he would be one of the last to eat. He didn't want it to run out. What had happened to the other pot he had seen?

"Those are my orders," he said, holding his hands up innocently. "If you have a problem with it," he jerked his thumb over his shoulder, having no problem throwing his coworkers to the wolves, "they are the ones that make the decisions."

After a moment's pause, the bigger guy marched toward the kitchen. The first person in line finally stepped aside, and Xander began serving the smaller portions, everyone grumbling as they received theirs.

Xander had to shut his ears so that he didn't hear each comment. The bigger guy finally returned from the kitchen and accepted his half-bowl begrudgingly. Xander wasn't sure what everyone had said in the kitchen to convince him to take it, but he was surprisingly relaxed about it.

Once everyone had been served, Xander returned to the kitchen for his bowl. There would be no need to clean the big pot today, because he had scraped it clean trying to get just a little more for the last few people in line.

Relieved, Xander picked up the cold bowl waiting on the table. His stomach grumbled, but Xander wasn't sure if it was in appreciation or disgust. He didn't care. He shoved the food down his throat and hoped that his stomach would stop threatening a rebellion.

The kind girl sidled up to him while he was eating. "I don't think I told you my name," she said. "It's Emily."

"Xander," Xander said, using his finger instead of his spoon to fully get out the chunks stuck to the side of his bowl.

"Please, after our shift will you show me the room? I won't tell anyone it was you that-"

Emily was interrupted by a screeching noise. Xander whipped his head up to the speaker in the ceiling as he gritted his teeth. "Emergency meeting in the dining room. Everyone currently on shift may leave their shift to attend the meeting, except for those in the bridge. Please go to the dining room immediately."

Xander glanced around at the others to gather some clue as to the purpose of this meeting. All of them looked just as confused as he was. Xander wiped his hands on a towel nearby and placed his bowl in the sink to be washed soon.

Then, he followed the others out to the dining room where most people were staring at their empty bowls longingly or hanging out in lazy groups since they didn't work until the afternoon. The room seemed too small for the number of people in it, but Xander was also fairly sure that it was the largest room in the place.

He studied the people entering and saw Eden come in. She was still wearing the white medical coat. Xander lifted his hand and waved, but she didn't see him. She stood against the wall with the rest of the medical team, crossing her arms and looking worried.

Finally, the flow of entrants slowed, and Xander looked around for someone to take charge. There was some movement on the other side of the room, and Xander craned his neck so that he could see a bit better.

A dark head of hair rose above the rest of the crowd, and Xander determined that the man was standing on the one table in the place. He nodded to everyone with one of those fake smiles plastered on his face.

"I hope everyone is doing well. Sorry to interrupt your daily schedules, but we have a problem that needs everyone's attention."

Xander's heart sped up as he realized that this young guy must be their "leader." No wonder such poor decisions were being made. Xander wasn't saying that older people made better decisions than young ones, but he looked like he could be Xander's age. No facial hair despite the fact that hair cuts and razors seemed few and far between, and his dark, curly hair looked like something an eighteen-year-old would sport rather than someone in a position of leadership.

The man held his hand up, and Xander remembered that someone had called him Roman. "The truth is that we have detected an asteroid headed in our direction."

Xander noticed how carefully he worded his announcement. He wanted to keep people from panicking, so he didn't give them the details that if they didn't change their course (and they had no ability to do so at the moment), then they would die.

"We have about a week until it reaches us, but we're hoping to break it up before that happens."

A couple of people close to Xander started whispering. Even though they were trying to be quiet, Xander could hear their conversation perfectly well.

"An asteroid? What's that?"

"It's something in space. It sounds like something we learned about in science class."

"You were paying attention in science? I never did."

Xander shifted away from the whisperers so that he could hear Roman better. "We aren't sure how to stop it, so we need every mind thinking about it. No idea is dumb or useless. It just might work. If you have an idea and it works, you'll be rewarded with your choice."

Xander heard the unspoken clause- if we survive. He took a deep breath and let it out slowly. This was exactly what they should do- get everyone focused on the problem at hand so that they had a hope of solving it.

"If you *do* have a suggestion, please bring it to the bridge at any time of the day or night." Roman paused and looked down, folding his fingers together in a steeple as the buzz rose around him.

Now that Xander knew who was in charge in this place, he wanted to talk to him face-to-face. He started shouldering his way through the crowd, though people were so distracted by the recent information that they didn't seem to notice him trying to push past them.

"Excuse me. Excuse me. Excuse me," Xander said so many times that it started to sound like a strange mantra.

"Xander?" Eden asked. Xander's eyes flicked to where she was; two bodies were in between them. Xander reached his hand toward her, but looked back at Roman while he waited for Eden to catch up. He didn't want to lose sight of him.

Roman still stood in the same spot. Xander could see that a couple of people at his feet were asking him questions, but he didn't appear to be answering them.

Roman cleared his throat, but it wasn't enough to break through the cacophony of conversation around them. He waved his hand, and a few voices quieted. Slowly, the rest of the occupants of the room followed suit until there were just a few voices still whispering in different parts of the space.

"There is another thing," Roman said. He looked up, and Xander could read his face a lot better now that he was closer. There was worry clearly etched into his features- the way his mouth trembled as he spoke and his eyes darted from person to person in search of comfort. "We don't have enough food to support the new arrivals and ourselves. We need a solution that will keep everyone fed. In two days, we will have another meeting to discuss your ideas. We'll also have a vote. We are open to anything."

Then, Roman stepped off the table in one smooth motion. "Hey!" Xander called out to him, not sure if the name he had overheard was correct. "Roman, I want to speak to you."

Xander wasn't the only one calling out to him, though. Others, too, were shouting questions like they were the paparazzi. "What about the people who have been disappearing?" someone asked.

"Are you going to kill everyone else to save yourself?" someone asked.

"We need a new leader!"

A couple of people cursed at Roman, and Xander understood why he disappeared without answering their questions. It wasn't as though he had conjured the asteroid himself or asked for a hundred or two of the eliminated to be shipped there.

All the more reason for Xander to talk to him up close and see how genuine he was.

"We're going to die!" someone wailed. "The asteroid is going to kill us!"

A couple of other people started panicking, and Xander didn't want to be there if a stampede broke out. He reached behind him and clasped Eden's hand. "Let's get out of here," he told her.

"What about our shifts?" she asked. "I'm supposed to be in the medical center until twelve."

"I'll walk you there," Xander suggested. He knew that Eden wouldn't break the "rules" even if no one else cared about them, but he sure wasn't going back into the kitchen to slave away at making gruel for nothing.

Once they were free from the main room, the rest of the station was surprisingly quiet. Xander didn't let go of Eden's hand as they walked.

"What are you going to do?" Eden asked. "I've seen that look on your face before. You're planning something."

"I'm going to talk to Roman."

"Ro-what?"

"That guy? I'm pretty sure his name is Roman. I'm going to talk to him and get all the details. I'm not going to die. I mean, I know I volunteered for that, but...I'd rather stop it if we can."

Eden looked down at the ground, and Xander studied her from the side. He could see the fear taking hold. "I'm scared about how that's even possible. The scientists from Earth obviously don't want us to come back. They've eliminated all of us, but what if we *did* come back? I mean, if our families knew that we were alive all this time, then they surely wouldn't make us go back, right? I mean, our families would stand up for us."

Xander could see Eden's vision. "Your idea makes sense, but the problem is the reality of it. How would we all be able to get back there? This thing doesn't have any controls."

"I don't know."

Xander heard the fear in Eden's voice, and he squeezed her hand. "Hey, don't worry. I'm sure we'll figure something out. We have to." He didn't want to think about the alternative.

Ahead, the medical center's door stood out against the others.

Xander stopped in front of it and squeezed Eden's hand again. "Good luck with your shift," he said.

"Thanks," Eden murmured. She slowly released her grasp on his hand, then pushed through the door. Xander stood there for a minute as his thoughts threaded through his brain, trying to put together a plan that made sense. He wasn't going to just accept this fate the way he had accepted so much from his superiors over the years.

Chapter 13

Eden was the only one in the medical center, and she looked around help-lessly. Where was everyone else? They still had another four hours of their shift, but she was the only one there. Even the guy who had been sched-uled for surgery had left the place to attend the meeting.

Eden settled onto a stool and waited for someone to come back and tell her what she could do. She hadn't finished her oatmeal-like substance, but she didn't really have the stomach for it right now anyway. She stared at her forgotten bowl forlornly.

The minutes on the clock ticked away, and no one entered the medical center's doors. Surely the rest of the medical team would be there in a couple of minutes. She stood up and went to a drawer, organizing its contents metic-ulously as a way to keep herself busy.

When she looked at the clock again, she saw that more than twenty min-utes had passed.

"Where *is* everyone?" Eden asked, peering out the little glass window beside the door. She could see movement in the hallway, so she opened the door, thinking she could usher the rest of the medical team inside. None of the people were coming toward her, though.

Eden stood in the open doorway, unsure what to do. She was *supposed* to be working, but where was everyone else?

Unsettled, Eden closed the door again and lay on one of the beds that was used for operations. Her mind wandered back to the announcement and what it meant for everyone. She had already had a day to digest the news, but everyone else was hearing it for the first time. They were probably panicking, but that didn't mean they could leave their jobs undone.

The door swung open, and Eden leaped up from the bed, trying to act as though she had been waiting at attention the whole time.

She saw that it wasn't one of the medics, though. It was someone else.

"Can you help me?" the guy asked.

Eden brushed her hair behind her ear and studied the guy from head to toe, trying to see if there was an obvious problem. The guy was clutching his hand and wincing.

"Come sit here." Eden pointed to the bed where she had just been lying. She tried to sound older than she was, but she really had no idea what she was supposed to do. She knew some basic first aid from taking care of herself, but she wasn't ready to see an open wound.

"What happened?" Eden asked, approaching the side of the bed where he had settled.

"My hand," the guy said, slowly uncradling it. Eden could see blood from a distance, so she immediately went to the drawer and started getting out some gauze and other basic materials that she could use to patch up the wound. But no way was she going to perform any sort of surgery.

"How did you hurt it?" Eden asked again, keeping her back to the mess.

"I fell when everyone was leaving the dining hall. A couple people stepped on it."

So, it probably wasn't broken...maybe. Taking a deep breath, Eden turned around with her materials and placed them on the bed next to him. "Give me your hand please," she said, feeling strange about just taking the guy's hand.

He slowly held it out to her, and his whole hand was shaking. "On a scale of one to ten, how painful does it feel?" Eden asked. That was something her mom always asked her. She didn't know if it was official hospital lingo, but it seemed like it would be helpful.

"Six, uh no, seven," the guy told her.

Eden held his clammy hand in hers as she wiped at the blood to see how bad the actual wound was. Once the blood was cleared away, Eden could see that his thumb bone was bent in a direction it shouldn't go. Bracing herself, Eden reached toward the end of his thumb and gently moved it back into place.

The guy screamed and yanked his hand away, holding it to his chest again.

Eden's whole body shook. She should just tell him that she didn't know what she was doing. She couldn't actually help him. He needed one of the medics here.

"Maybe we should wait until the other medics return," Eden suggested.

The guy didn't engage in conversation with her. He just cradled his hand and closed his eyes, rocking back and forth slightly. Eden paced to the door of the medical center, hoping she would see one of the other white coats just outside. However, when she looked outside and saw a couple of people running down the hall, none of them toward her, she panicked.

"I actually don't know where they are. They must have gotten sidetracked on their way back here," Eden suggested, trying to keep her voice panic-free.

"Do you have anything for the pain?" the guy asked, and Eden went to the drawers where the cups of liquid were, the ones they used to trick people into thinking they were giving pain medication. Eden touched the base of one. Should she be honest or help him in the only way she might be able to?

"No," she said, turning around.

The guy's eyes flickered open. "Nothing?"

Eden swallowed and shook her head. "I'm sorry," she apologized. "This is my second day here. I just came with the other eliminated, so I don't really know much about this place."

The guy muttered something that Eden couldn't hear. She leaned forward a little bit. "What was that?"

"Just my luck!" he almost shouted. "I can't even enjoy my last few days because my thumb is broke!" He clenched his teeth and folded into the bed. Eden glanced at the door again, but no one was coming to save her.

She decided to have a look through the cabinets to see if there was really nothing that could help him. Besides, that was better than standing beside the bed and staring at the guy as he suffered.

After sorting through some cabinets, Eden realized how few medical supplies there were. Even some of the basics like rubbing alcohol and painkillers were nonexistent. This place really wasn't designed to be able to last very long.

The guy wouldn't stop groaning in pain, and Eden needed someone to help her deal with this. She couldn't just leave him there, but she also couldn't just while away her shift with someone in pain.

"I'm going to go find some of the other medics," she said, feeling nervous about leaving the medical center during her shift. "I'll be back. I don't know how long it will take me, but I'll be back, okay?"

The guy didn't respond, but Eden was pretty sure he had heard her. Pulling her white coat further around her shoulders, she stepped out of the medical center and decided to do a methodic sweep of the place. It shouldn't take her long if she walked up and down the hallways one by one. She might not be able to find everyone, but she should be able to find at least one medic.

Eden started down the main hallway of the first floor, peeking down the side hallways as she went. She was halfway down the hall when she realized that the medics might not be just hanging out in the halls. They could have gone into their rooms or given up altogether.

Forcing herself to remain calm, Eden continued her sweep of the place. When she was almost done with the first floor, she heard a familiar voice down the hallway to the left. It was Xander, and Eden already knew what was down that hallway- the room with all the bodies.

Eden turned down the hallway and followed Xander's voice. What was he doing out of the kitchen?

"...don't remember the code."

Eden turned the corner of the side hallway and saw Xander standing in front of the off-limits door with another girl. She blinked a time or two like maybe the image would disappear if she just cleared her eyesight. But it didn't.

"I thought you said there was a window."

"I never said that. The truth is... someone let me in, but I can't tell who that is or I might get in trouble."

Eden opened her mouth to say something, but nothing sounded right. She was still working her jaw up and down when Xander turned and saw her.

"Oh! Eden!" he said in a weirdly high voice, a voice that didn't belong to him. The girl turned around, and she was just as beautiful as she had looked from the back. She had long, blonde hair and the kind of large eyes that made her look like some sort of Barbie.

"What are you doing here?" Xander asked.

"I'm...looking for the doctors," Eden explained, answering his question like the good little girl she was instead of asking her own.

"Nobody on here is really a doctor," Xander mumbled, but Eden wasn't looking at him.

"What...are you two doing here?" she asked.

The blonde girl looked at Xander as though waiting for his permission to give information. It hurt, it really hurt, the clear camaraderie between the two of them. How had they managed to become such good friends when they had only been here a couple of days? Unless...maybe Xander had known her before. Was she recently eliminated?

Eden's panicked thoughts were interrupted by the girl. "Xander was just showing me around the place. Do you know Xander?"

"I need to...go find the medics," Eden said, dropping her eyes and turning to go back to the main hallway. A few people passed by the entrance to the main hallway, almost bowling her over. Eden took a step back to avoid losing a toe or two, and Xander used that time to catch up to her.

"Emily, I'll see you later," Xander told her, calling over his shoulder. Her name was Emily. Eden stored that information away for later.

"I have to find the medics," Eden told him instead of engaging him in conversation.

"Are you okay?"

"It's not me. Someone has a broken bone, and I can't take care of that on my own. I don't know where they went." Eden's worst fear was being left alone, and even though there were people all around her, she had never felt more alone than right here- in the middle of a situation where everyone else had more important things on their minds.

"I'll help you," Xander announced, and he walked beside Eden as they climbed the stairs to the second floor. There wasn't much to see on that floor besides a few open doors to the bedrooms. Voices floated out, and all of the discussions were about the same topic- one Eden wanted to push out of her mind.

"So, what happened?" Xander asked her as they walked. Eden peered into a room they were passing. Were the medics still in the dining hall? She should have looked in there first. She made a move to turn around, but Xander touched her elbow and guided her to keep going.

"This guy hurt his hand. That's all I know."

A couple of people ran past them, brushing into Eden so that she stumbled. Even though she would normally consider herself the more forgiving type, she threw the group a dirty look as she brushed at her jacket and kept going.

"I mean with you. You look...upset. I get it. There's a lot going on right now, but we already knew about all this."

Eden wanted to snap back with a smart comeback about how she hadn't known he had another girlfriend, but she didn't say anything. Her mother had drilled into her head the saying that if she didn't have something nice to say, then she shouldn't say anything at all. Right now, Eden's mouth was glued shut, because only mean things were passing through her head.

"Eden? Hello?" Xander's voice had changed from concerned to irritated. Eden had seen him ticked at people before- other students, competitors, teachers, his parents... but never her. She just shrugged.

"I don't know what's going to happen, okay? We could die in a few days, but we might not."

"It's bothering me too," Xander responded in a gentler voice.

Eden glanced over her shoulder. She felt like Emily was still watching them. There were lots of people in the hallways running from room to room, but no Emily.

"Who was that girl?" Eden finally asked. She could hear the annoyance in her own voice, but it was the calmest tone she had at the moment.

"Oh? Emily? She works with me in the kitchen. She said that her best friend disappeared, so I told her about that room. I thought her best friend might be one of those...people."

Eden's eyes widened not because he thought it was a good idea to just share Matt's secrets, but because she was worried about his collusion with Emily. It wasn't like the two of them had been holding hands or kissing or anything. Still, she hadn't liked how close they were standing. Why hadn't he told her about working with Emily yesterday?

At the end of the second floor, they climbed the stairs to the third floor. Eden spotted a white coat on the floor almost immediately. She stepped forward and picked it up, looking underneath it as though one of the medics might be hiding there.

"Where are they?" Eden asked. As far as she could see down the main hallway of the third floor, there were no medics. For the first time, she wondered what she would do if she had to return to the medical center without a medic in tow.

"I don't know, but Eden, even if you find one of them, they might not be willing to help."

"What do you mean?"

"I mean that they're going to die in a few days. Everyone probably will, and that makes people crazy."

"So they just give up? That's not fair! They should still take care of people!" Eden clutched the white coat and marched down the hallway, angrily glancing in the public rooms and peering in the windows of the locked ones.

"Nobody. Nobody!" she said once she got to the end. She knew that she was getting worked up now, but she couldn't help it. All she could think about was going back downstairs to the medical center and having to face the guy and tell him that there weren't any medics willing to do their job.

"Eden, you just have to let this go," Xander told her. "You've tried your best. You just have to accept that you can't help him right now."

Eden shook her head. She wasn't sure why this bothered her so much. It wasn't *her* bone that was broken, but she imagined him waiting and waiting and waiting for her to return with some help. Maybe she could try to fix it after all. She had learned a little bit in biology class. She had never set a bone before, but she knew there was some pushing, then using something to hold it in place. That was all medics normally did, right? Sometimes, there would be stitches, but she would just skip that part.

"Well, he shouldn't have to be alone," Eden said. "I'm going back down there. I told him I would come back, and I'm not going to just walk away from that."

"Okay." Xander glanced back the way they had come. "I'm going to speak to my brother. I'll see you later, okay?"

Eden didn't want him to go just yet. "When?" she asked, wondering if he would be impossible to find like the medics.

"I'll see you at lunch in the dining hall, okay?"

Eden nodded, and Xander headed back down the hallway while Eden went to the stairs. Her stomach reminded her that she hadn't finished her portion of breakfast, the portion that had seemed smaller today than it had been yesterday. Maybe she was just imagining things, but it worried her.

When Eden reached the medical center again, she braced herself before going inside. The guy was still lying there, but his groaning sounds had lowered in volume. Eden approached him on tiptoe, and his eyes snapped open. Of course he hadn't been asleep. What had she been thinking? When someone is in that kind of pain, they can't just drift off.

"Where are the medics?" he asked gruffly.

Eden held up the discarded coat unhelpfully. "I couldn't find any of them. I looked everywhere."

The guy stood up and shook his head at her, then pushed his way out of the medical center. The door swung shut harshly behind him, and Eden was alone once more. She had tried; she had really tried. But that didn't matter. She hadn't been able to help him. Now, Eden was left on her own again, and all she could think about was the giant ton of rock that was headed in their direction at this very moment.

Chapter 14

Xander knocked on the door to the bridge. A group of people were milling outside the door, and he could feel them staring at him as he waited for the door to be opened.

"You have an idea?" someone asked him. "Are you some scientist or something?"

Xander folded his arms. "No, but I have an idea."

"What?" someone else joined the conversation. Xander glanced at each of them, and he could feel the desperation in their faces.

"I have to see what sort of supplies are on this ship, before I know if it would work or not," he responded, purposely keeping his answer mysterious.

He actually had *no* idea. He just wanted the chance to talk with his brother, Matt. The sound of voices and movement filtered through the door, but no one opened it.

Xander made a fist and gave three more hard knocks. After another short wait, the door finally opened. The face behind it wasn't Matt's, and the woman didn't look amused.

"Can I help you?" she asked.

"I need to talk to Matt," Xander said, trying to see behind the woman.

"I'm taking all ideas," the woman told him in a bored voice.

"I understand that," Xander responded, keeping his tone even. "I'd just like to speak to Matt when he's available. If I need to wait a few minutes, that's fine."

The woman shook her head. "This isn't a party. We're actually doing real work in here. I don't know why Roman..." she muttered something Xander couldn't hear.

"Matt?" Xander asked in a somewhat loud voice. Maybe his brother would hear him and come out.

The woman just narrowed her eyes at him and shut the door. Xander marched back across the hall, narrow though it was, and found a place to settle against the wall.

Someone who looked vaguely familiar sat next to him. "They don't seem too happy to answer any questions, do they?" he asked.

"No," Xander responded. He needed to think, not talk to someone, but this person insisted on invading his personal space and thoughts as well.

"Maybe if we stormed the door, they would have to listen to us."

"The last thing anyone on this space station needs is to get desperate," Xander told the other guy. "We're already pretty miserable, but if everyone starts going crazy, then people could end up dead."

The guy's eyes widened. "Whoa! You serious?! Dead?" He kind of laughed. "I guess it doesn't matter when everyone's going to be dead in a few days anyway. I could stab you right now, and you would bleed out on the floor and die. But hey, maybe that's a better way to go than having an asteroid slam your face in."

Xander didn't like the glint in the guy's eyes, and he stood up to put some distance between the two of them. "I guess you could," he said, entertaining the guy's bloody scenario. "But the thing is that I don't die easily."

The guy laughed, one of those laughs that showed he wasn't really enjoying himself but desperately searching for some sort of fun. "I guess..."

"Besides, if you did that, it would guarantee your death even if this place did survive the asteroid."

"You think there's a chance?" the guy asked.

"There's a chance," someone else answered. "If they didn't think there was a chance we could be saved, then they wouldn't be asking us for ideas. They're hopeless, but they must think it's possible."

Xander glanced at the closed door again. He wasn't willing to wait with this strange collection of people any longer. He approached the door to the bridge and knocked, trying to make his knock sound distinct from his last one. He heard a raised voice behind the door, then it opened.

This time, it was Matt.

"Can I talk to you?"

Matt glanced at the people behind Xander before his eyes rested on him again. He shrugged. "I guess." He stepped aside just enough for Xander to slip into the bridge, and he did, not wanting to give anyone behind Matt the chance to intercept him.

Matt secured the door behind him while Xander took in the room. There was a big panel with an array of buttons on one side of the room. A large screen with several different camera views rested above the panel. Xander's eyes skipped from one image to the next.

Each one displayed a different angle from outside the space station. One was pointed back at the station itself. But in one, a view that must have been purposely made larger than the others, Xander could see something that looked like a rock hanging there in space. It wasn't very big, but he wondered if this was the asteroid that had everyone panicking.

The woman who had refused him entrance narrowed her eyes at him but didn't say anything about his presence.

"Why are you here?" Matt asked, returning to his seat at a computer. Xander stood behind his brother. He could hear the exhaustion in his voice. It had not been an easy day for him.

"Roman, that's his name, right?"

Matt nodded in the affirmative.

"He made a nice announcement. I didn't see you there, but I'm assuming you know about it."

"Yes, we couldn't leave this part of the ship unattended, and we already knew what he was going to say anyway." Matt rubbed at his forehead.

"So...that has started spinning everything out of control. Eden is losing her mind because people have dared to not return for their shifts." Xander chuckled, even though the end of the world wasn't funny. "Has anything come of Roman telling everyone? Any ideas?"

"One of the new guys stepped forward." Matt pointed to the corner of the room where someone was working hard hunched over a computer. "It seems like he's pretty smart after all."

Xander thought about Colt. Colt had been a genius, but he hadn't won a medal. Even though he had gone his whole life thinking quite differently, Xander now believed that the Olympics didn't accurately measure someone's potential to contribute to society.

"So there's hope?" Xander asked, trying to see what was being done on the computer.

Matt shrugged. "I don't think I've ever let go of hope completely, but I also can't let go of reality."

"And reality is..."

"We're going to die, man. If it's not this, it will be something else."

Xander was about to say something about how it sure seemed like Matt had let go of hope completely, but he could see the fear in Matt's eyes. He was scared of what was going to happen, and that sent a bolt of fear through Xander as well. Matt had always been someone who knew what he was doing. Now, he looked lost.

"You can't think like that." Xander put a hand on Matt's shoulder. He glanced back at the camera with the rock-like thing in the middle of its view. It didn't look like it had moved. "Look, I want to help. I'd be more help here than in the kitchen stirring the gross stuff they call food."

Matt's lips formed a grim smile. "I don't think there's any way you can help," he said. "We can't do anything. We aren't equipped with any weapons. I mean...there *were* some here at one time, but whoever brilliantly decided that we should occupy this place dismantled them before letting us on board. I guess they couldn't take the chance that we would shoot the rockets back at them."

"Wait? So there are rockets somewhere?"

"Are you listening? They've been dismantled."

"Yeah, but something that's dismantled can be put back together." Xander leaned forward, searching Matt's computer screen shamelessly as though it held the answer to his question.

"Okay, then, dismantled isn't the right word. Destroyed? Does that work? They're not functional, and no amount of mechanical engineering is going to change that. The only thing that might still work from them are the thrusters."

The guy in the far corner jumped up and pumped his fist in the air. Everyone in the room turned to him, waiting for an explanation as to his celebration.

"I think it will work," he said sheepishly when he realized everyone was watching him. Xander drifted over after the others as they waited for his explanation. "Based on the materials you said are here, we could build a ship, a small one, and use the thrusters from the old rockets to power it."

"But will it be strong enough to destroy the asteroid?" someone asked.

"No," the speaker shook his head. "But that's going to be impossible. I mean, we don't know how big it is, but based on what you guys showed me, it's pretty big."

"So, you're thinking it's a rescue ship?" someone else asked.

Xander was equally as confused. What was the point of building a tiny ship if it wouldn't accommodate everyone or destroy the asteroid?

"No...I think if the thrusters give it enough power, we can change the asteroid's course."

Matt shook his head and made eye contact with Xander. He leaned closer and whispered. "This guy doesn't have anything. We've thought of that before, but the problem is that we have no way to steer it."

"Can we aim it toward Earth?" someone asked.

Another person laughed, but Xander was thinking. He wasn't supposed to be there, but he had to know more about this plan. "Are you saying that you can build this thing?" he asked. "Or you just think it's possible?"

"I mean...I've never used a hammer before," the guy responded sheepishly. "But I know it could be done. The problem is that there would be no way to control it from here. A group of people would need to go in the...rocket or whatever you want to call it and guide it toward the asteroid."

"But won't the rocket be destroyed when it hits the asteroid?" someone else asked.

"Yes," the guy nodded. There was no question about it. He was asking for someone to sacrifice his or her life. At first, the idea hit Xander hard. No one here would be willing to sacrifice their life, but then...everyone would die if no one stepped up.

"How fast can you build it?" someone else asked him.

"I...can't build it, but I can draw up the plans. Someone else can build it," the guy looked hopeful.

"Okay, I'll bring Roman here, and you can explain it to him," someone said. The woman hurried out of the room, and Xander melted into the back of the crowd, considering what this new plan was.

"How many people will need to be on there?" he asked.

"Two," the guy held up his fingers as though Xander might have trouble deciphering spoken numbers. "It could probably fit up to four or five." He shrugged. "But why take more than you need?"

Xander nodded. Why indeed?

Matt grabbed Xander's arm and pulled him over to the corner. "Roman is going to ask for volunteers to man the rocket," he said. "Volunteers to die."

The words cut through Xander, but he nodded. It made sense. If they selected someone who deserved to die, like Derry, then he would just steer the rocket off course and let them all die. It had to be someone who was willing to give up his life for others.

"Do you think it will be hard to find volunteers?" Xander asked.

Matt cocked his head for a second. "I don't know. But I think we should do it."

Xander's heart automatically sped up, and he studied his brother. "You want to...you and me? I don't know about that."

"Scared?" Matt asked.

Xander took a deep breath and shrugged. "Not scared, just not sure I can choose death knowing there's no chance of it not ending that way."

"You chose to be eliminated. Isn't that the same thing? You got a few extra days to live. Now, I'm asking you to do it with me."

"Why do you want to do it?" Xander couldn't understand his brother's reasoning. The kind of person who would volunteer his life for others...well, that didn't strike him as who his brother was. But then again, he had seen the constant lack of hope hanging around his brother's head. Maybe his brother was ready to be done with his life.

"It's better to go out as someone respected, right? A name that will be remembered by everyone here is better than to just die with everyone else?"

Xander took a deep breath. "Can I think about it? Do I have to agree right now?"

"It would be better if we had already agreed to it before Roman gets here and takes this guy's idea."

"Okay," Xander finally said, wondering if there was an escape clause. Maybe since he had just said "okay," and not "I'll do it," then it didn't really count as agreeing?

"Let's see if they can get it built first."

The door flew open, almost hitting the opposite wall, and Xander got a close-up look at Roman. "Tell me about this solution," Roman commanded.

Matt stood next to Xander as the scientific nerd explained once again what he thought. Xander thought over Matt's proposal. If the asteroid was set to hit the space station in a week or so, they would probably need to leave in the next day or two. That meant that he didn't have very much time with Eden left.

"Let's do it," Roman said with a nod of approval. "Does anyone know someone who could follow his directions and build the thing?" He looked around at the group.

No one said anything, and Roman rolled his eyes. "Right, because all you want is someone else to save you. I'll find someone to build it," he said. "But then, we'll need two volunteers. You said, two, right?"

The science guy nodded.

"Two volunteers. If no one steps up, I'll have to select someone." Roman was starting to go on about how everyone would die if no one was willing to do it, but he didn't have to conclude his speech.

Matt stepped forward. "My brother and I will go," he said.

The group's eyes turned from Matt to Xander, and Xander felt the pressure of their gazes.

"Well, that was easier than I expected," Roman said. He stepped over and clapped them each on the shoulder in turn. "We'll see how fast we can get this built. Meanwhile...you two are off duties."

Xander wanted to laugh. They were going to sacrifice their lives, but at least they didn't have to work for the next couple of days. What was he thinking?

Chapter 15

When the clock finally showed that Eden's shift was done, she slowly took off the white coat and mask that she was supposed to wear. She hung them neatly by the door for the next shift, though no one was urgently pushing through the door to face their responsibilities.

Other than the one person she hadn't been able to help, no one else had come into the medical center during her shift. Still, Eden felt as though she had to fulfill her duty and be there for the hours she was assigned.

A bell sounded in the hall, and Eden was reminded of school as she hurried to the dining hall, not sure what might be served at this meal. She was looking forward to seeing Xander though and nervous that she might see that Emily chick again.

The dining hall was swarming with people, and everyone was talking about the asteroid. "If we're going to die, what's the point of this?" the person in front of Eden asked. Eden looked away so that the girl wouldn't direct her comments toward Eden. "I mean, what are we doing waiting here like sheep to die? I'm not just going to wait around and die."

"What? You're going to die early? Maybe then I can enjoy my last few days to live," someone else said.

The first girl shoved the other one, and Eden stepped aside as a shoving match quickly turned into a weird sort of fight that looked nothing like Xander when he wrestled with someone. There was a lot of scratching and squealing.

"Hey! Hey!" a male voice shouted from the other side of the dining hall. The lines had curved to give the girls some space, but everyone continued to move forward and take their ration. The guy made his way over and finally succeeded in pulling them apart. He started lecturing them on how to treat others, and even Eden rolled her eyes.

The girl tried to take her place in front of Eden again, and Eden stepped back to allow her space. She wasn't about to criticize this girl for "cutting."

The girl breathed heavily as she grabbed a bowl of food. "Can you believe this?" she asked, showing Eden a long, red scratch down her arm. "She just attacked me. Apparently, freedom of speech isn't a thing anymore."

Eden nodded to show the girl that she had heard her, but she had nothing to say to this girl, especially considering that the girl had been the one to start the fight. Turning away, Eden searched the dining hall for Xander. She didn't see him anywhere. Just as she was turning back to take her bowl of lunch mush, she realized that she didn't see Emily anywhere either. Where were they?

"Want to sit with us?" Nicole asked Eden as she wandered aimlessly around the room.

Eden nodded and plopped down, grateful to have a place, even if she didn't have anything to say. Her roommates were okay, and it helped that they barely saw each other since they worked opposite shifts. Eden still hadn't really met Jazzy as anything other than a dark-haired head sleeping on a pillow.

"Please tell me you're some sort of genius," Nicole begged as Eden took her first bite. The taste turned her stomach. Even though she had only been here a few days, eating the same nauseating thing so often made her feel sick at just the smell of it. She closed her eyes and forced herself to swallow. It was sustenance, and she couldn't say no to it.

"I'm not," Eden responded, her eyes popping open.

"Ugh, I'm not ready to die," Nicole complained.

Avery looked at the ground sadly. "Maybe there's some sort of afterlife. I keep wondering what happened to Maya, and maybe if there *is* an afterlife, then she's there already, waiting for me."

Avery's somber mood hung over Eden as well now. She wondered who would be waiting for her if she died, not anyone she wanted to see- that was for sure.

Should Eden apologize again for Avery's twin disappearing? She wasn't going to explain what she knew about the bodies in stasis, because at this point, it didn't really matter. In fact, maybe Maya was better off since she couldn't dread what was coming.

Eden scanned the hall again. Most people had received their food now, so they were sitting down. Of the few people standing, none of them were Xander. Where had he gone? How could he have forgotten that he promised to meet her?

"What do you think, Eden? Ready to die?" Nicole asked.

Eden shook her head. "No, but who is? I mean, it's not like we can really do anything about it now."

"You just say that because you thought you were going to die a few days ago. But once you get used to living here, there's something beautiful about it," Nicole said. "There's so many things I have left to do before I die anyway."

"Like what?" Eden took the bait.

"Like...find a boyfriend and see what...that's like."

Eden's cheeks reddened. How could Nicole think about that right now? Eden was still trying to grasp the fact that she might only have a few more days left, and Nicole was looking to have a good time.

"I'm sure some guy will be happy to take you up on that," Avery responded.

"Don't *you* have a boyfriend?" Nicole asked Eden curiously.

"I don't..." Eden stopped herself. Technically, before they had been eliminated, Xander had asked her to be his girlfriend. To be honest, she hadn't thought about that in days because this wasn't the typical next step in a dating relationship- confirm boyfriend/girlfriend titles, kiss, be eliminated, be threatened by a giant asteroid. "Well, yeah, I do," Eden finished answering.

"You don't seem very sure about it." Nicole wiggled her eyebrows and leaned in for the juicy details. "Tell me about him. I've seen you with that one guy. He's got that gorgeous tanned skin, brown hair, and he's well-built. What did he train for?"

"He won a medal in wrestling," Eden told them. She wasn't sure why she wanted the record to be set straight, but Xander...he shouldn't have been eliminated. "And I'm actually supposed to be meeting him right now. The fact that he's not here worries me, so I think I should go look for him."

"Go find your Romeo!" Nicole called after Eden as she rose and forced herself to take the last, large mouthful of food. A couple of heads turned, and Eden lowered her own head so that she didn't have to see the stares.

Once she was out of the dining hall, Eden headed directly toward the off-limits door on the first floor. That was where she had last seen Xander, and she just imagined him standing there again with Emily, trying to break the code on the door for her.

However, when Eden rounded the corner to the door, the hallway was empty. She breathed a sigh of relief and headed toward the bridge. Xander must be with his brother, though if Matt worked a morning shift, Eden wasn't sure why he wouldn't be off yet. Still, it was the only other place she could look, because she couldn't remember Xander's room number.

A few people were gathered outside the door to the bridge, and Eden stopped on the edge of the group, waiting for someone to either move and give her a clear pathway to the door or for someone to let her know what was happening. She remembered that the leader had asked them for ideas to save the station. Maybe all of these people were waiting to share their ideas.

So, Eden leaned patiently against the wall as she waited for something to happen.

Not more than a few minutes later, something *did* happen. The door flew open, and Roman strode out. A mousy guy followed him along with two others. A couple of the people waiting tried to talk to Roman.

"I have an idea," someone said.

"Are we all going to die?"

"Why didn't you tell us about this sooner?"

Roman didn't answer any of them, even as they followed him down the hallway. Only one other person and Eden were left after the group disappeared down the hallway. Eden cautiously approached the door and knocked. No one opened it. She swallowed nervously and knocked again.

Inside the room, she heard a laugh- a familiar laugh. Xander was in there. He had to be. It was all she could do to keep from pounding on the door. This wasn't an emergency. She could wait, but he was right there!

After a few minutes of glancing at the other person waiting and trying to figure out what was the best and most polite thing to do, Eden knocked again at the door, just three little taps, and waited.

She heard something from inside, and Matt's face appeared in the opening between the door and the frame. He looked over his shoulder. "It's your girlfriend," he said.

Eden's face warmed at being called Xander's girlfriend, but that's who she was, right? She couldn't get all embarrassed about it every five minutes.

Matt stood aside and let her through the doorway. Eden was distracted by the tools in the room- the screens, the buttons, and the controls. She didn't look at Xander immediately, but he was already wrapping his arms around her.

"I just remembered that I was supposed to meet you," he said.

Eden snapped back to the reason she had come even though she continued to look at the pictures of...was that outer space?

"Yeah," she said, finally turning her eyes to Xander. He looked sincerely sorry, but then she remembered Emily. "I kept looking for you. I was worried that something had happened. You didn't go to your shift, and..." she let her voice trail off, but she hoped that he caught the disapproval in her voice. Just because an asteroid was threatening them didn't mean that everyone could give up on their jobs. The station would cease to run if they did that.

"Sorry about that. I got caught up talking to Matt and... Roman. Somebody has a plan that might actually work."

Eden stood a little straighter and looked directly at Xander, searching his face for some sign that he was joking. "A real plan? Do *you* think it will work?"

Xander's eyes flicked to Matt. "Yeah, I think so. I'll tell you about it later. Do you want to...take a walk?"

Eden shrugged. "I guess so." Her eyes flitted over all of the equipment again, curious as to what it all did. She had never *loved* science, but the idea of being able to peer out at the stars and...

"Is that it?" she asked, stepping closer to one of the camera views. There was something in the middle of the speckled sky that looked out of place. The rock was an orangish/tan color and didn't seem to be moving.

"I think so," Xander said, coming to stand next to her.

Someone was sitting at the keyboard in front of them, and he turned to give them a dirty look. Xander shrugged and pointed toward the door. Eden started toward the door, and Xander stopped to talk to his brother for a moment. Eden gave them a moment alone as she took her time opening the door, keeping it cracked, even though she had already passed through.

Finally, Xander appeared and swung the door wide open. "Let's go," he said, ushering her outside the bridge.

Once the door thudded shut behind them, Eden looked down the hallways on either side. "Let's go this way," Xander suggested, taking the lead as though he had been on the station a lot longer than she had.

Eden didn't mind. His hand brushed against hers, and she grabbed his fingers, securing his hand in hers. They walked in silence for several minutes. "At least they have a plan they can work toward now," Eden finally said, her thoughts on what Xander had told her about a way to stop the asteroid. "Are you allowed to share what it is?"

In this case, rules or no rules, she wanted to know if the plan was as good as it sounded in theory. She wanted to know the details so she could either rely on it or keep thinking of something else.

"Basically, this guy thinks he can build a sort-of rocket. The rocket will run into the asteroid and turn it off course."

Eden considered the plan for a moment. "You say 'thinks' with a little bit of doubt." She smiled at him. "I know you. You don't think it can really be done."

"It's not that…it's just that I don't know the guy. Why *should* I believe he can do it especially when people have lived here for years and never built anything to leave?"

"I guess they've never been desperate enough. Besides, I'm sure whatever he's building wouldn't really be habitable, for people anyway. He's building it to basically self-destruct, right?"

"Yeah, that's my understanding," Xander responded quietly. Eden had to almost strain to hear him. They turned down a busier hallway, and Eden kept her mouth closed, not sure how much she should say when others might hear them.

Finally, they reached the quietest hallway. At least, it was normally the quietest. Today, though, there were a couple of people running back and forth down the hallway, going toward the door that had remained shut since their arrival.

Eden settled into the carpet anyway, wanting to chat with Xander without walking past everyone's roving eyes. This was as private a place as they were going to find. Xander settled next to her after watching the bustle of activity for another minute.

"Do you think they're working on it right now?" Eden asked in a low voice.

Xander nodded. "I think they're trying to build it as quickly as they can. If it doesn't work...they'll need time to try something else."

"How long is this going to take?"

"Two days."

He sounded so confident in his answer, so sure that he was right. Roman must have said something when Xander was in the room. "Good thing he came along then," Eden said. "Or we might not have figured that out. He'll be some sort of hero if it works."

"I guess." Xander shrugged.

Eden thought she detected something like worry in his voice. "Are you doing okay?" she asked. "You seem weird."

Xander smiled his familiar, lopsided grin. "I'm always weird, but I appreciate you noticing today."

Eden nudged him with her shoulder. She thought about what Nicole had said about wanting to take advantage of the last few days of life. She had barely felt comfortable *kissing* Xander. There was no way she would take it further. Besides, it seemed like they weren't going to die after all.

Eden watched Xander watch them work. "What if..." Eden started as someone came down the hallway carrying a few squares of metal that she recognized as the paneling on the ship that had brought her here. "What if they have a really good idea, but they don't build it correctly?" Her eyes flicked to the long row of windows, but she couldn't see anything from here- no menacing-looking rock headed in their direction.

"Let's hope that's not the case."

Eden leaned her head against Xander's shoulder. Something was up with him, but everyone deserved a day to be broody after being eliminated, then shoved on a space station they had never known existed and told they were going to die in a few days.

She just sat in silence with him, hoping that the silence was what he needed.

"What do you think it will be like to live here?" she asked after a long silence. "I mean, let's assume that the asteroid is destroyed and everything. Do you think you'll work in the kitchen forever?"

"No," Xander answered.

"No?" he sounded so ominous. "Where do you want to work? I mean, if you got to choose. And I think we should be able to choose, at least somewhat."

"Eden," Xander said, and she detected a note of exhaustion or frustration in his voice. "Eden, I don't think this is what you're wanting."

"What do you mean?" She lifted her head from his shoulder and studied his face.

"I mean that I don't want to talk about the future. The future may not even exist. Let's just focus on these next couple of days."

"I thought we had at least a week until the asteroid is here. Do they think it's sooner now?"

Xander sighed, and Eden knew that she was frustrating him, but she wasn't sure why. He was acting strangely, and she didn't appreciate it. "Okay, here's the thing. This rocket or ship or whatever you want to call it that they're building can't be powered from here. It has to have someone inside to power it- two people according to the person who has designed it."

"O...kay," Eden responded, frowning. That didn't seem like a brilliant plan. Let's build something that will be destroyed but put people in it while that's happening.

"And Matt volunteered to go. He asked me to go with him, and I said yes."

Eden blinked as she tried to understand what Xander was saying. "Are you telling me that you volunteered to *die*?" she asked, gripping his arm tightly.

Xander slowly pried at the tips of her fingers so that she let up on the pressure. "You could put it that way."

"But you can't!" Eden stood. She couldn't stay seated after being told something like that. "Why would you do that?"

"I've done it before. I mean, being eliminated was as good as...death." Xander slid up the wall so that he was standing too.

"Yeah, but that was different."

"How?"

Eden didn't like the way he was challenging her, as though she were seeing everything wrong, and he was the only one who understood things correctly.

"Because...you were doing it with me. And...I wouldn't have let you do that either if I had known you were doing it."

"Glad to know what I would or wouldn't have your permission to do," Xander said. He was joking with her, but this was *not* something to joke about.

"Xander!" Eden said. Someone who was walking down the hallway gave them a strange look. Eden stepped around Xander so that her back was to the main part of the hallway and Xander was between her and the wall. "You can't do this. Come *on*! How am I going to survive here without you?" She hated to sound desperate, but he couldn't just give up on life like that.

"Look, someone has to do it. If no one does, then this place doesn't stand a chance."

"Let someone else do it," Eden suggested. "There are hundreds of other people in this place, probably a thousand. I don't know. Just let someone else volunteer."

"And what if no one does?"

Eden's heart beat loudly in her ears, the rushing of her blood sounding like the end of the world rushing in on her.

"Someone will," she said, trying to sound like she fully believed her words. "But *you* can't."

Xander reached for Eden and pulled her into a hug. It wasn't what Eden was expecting. She would have thought he would have kept arguing, but she melted into his arms, hiding her face in his shoulder. She wasn't going to cry. That wasn't going to happen, but she could at least let her emotions pass through her. She had to calm down and talk this through rationally with Xander so that he could see how ridiculous he was being.

She stood there a long time in his arms, his body pressed against hers. Finally, she thought she had enough strength to step back and talk sense into him.

"We were *just* eliminated," she said. "Let someone who was eliminated years and years ago volunteer. They've already had their extra chance at life. We haven't."

Xander placed his hands on both of her shoulders and looked directly into her eyes. "Eden, I'm going to go. I've made up my mind, and I've promised my brother and Roman. I'm not going to go back on that and be a liar. Someone has to do it. This time, that someone is me."

Eden bit the insides of her cheeks in an attempt to not cry, but the tears welled up within her anyway. "Please, Xander. Just think about it. I'm sure someone else is willing to volunteer."

Xander shook his head, stubborn as he had always been. Eden clenched her teeth, trying not to cry, but this time, she failed. A few tears escaped and made their way down her cheeks. She just wanted to be alone, but even her room wouldn't be vacant. Still, it was the only place she had.

"I just...need a few minutes," she said. Turning away from Xander, she hurried to the solace of her bedroom.

Chapter 16

When the alarm went off the next morning, Xander fumbled around to turn it off, his hand missing the thing the first two tries. So much for not having his duties. He still had to wake up at the same time as everyone else. As Xander climbed back into his bed, he could hear the rustle of hurried movement in the hall as everyone rushed to the bathrooms to get ready for their morning shift.

"Get up, man!" Connor urged him after he thumped to the floor. "Time to work."

Xander slurred out an excuse. "Today is my day off."

"Day off?" That woke Connor up even more. "I didn't know we have those."

Xander shut his eyes and tried to sleep again as Connor left the room, but he was already awake. His thoughts started racing. If everything went according to plan, this would be his last day at the station. Tomorrow, he didn't yet know what time, he would follow Matt into this newly built spaceship and hope that it was sophisticated enough to let them complete their mission.

Even though he knew it wasn't a good idea, Xander allowed himself to run through worst-case scenarios. He imagined the ship blowing up as soon as it got away from the space station. They would have sacrificed themselves for nothing.

Then, Xander imagined crawling into the ship and waiting for something to happen, but nothing did. It didn't work, so he would be stuck on the space station dying with everyone else.

Xander shook his head and got out of bed. He had to do something with himself to get his mind off what little of his future was left. The exercise room was calling his name, so he walked briskly down the hall to the machines, planning to see Eden in the medical center after he had received his bowl of slop.

Once in the exercise room, Xander approached the weight-lifting machine. No one else was in the room, and Xander felt like his thoughts had room to expand. He started talking out loud like a lunatic.

"Tomorrow is your last day, but that's okay. A lot of other people will get the chance to live."

Xander shoved the weights above his head and held them there as his arms strained, wanting to push himself past what he normally did. His back protested, but he didn't care.

"Every person you see today gets to live. That's worth it."

Another big push. His arms trembled as he held the weights above his head. Then, he had to focus on breathing as he lifted, and his conversation continued itself in his head.

You were going to die anyway when you gave up your medal. You got a few days extra. Eden will be fine. She'll be fine. Xander echoed that sentiment multiple times as he remembered how she had turned away to hide her tears. But he had known. He had already seen the shining in her eyes as she had tried to hide her face. He knew that he was hurting her.

Part of Xander wanted to grab her and bring her with them, but that would negate the whole point. He was doing this to give her, and everyone else, another chance. He had to be strong and give her that second chance.

Finally, Xander's arms trembled with the effort of lifting the bar over his head again and again. He set the weights down on the ground and stretched out his arms, feeling the burn. Part of him told himself that it was dumb to spend time working out when he wouldn't see the effects of the workout anyway, but the other part of him knew it was the only way to stay sane.

The clock on the wall indicated that it was time for food, and Xander needed sustenance, disgusting or not.

When he reached the dining hall, there were already groups of people sitting around and staring mournfully into their bowls. Xander got in line and shuffled forward slowly as he waited his turn.

When he got to the front of the line, the girl behind the pot gave him a dark look. "What? You're too good to work anymore? You shouldn't get any if you don't show up for your shift."

"I don't have to work today," Xander told her, holding out his bowl.

She narrowed her eyes at him. "We don't get days off."

Xander glanced over his shoulder. Apparently, no one had thought it would be important to inform Matt and Xander's workmates about the whole "no duties for the last two days of your life" thing.

"You can ask Roman." Xander finally shrugged. An animalistic urge to grab some food and go almost overcame him. He was hungry and wanted to eat right then. If he didn't get something in his cavern of a stomach, then he wasn't sure he would be responsible for his actions.

"I'm hungry," he told her. "I need to eat." He held his bowl out a little more forcefully, almost in her face.

"I don't know about this," the girl said. She looked at the almost empty pot, then the line of people behind Xander. "I'm going to ask Sarah." Then, the girl disappeared into the kitchen.

Xander shook his head, not about to wait for her to come back with some stupid answer. He grabbed the big spoon himself and served what he thought was a normal portion. He wasn't going to take more than his fair share, but his stomach needed something.

Breakfast in front of him, Xander found a piece of unoccupied wall and sat down to eat. A minute into eating, the woman emerged from the kitchen again and seemed shocked that Xander was gone. He thought about waving kindly at her, but that might be over the top. He had gotten what he needed. Being nasty about it would serve no purpose.

Once he had eaten, Xander meandered toward the medical center. He had never noticed how many clocks there were around the place. Now, each one seemed to stare down at him and let him know that a few more precious minutes had passed. Each minute filled with sixty seconds seemed like a sacrifice.

Finally, Xander stood in front of the medical center door. He didn't remember seeing it at the end of the hallway or approaching it. He had just been walking, then the door was in his path.

Blinking, Xander pushed open the door. A low murmur of voices greeted him. So Eden wasn't the only one who had reported for duty today. Xander slid into the room so he wouldn't interrupt the conversation.

He peered over a half-wall partition that separated a bed from the rest of the room.

"That should keep it from getting infected," Eden told the girl. Xander glanced between the two of them as the girl looked at a bandage on her leg. Both of them looked up at Xander, and he gave a little wave.

"Well, I think that's all I can do for you," Eden told the girl. The girl's face was streaked as though she had been crying in earnest. The bandage didn't look big enough to be hiding the serious wound, but Xander averted his eyes anyway as the girl left the room.

Xander took the girl's place on the bed, and Eden shifted her position.

"I see you actually have something you can treat today," Xander commented.

"Yeah." Eden was avoiding eye contact. Xander gazed at her, his eyes searching her face as he tried to understand what she was thinking beneath her mask.

"I wanted to spend the day with you since..." Xander trailed off, not sure exactly how to phrase the situation. Since it was his last full day alive? Since he would never see her again?

Eden just shrugged. Then, she reached for the roll of bandages and neatly packaged everything away in a tiny box before storing it in a large drawer.

"So you're still planning to...do it?" Eden asked.

Xander stood and followed her to where she stood at the counter. "Yes," he responded, even though his insides were warring. He wanted to stay alive-didn't everyone? He wasn't sure if his bravado would fail him tomorrow, but today, he was continuing to nod his head and agree to this crazy plan.

"Matt is willing to do it, and I'm going to do it with him," Xander explained. His brother had always been his role model, and if Matt could give up his life, then Xander could too.

"So...I don't know what you want me to say." Eden shrugged, a tiny movement of her shoulders. "I mean, I'm not going to tell you I'm okay with it, because I'm not. I think it's too...extreme. And I'm not going to go with you."

Her voice broke on the last word, and Xander wrapped his arms around her from behind, giving her an awkward hug over her shoulders.

"No one is asking that of you. Only two people are needed, and we've got those two. Just...the only thing you need to do is stay here and find your place on the station. It seems like you're already doing a lot."

Something blared out over the speakers, and Xander winced at the sudden loud noise.

"Please pay attention. We have a promising solution to the asteroid problem," Roman's voice sounded old over the speaker system, like he had aged ten years. "A ship is being sent out to collide with the asteroid and change its course. This ship will be sent tomorrow at 10:00 a.m. Matt and Xander Coxon will be manning the ship. Please give them your thanks."

The speaker blared out, then the sound disappeared. The silence seemed louder now, and Xander wondered why Roman had announced their names over the speaker. Was he trying to make sure Xander didn't back out of it? If he did, then everyone would remember him as the guy who hadn't had the guts. Or maybe Roman really was grateful and wanted to make sure everyone knew who to thank.

Xander shook his head at the announcement. "Anyway," he said, turning his attention back to Eden. She swiveled in his arms so that she could give him a proper hug, and they embraced for a few moments. Xander closed his eyes and rested his cheek against the top of her head. He wished he knew what to do to make her feel better, but he was just as lost as she seemed.

"So, this is it, then? The last day," Eden commented.

Xander raised his head so that he could nod. "Yes, the last day, but don't think about it like that. Think about it like...an opportunity for just you and me. We get to say goodbye. I mean, a lot of people don't get to say goodbye when someone dies."

A sudden knot rose in Xander's throat, and he had to swallow it down as he thought about his mom. How was she doing right now? Was she still working?

Or had the worst happened?

Xander took a deep breath and slowly let it out. He had to stay cheerful. He could let his emotions out once he and Matt were packed away safely in this ship or whatever it was.

"I guess," Eden mumbled. "But people aren't supposed to die at our age. I mean, once we get past the Olympics."

"Let's do this," Xander suggested. "Let's *not* talk about death or tomorrow or ships or asteroids all day today. Can you do it?"

Eden busied herself at the counter rearranging instruments in a new order. "I'll try."

"Try is a lie," Xander said, the way his father had instilled in him. But even as he said it, he didn't know how true it was. He was asking Eden to just accept that her closest friend here, her *boyfriend* if he wanted to get technical, was going to die and not talk through her emotions.

Eden shoved him away as she continued to organize things. Xander wanted to take his words back, because they seemed a little harsh, but Eden was already speaking. "Well, I *will* try, but I'm not going to promise anything. It's the only thing I can think about, so we'll see how well I'm able to filter what comes out of my mouth."

Xander nodded. "Are you planning to stay here until twelve?"

"That's my duty," Eden responded. She finally turned around and looked at him again. Xander wasn't trying to be dramatic, but he also wanted to remember every detail of her face- her freckles, her slightly wavy brown hair, even the way the sadness crept into the corners of her eyes.

"Sure, yeah, and if this station is going to survive past our mission, then everyone should keep going."

"You know, I'm pretty sure you just mentioned one of the things you told me I'm not allowed to mention."

Xander caught the teasing note in her voice, and he swung his arm forward to poke her in the side. She dodged, her elbow clattering into the instruments she had just arranged so neatly.

"Well, now I know what I'm going to be working on for the next thirty minutes," Eden said. Xander could tell that she was trying to make him feel guilty as she began rearranging again. He noticed that she didn't use the same pattern as before.

"Hey, if you're going to continue working in here, I might as well give you something to do."

"You're so kind." The sarcasm was heavy.

Xander pulled himself up onto the counter, swinging his feet in the empty space underneath.

"Any*way*, what I was going to say," she said, "is that if everything succeeds, you know, in the thing that shouldn't be mentioned, then that doesn't solve everything here. They've cut back the amount of food they're feeding us. There are still bodies in a room that people act like don't exist."

"You're right." Xander's mind raced trying to come up with an easy solution. "But...they've figured this one out, so I'm sure someone will figure that out too."

The metal of the instruments clattered against the silence and filled the space. Xander watched Eden's hands as she arranged them. He wanted nothing more than to hop on his bike and ride down the hill to the edge of the sea, the way they had so many times in Greenland when they needed to clear their heads.

Now, though, that would be impossible. The station seemed smaller than it had in the last few days. "I'm going up to the game room, and I'm going to grab some cards," Xander replied. "You're going to play them with me and not insist on organizing everything in here."

Eden rolled her eyes, but Xander could tell that she was going to agree. "Fine, but if someone comes in, and they're hurt, I'm going to try to help them."

"Deal."

Xander hurried to the game room, trying to think of other ways to make this day unforgettable, at least for Eden. He, on the other hand, wouldn't have a chance to forget it in the few days he had left.

When he reached the game room, Xander saw a familiar dark head of hair, and he gritted his teeth- Derry. Xander wasn't one to hold grudges, but every time he saw Derry, his back ached just a little bit.

Xander pulled open a drawer hard, harder than he meant to, and it came out of the cabinet. A couple of people looked over at him including Derry. Xander grabbed a worn box of cards and spent his time wiggling the drawer back into place.

"Want to race?" Derry asked Xander, waving his controller at him.

"No," Xander responded darkly, gripping the cards so tightly that the box bent. He marched out of the room, resisting the urge to touch the bandage on his back. Even though Eden had cleaned it up, he couldn't see it well enough to judge if it was healing or not. At least the pain was just a dull ache at the back of his mind and nothing worse.

When Xander returned to the medical center, Eden had finished her self-assigned job and was waiting for him on one of the beds.

"Bring them over here," she suggested.

Xander thought her voice might even sound a little cheerful. He brought the cards over and started shuffling them. "What game do you want to play?"

"Solitaire," Eden said, taking the cards out of Xander's hand and shuffling them herself. She shot him a grin, and Xander was glad that she could still joke. Even though he had told her not to bring up certain subjects, he couldn't help thinking about them. They were on his mind all the time as he struggled with what he had decided to do.

An hour of card games later, they were starting to get bored. Xander carefully packed the cards back into the box, wondering who had put them in the station and who they were meant to be used by.

"I'm hungry," Eden said, touching her stomach.

"Me too," Xander agreed. "We still have almost two hours until lunch, though. There aren't any snacks around here, are there? You know, in case someone isn't feeling well or something?"

"I don't think so." Eden stood up and stared in the direction of the countertop she had recently rearranged. "Besides, if there are, we shouldn't take them. They weren't meant for us."

"Yeah, but I think a little bit won't matter." Xander started opening and closing doors. He didn't know if he was right, but it seemed possible. And his empty stomach was driving him to hope.

In one of the lower cabinets, he found a stash of freeze-dried fruit, definitely something that hadn't been grown here. Xander snatched up a package of it and held it greedily as he hurried over to Eden.

"Look at this!" he cheered.

"I don't know," Eden said, but Xander could see how she was eyeing the package. "What if we get in trouble for taking that?"

Xander studied the package. He could see through a small plastic window that there was a mixture of dried bananas and orange slices inside. Then, he saw the date. "Well, it expired three years ago," he said. "So I'm guessing that no one can get mad at us for...getting rid of it."

"Really? Three years ago?" Eden looked concerned. "I'm not sure we should eat it then. What if we get sick from it?"

Xander shrugged. "I'm going to get sick if I *don't* eat something." He ripped the bag open and forced himself to only grab one of the pieces. Placing the slice of orange in his mouth, he waited as his saliva did its work. Suddenly, flavor burst into his mouth, the sour/sweet taste of orange reminding him that food could still be enjoyable.

He grabbed a handful of the stuff and shoved it into his mouth, his stomach begging him to fill it immediately. He pushed the bag toward Eden. "You better take some before I eat it all."

"I'm waiting to make sure you're not going to keel over before I try some," Eden said, though Xander could see the way she was looking at the bag. She was just as hungry as he was.

Xander waved the bag in front of her face. "Fine," she said, accepting it. "I'll take it." She reached in and cautiously extracted one piece.

Thirst filled Xander's mouth as he chewed the fruit, and his stomach begged for him to feed it faster. Xander hurried to the sink and filled a cup with water, taking the sips slowly as his stomach realized that food was on the way.

He opened the drawer again and began sorting through the packages of food. "I don't think these actually go bad," he commented. "I think they just have to put some sort of date on there for suing purposes."

"Well, I'm pretty sure even if something bad did happen to us that we wouldn't start a lawsuit from up here."

"Pretty sure but not 100%."

Eden reached for another piece of fruit as Xander counted the bags. There were fourteen.

"I wonder why no one has ever eaten these," he said. "I mean, obviously there aren't enough to share with everyone here, but you would think the medics or whatever they want to call themselves would have eaten them already."

Eden shrugged. "Maybe they were doing the right thing, not like us."

Xander shrugged too. He took another handful and walked around the room, suddenly with more energy than he had had before. Morally, was it right to eat the hidden fruits and not share them? No, but did he care about morals at this moment? His stomach certainly didn't.

Xander stopped himself from opening another bag, even though his stomach assured him it could fit two or three more bags. When he and Eden finished the bag, he placed it back in the drawer with the others.

Eden bit her bottom lip. "I kind of feel bad about that."

"But be honest. Your stomach feels a lot better about it."

Eden smiled as Xander sat beside her. "Okay, yes, that's true." She leaned her head against his shoulder. "I'm going to miss you," she said.

Xander put his arm around her shoulders. He almost echoed the same thing before realizing how ridiculous it was. How could he miss someone when he would no longer be alive? Part of him wondered if there was some small chance that he could survive. Maybe the ship would collide with the asteroid, but people survived car crashes all the time, right?

There had to be some way to get back here. Xander had to talk to the people responsible for building the thing, but right now, he just wanted to enjoy a few minutes with Eden.

Xander kissed the top of her head, and she turned her face up to him. Xander hesitated, but he didn't want to evaluate his feelings right then. Instead, he leaned down and touched his lips to hers, hoping that he could promise her comfort even when he wouldn't be there any longer.

AFTER AN AFTERNOON and evening that sped by far too quickly, Xander found himself sitting across from Matt in the deserted dining hall. Dinner had ended three hours ago, and a lot of people who had to get up early were already going to bed.

Xander didn't think he would be able to sleep, even though he had used that excuse with Eden so that he could have a chance to think things through. There was something about the end of his life approaching rapidly that made him want to evaluate the way he had spent the last eighteen years.

Matt leaned against the wall and closed his eyes. Xander copied his movements. This was it. The final night of his life.

"I know it's dumb, but sometimes, I wonder what the people back in Sisimiut think of me," Xander said.

Matt nodded. "I guess it's normal. You have this whole life, then suddenly you don't. Some people continue with their lives, get married, and have kids, but we just stay here...stuck."

"Is that why you volunteered?" Xander asked. He would never have called his brother a coward, but this kind of volunteering went beyond the type of duty anyone could be expected to perform.

Matt opened his eyes and looked around. "Yeah, I guess you could say I'm tired of life here. I've been here three years, and nothing has changed. There's not enough food, and I don't want to deal with the kind of solutions that will be proposed. You think anything good is going to happen here after we're gone?"

"You think it won't?" Xander didn't like the pessimism in his brother's voice for Eden's sake. She was going to be left here to deal with this place.

"No way." Matt shook his head. "Nope. I know Roman too well. I know that he's not going to die. That much I know. But everyone else?" Matt shrugged his shoulders, his hesitancy coming through. "I think the bodies in stasis are going to be dumped when they don't have enough food. More people will be put in there, maybe real volunteers this time."

The bitterness in Matt's voice gave Xander the courage to let his older brother keep talking.

"Maybe not. I think that Roman is going to cull the group until it's only a few people that trust him and believe in him. None of the people who have questioned his leadership, like me, will still be here in a year. Then, when it gets down to that small group, someone is going to turn on Roman. He's going to die painfully."

"Answer me something. How was Roman chosen as the leader?"

Matt shrugged. "I don't know exactly. He was the leader three years ago when I got here. He seemed confident, and he's one of the oldest here. No one else wanted to be in the decision-making position, so it worked. But as more of the eliminated arrive, he's become stricter and stricter. That nauseating stuff they call food...that wasn't here until a year ago."

Xander just listened. He had been so eager for another chance at life that he hadn't thought about how terrible this chance might be. Xander reached back and touched the fresh bandage on his back. He pressed into the skin and felt a sharp jab of pain. It hadn't healed yet.

"So death is better?" Xander concluded.

"Yes," Matt replied. His eyes had closed again, and he looked the picture of an exhausted man. His beard made him look older, but Xander didn't think he was old enough to die. None of them were, but he would stick by what he said. In twelve hours, he and Matt would leave this world in the air and start their journey to the asteroid.

Chapter 17

Feeling guilty, Eden didn't report for her shift the next morning. She had found Xander at breakfast and stuck by his side, even though they didn't converse much. Roman had pulled Xander and Matt aside, and Eden had been left on her own for the last hour.

Now, a lot of people were gathering in the first floor hallway to see Xander and Matt leave. Eden pushed her way from the edge of the crowd into the middle of it. Who were all these people and why did they care about Xander?

"Excuse me," Eden said, trying to still be polite even as she liberally used her elbows. A couple more people let her pass, but others firmly stood their ground.

What if she didn't get the chance to say a final goodbye?

"Xander?" Eden called above the excited murmurs.

She could hear plenty of conversation but not Xander's voice.

"Do you think this is really going to work?"

"I can't believe those guys are willing to die for us."

"Especially the new one."

"Better them than us."

Eden clenched her jaw and peeked through an arm and a shoulder. There, Roman was pushing his way through the crowd, and everyone was letting him. They stood aside as he passed, and with him were Xander and Matt.

Reaching out her hand, Eden grabbed Xander's arm as he passed by. Xander started to yank his arm away, then he must have seen who it was pulling at him. He smiled, and Eden sensed sadness in his smile.

"You're leaving right now?" she asked.

Xander glanced at where Matt and Roman were striding ahead. Matt held his head high like he couldn't hear the comments around him.

"I can take a few minutes," he said. He glanced at everyone around them, and Eden knew that this wouldn't be a private goodbye. They had had that the day before. Still, she wrapped her arms around him and tried to pretend that there weren't people staring as she buried her face in his shirt for the last time. He smelled so familiar. She wasn't sure how else to describe it, but the tears welled up within her anyway.

She wanted to say something meaningful, but nothing came to mind. The words either seemed too extreme or not enough. "Xander, I'll miss you, and...thank you for doing this."

She squeezed him tightly for another few moments, then let go as other people started patting Xander on the shoulders and thanking him. He was a real hero, Eden realized as she craned her neck for one more view of him. The other people in the hallway surrounded him, and she watched as his brown hair bobbed away until it disappeared altogether on the far end of the hall.

He was gone. He was really gone. This was the end of their story. Eden turned so that she could see out the window. The glass felt cool against her fingers, and she wondered at how this piece of glass could keep the atmosphere in this space station pressurized in just the right way. If one tiny hole were to be made in the glass... everything would fall apart.

A few people drifted away, the excitement of the moment over, but Eden was still waiting, hoping for one last view of them as they drifted away into outer space. She searched the airspace directly below the station, as far as she could see anyway. Then, she gazed out into the distance, looking for that asteroid that was coming for them. She didn't see anything, so either the station had really good cameras or the asteroid was coming from the other side.

As Eden listened, she could hear an engine rev in the distance. That must be the ship that Matt and Xander were piloting away right then.

Roman appeared again in the crowd. "Go back to your duties," he said. "We'll know in about twelve hours if they've been successful or not."

"How are we going to know?" someone asked him.

"Can you communicate with them in there?"

Roman stopped and turned, looking like he was preparing to make a speech. "I appreciate all of you coming to show your support for Matt and

Xander. I know that they appreciate it as well. We will not be able to communicate with them, but our camera will be able to view them until they make contact with the asteroid."

Eden clenched her fists when he said it like that. "Make contact with the asteroid" sounded like they were going to have a conversation with it, wish it a happy birthday or something.

"Once they have made contact with it, we will be able to judge if it was successful based on the asteroid's angle of movement. Until then, I need everyone to keep working as they've been assigned or this station won't be able to function."

Eden took a deep breath. Roman might be able to tell everyone that, but he didn't seem able to make them show up for their duties. She had been the only one in the medical center yesterday. Now that Xander was leaving, she wasn't sure if it was stupidity or hope that made her head to the medical center for the hour and a half left in her shift.

Once there, she paced back and forth in the room, glancing at the door every second turn as though someone might burst through and demand her assistance. She should have gone with Xander. Maybe she could have figured out a way for them to survive.

The time on the clock ticked away slowly, and Eden's legs were growing tired. She settled onto the edge of the bed and thought about snacks in the drawer. The breakfast that had been delivered that morning had been small portions just like yesterday, but five portions had been delivered. She was the only one there, so she had eaten two and a half, feeling guilty about it as she soothed her stomach.

For the last ten minutes of her shift, Eden stared the clock down, watching as the hand tick, tick, ticked past.

Seven minutes left.

Five minutes left.

The door burst open, and Eden stumbled backward.

"I need a doctor!" the girl shouted, and Eden looked behind her to see if one was there. But she was alone, and she knew that. She straightened her shoulders and tried to appear as strong as she could.

"What's wrong?" she asked, glancing at the girl's visible body parts. She didn't see any blood or crooked bones. The girl's face reflected more fear than pain anyway.

"Not me," the girl said. "This...person."

Eden nodded. "Are they too hurt to bring here?"

The girl nodded soundlessly, her eyes wide. Eden glanced at the clock again that told her she only had three minutes left. Still, she would try to help however she could.

"Let me bring a bag," she said, trying to sound official even though she had no idea what she was doing.

"You have to be fast," the girl said, glancing over her shoulder.

Eden stuffed things haphazardly in the tiny bag at the end of the counter before turning to the girl. "I'm ready," she said. Finally, she might be able to help someone. She could be useful instead of thinking about how far away Xander might be from the space station at that point. What was he thinking as he stared at the asteroid?

The girl hurried in front of Eden, almost running, and Eden jogged to keep up. The girl turned down a hallway to the left, then to the right. The hallway ended abruptly in front of a door, a door that Eden recognized too well. It was the one that held the station's biggest secret, at least the biggest secret that she had discovered since living there.

But in front of the doorway was another girl, her blonde hair half-covering her face. She wasn't moving, and her body was lying in a weird, uncomfortable angle.

"Okay, what happened?" Eden asked, stepping forward an inch at a time as she tried to get up the courage to help the girl. The girl wasn't making any sounds of pain, so she must have passed out. Eden wasn't sure how she felt about helping someone who wasn't able to answer her questions or tell her what hurt.

"I don't know," the other girl said from just behind Eden's shoulder. "I always walk the whole place every day for exercise and, and I saw her there. She wasn't moving."

"Okay." The word seemed to be as much to soothe herself as to acknowledge that she was listening. Eden was now close enough that she had to bend forward and look at the girl more closely.

She moved the blonde hair away from the girl's face and recognized who it was immediately- Emily. Eden jerked her hand back, but Emily didn't move. The skin on her face had a strange pasty hue that made her look almost...not real.

Eden felt like she couldn't breathe, but she forced herself to take deep breaths as she pressed the medical mask against her face. It was okay. Things were going to be okay. She needed to ask more questions. Yes, questions. She just had to keep talking and not think about what had happened to Emily.

"I'm going to just..." Maybe she shouldn't announce that she had no idea what she was doing. "Okay, you said you just saw her here. Did you see anything else? Did she say anything?"

The other girl shook her head vehemently. "No, I just saw her laying there, not moving. I asked her if she was okay, but she didn't answer. I thought a doctor could help her better than me. I'm not good with this sort of thing."

Neither am I, Eden thought, but she couldn't say that out loud. She knew that this girl held some sort of illusion that Eden could help, even though Eden knew how truly unqualified she was in this situation.

"Okay," Eden repeated. It seemed like it was her favorite word now. "Let me just..."

A sudden thought occurred to Eden. Emily was still, too still. Eden slowly reached her hand forward, hovering her fingers just under Emily's nose. She didn't feel a puff of air that would indicate she was breathing.

Eden's eyes went wide, and she pulled her medical bag open, looking for something that would help her. Should she do CPR? She wasn't really sure of the steps, but she thought she could do it.

Trying to sound brave, she gave the watching girl instructions. "I need you to go to the bridge. Tell them to get Helena down here now. They can make an announcement or something." Eden couldn't remember the names of the other medics, and she didn't want to use the term "a real medic."

The other girl scurried off, and Eden pulled out a plastic barrier device like what she had used when they practiced CPR in school all those years ago. This was not nearly as fun as it had been when she was laughing with Xander about the plastic dummy. Tears filling her eyes, Eden placed the film over Emily's mouth, tilted her head back slightly, and breathed into her lungs.

Then, she sat back on her heels and pushed on Emily's chest ten times. She wasn't sure if she was pushing in the right place, but she didn't know what else to try.

As she repeated this process, Eden wondered what the point was. Emily was obviously dead. Eden couldn't bring her back to life. No one could. But the thought that made Eden look over her shoulder after each deep breath was what had happened to her, how she had ended up like this.

Running footsteps broke into her thoughts, and Eden sat back in relief when Helena appeared. Helena stepped forward and took Eden's place without saying anything to her. Instead of continuing CPR though, she tilted Emily's chin toward her ear, listening.

Helena touched Emily's wrist before shaking her head.

"She's gone," Helena announced. "Look at her coloring."

Eden looked at Emily's coloring. She knew it was wrong, but she didn't know why. Helena stood back and stared at Emily, and Eden leaned on the wall for support. Then, Helena turned and drilled Eden with a look. "What happened?" she asked.

Eden shook her head. "I don't...I don't know. She found her, but she doesn't know what happened."

Helena shook her head. "She didn't just pass out. Someone killed her."

"Wh-what?" Eden couldn't quite get the word out of her mouth, but Helena looked so sure. Suddenly, the thought that Emily might have had some sort of heart condition or something else fatal seemed silly. This was much more serious than what Eden had thought.

Chapter 18

The ship was small. There was barely enough room for both of them to exist without hitting each other, made harder by the fact that there was no gravity. With each lurch forward, Xander was sure that the whole contraption was going to fall apart.

"They could have at least let us die in style," Xander said as he looked at the two water bottles that had been strapped next to the control booth. He recognized them from his journey to the station.

There was a long length of material for each of them to use as a seatbelt, and Matt had tied himself next to the control panel as soon as they had entered. Since he had no knowledge of the buttons and controls, Xander had no problem letting Matt control things. Matt barely glanced at the bottles of water. "Doesn't matter," he said, still fidgeting with the controls.

Xander pushed himself off one of the walls, gliding through the air for only a few seconds before bumping into the opposite one. That was all there was room to do. This thing was built as small as a coffin, and it would serve as theirs.

Xander finally strapped himself down before he stared at the tiny screen in front of Matt. "I can't believe they built this in two days," he said, but once again, Matt basically ignored him. There was a tiny clock in the corner of the screen, but Matt's shoulder blocked it. Xander would guess that they had been in the ship for at least an hour.

And honestly, the longer he sat there, the more he wondered why it had been necessary for two people to come. Matt seemed more than capable of doing this himself, and if he was willing to make the sacrifice, why should Xander do it too?

He knew that he was going crazy as his death approached, but he couldn't help it. His thoughts continued to circle and circle, and he couldn't get out any of his energy with exercise unless he could count bouncing back and forth against the walls as exercise.

Xander grabbed the back of the chair to keep himself from floating away and peered over Matt's shoulder. "What are you working so hard on? I would think that the techy guy would already have things aimed us in the right direction."

"Yeah, he did," Matt muttered, pressing something, then glancing at the screen again. Xander could see a projection of the ship as it moved forward quickly in time. Matt shook his head and adjusted a few more things, then looked at the newly changed projection.

"So what are you doing pressing everything, then?" Xander asked. "You're going to mess us up and make us miss the asteroid or something."

"That's the point," Matt said. "I'm not about to die."

His words froze Xander. Xander tried to look at Matt's face, but Matt was too busy with all of his buttons.

"Stop! Hey! What are you doing?" Xander asked even though Matt had just made it pretty clear what he was doing.

"Man, please stop distracting me. I only have a few hours to get this right, and it's not like I've had time to practice."

"You can't...you can't change our course," Xander said, trying to comprehend what was happening.

"Yes I can, and that's what I'm going to do."

"Stop!" Xander shouted. His voice bounced off the walls and seemed to echo back more loudly.

He had never been in a physical altercation with his brother. Sure, they had wrestled some as kids, but Xander didn't know what to do right now. He hovered behind Matt's shoulders as Matt continued to press buttons, then play the same projection video over and over. It kept showing the ship crashing into the asteroid in a few hours' time.

Matt swore as he thumped the keyboard. "I don't know enough about this stuff to change it!" he said. He pushed back out of his chair, the lack of gravity causing him to float toward the ceiling headfirst.

Xander kicked backward and crashed into the wall. His back reminded him that it hadn't fully healed as he found a place where he could attempt to stay motionless. "So, we're still going to hit the asteroid and take it off course like we're supposed to?" he confirmed.

"Why are you trying to be so noble? What's the point?" Matt said, slowly spinning around to face Xander. "Do you actually want to die?"

"Well, yeah, I had kind of accepted that it was going to happen since that's what we signed up to do."

"But we don't have to die," Matt said. "We can have a chance to live. Look, what if we go back to Earth? We'd have to be sneaky about it, okay? But we could go back and figure out a way to live. It's got to be better to live as fugitives in Greenland than on that thing back there." Matt jerked a thumb over his shoulder, and Xander could see the disgust on his face.

He had to think things through. "There's just a couple of problems. We're two people, *two* people. I don't want to die, but I also don't think it's fair to take away their chance of living. I don't know how many people are on that station, but they trusted in us to do this."

Xander remembered the cheers and the claps on the back he had gotten as he had followed Roman to this ship. It wasn't that he was doing it for the attention, but knowing that people were grateful for what they had done made a difference. For once in his life, he was doing something for someone else rather than just himself.

"I know they trusted in us, but the truth is that they're all going to die anyway."

"Aren't we all? I mean, I don't know anyone who's lived forever."

Matt rolled his eyes, and Xander could see his anger calming down as he thought about the whole thing rationally. "You heard Roman. He was willing to make the problem of rations public because they are *that* desperate. They've been working on some garden. It's supposed to replenish itself, but we've been eating through it too quickly. There isn't enough, not for everyone."

"But what about putting people in stasis?"

"I don't know if it's working." Matt shrugged his shoulders. "Who knows? I mean, they haven't complained. But we could take them out, and find out they're dead anyway."

He said it so casually that Xander had to question how much he really knew about his brother. He knew Matt as his hero, the guy who had always had a joke for every situation, the one who had worked hard and made his parents proud, who had never tried to kick Xander out of the way like some older siblings did.

Xander took a deep breath, wondering for the first time how much oxygen was in this thing. Physically, did they even have the ability to make it down to earth? He couldn't believe he was considering it. It wasn't that he wanted to die. Who did? But the thought of being able to live, even if it wasn't the life he had dreamed of having, it had to be better than just...nothing, right?

Then, Xander remembered Eden back on the space station. He shook his head. "I can't do it," he said to Matt. "We can't leave them all to die. It's not right."

Matt shook his head and pushed off the wall to the controls again, strapping himself in securely and trying with renewed vigor to figure out what had gone wrong before. Xander couldn't stay still. He pushed back and forth off the walls, his mind turning over the problem. He didn't have the brainpower to change anything about the ship. He had barely paid attention in his academic classes, but even if he had, he highly doubted that they had covered powering a spaceship.

If only Colt were there, he would probably be able to figure things out right away.

Xander stopped bouncing off the walls for one second, glancing at Matt to see if he had made any progress. Then, he propelled himself to the window that faced out the front of the tiny ship. He could see the asteroid in the distance like a tiny rock. It hardly looked threatening, but he knew that it was a lot bigger than it looked right then. Xander craned his neck and changed his angle, trying to see Earth. It had to be somewhere below them, right? He didn't see anything that resembled the green and blue ball that was used in class to depict Earth as a planet.

"Do you even know where we are in relation to Earth?" he asked, coming back to where Matt continued to press buttons and turn knobs.

"Kind of," Matt responded. "I know in relation to the space station, but the further we get from there, then-" he stopped abruptly and leaned back in his chair, staring at the screen.

Xander turned so that he could see the screen too.

"It's worked!" Matt exclaimed. He threw his fist in the air, but his fist hit the roof. Xander heard his knuckles crack, and Matt clenched them while laughing. "I can't even celebrate in here without being punished for it."

The ship lurched, and Xander pressed into the side of the ship. The thing hadn't been outfitted with handles or other important necessities, so he did the best he could to not hit his head while the ship changed direction.

"You did it?" Xander asked even though it was clear what his brother meant.

"We are going to Earth, man!" Matt said.

His smile was so wide, so genuine, and Xander could hardly believe that it had happened. He had been mentally preparing himself for death for the last forty-eight hours. Once he had found his balance again, Xander fumbled his way to the window. The tiny rock that he had seen in the distance had disappeared from view, and he could see the distinctive green, red, and blue ball in the distance. It looked bigger than the asteroid did, and Xander's stomach did a weird, excited flip.

"We're actually going back there," he said out loud.

"Yes we are!" Matt cheered, thumping Xander on the back harder than necessary.

Xander winced. Even though Matt had missed his wound, his whole back still protested the movement.

"I better aim for Greenland, though, or we might end up in South America or something," Matt winced.

Xander knew that the red blazes that spotted the perfectly round Earth were from the unquenchable fires that started up every now and then. Eventually they died when they ran out of fuel. Other parts of the earth had lava flowing over them. Seeing it like this made him realize how sick their planet really was.

Matt sat down at the screen again and began punching buttons more slowly. He was taking his time.

"When will the people back at the station know that we've changed our course?" Xander asked.

Matt shook his head. "They might already know, depends on if they're watching the asteroid camera or not. I mean, they've been watching it since it first appeared, so...my guess is they know."

Xander closed his eyes and imagined the panic. Everyone would know that these two "heroes" had changed their minds and headed toward Earth. Xander wasn't a liar. He had always been trustworthy. Part of him told himself that he had to convince Matt to turn the thing back around, but the other part just wanted to live.

Chapter 19

Eden folded her hands in her lap as she felt Roman's eyes boring into her. Helena sat on Eden's right side, and the girl who had reported the whole thing to Eden sat on her left. Eden still hadn't caught the girl's name.

"I need to know what happened," Roman said in an even voice. "People don't just die. Helena, you've already made your report, and you obviously weren't there when it happened. You can go back to the medical center."

"My shift is over," Helena murmured, and she left as she said something about the dining hall. The buzzer for lunch had rung fifteen minutes ago, and Eden's stomach rumbled. Perhaps this was her penance for eating all of that extra oatmeal for breakfast.

Roman turned his gaze on the two of them. "So?"

Eden glanced at the other girl. "I was in the medical center, and she told me something was wrong. I followed her to that part of the station. When I found the girl, I started giving her CPR."

"But you were alone with her." Roman pointed an accusing finger in Eden's direction.

"I wasn't...I mean, I was for a minute while she went to get more help. I just started in the medical center, and I don't know a lot about what I'm doing. I thought it would be better if a real medic took over."

"So why did you go with her if you weren't prepared to handle the situation?" Roman asked.

Eden hated the guilt that seemed to be eating away at her insides. She hadn't done anything wrong!

"I was the only one in the medical center."

"Where were all the other medics?" Roman asked.

Eden shrugged. "I don't know. They didn't come for their shifts."

Roman frowned and made some sort of growling noise in his throat. "So you haven't done any operations today?"

"No one came for them, and I don't know how to do them anyway," Eden explained. Her answer only seemed to infuriate Roman further. He clenched his hands into fists, but at least he decided to turn his questions in the other girl's direction.

"And what were you doing going down that hallway anyway? There's nothing down there for anyone without the passcode."

"I was just walking. I like to exercise by walking down every hallway every day. My shift isn't until, well, right now, so I wasn't skipping my duties."

Roman huffed, and Eden shared a glance with the girl. She seemed as worried as Eden. Then, she spoke up again. "Emily didn't look dead. I'm pretty sure I saw her move when I first looked at her, but she didn't say anything when I called her name. I knew she was hurt or something."

"Not dead?" Roman asked.

Eden's eyes widened. Was the girl trying to get *her* in trouble? Eden hadn't killed her. Even though Emily wasn't her favorite person, she had done CPR and whatever she could think of to help her. Eden wanted to raise her hand and deny any culpability, but she knew that wouldn't help her case.

Roman muttered to himself, and Eden glanced at the door behind them. This felt awfully similar to being called into an office and questioned by the officials at the Olympics. Except this time if she were decided guilty of a crime, then she knew Roman wouldn't have any mercy, not with the ration shortages on the station.

He finally turned and looked directly at both of them, staring at them so that Eden felt like he could see through her skull to her brain and all of its thoughts.

"You're both going to stay here until we figure out what happened," he decided.

"But I went to help her!" Eden protested. She rose partly from her chair, but Roman's look sent her back down into it.

"She could have been alive when you got there, and you were left alone with her for several minutes. I'm tempted just to call both of you guilty for it just to lighten this place a little bit."

"But-" the other girl protested.

"But that wouldn't be fair," Roman finished. "So, I'm going to see if I can figure something else out."

"What about lunch?" the other girl asked as Roman strode toward the door.

"I'll send some in." He rolled his eyes. Then, he opened the door and pressed something on the other side. Eden could hear a lock sliding into place.

Suddenly, the room felt a lot smaller. She looked around at the table that was in the center of it along with two chairs and a tiny window on the far side. She didn't have anything to say to the other girl, so Eden went to the window and looked out. She could see the stars, glowing orbs in the sky, but that was it. It didn't provide her with a real view. Still, she stayed there because pretending to look out of it gave her something to do.

The other girl finally spoke. "What do you think really happened?"

Eden turned around and studied the girl's face. She didn't think she looked "evil" per se, but Eden wouldn't be able to like her because she had brought her into this whole situation. What if Eden had refused to go with her or hidden out like everyone else had instead of going to the medical center?

"I don't know," Eden said, keeping her voice even. "I wasn't there."

"Neither was I!" the girl protested. "I was just walking. I mean, if I hadn't been there, then someone else would have found her."

Eden tried to remember exactly what the girl had said when she retrieved Eden, but she couldn't remember her exact words. She just remembered the girl's eyes and how fearful they were. Why was she so afraid? If she just thought someone was hurt, not dead, then she might be concerned. But afraid?

"What do you know that you're not telling me?" Eden asked. She knew that she couldn't sound threatening. She just didn't have that kind of face or build, but maybe if the girl thought Eden knew something, then she would be more likely to tell the rest of the story.

"I don't...I just saw her and got help." The same story.

The door opened, and someone brought in half-bowls of mush. Eden didn't care how tasteless it was. Her stomach rumbled and begged her for more as she dove into the bowl, forgetting the other girl for a few minutes.

All Eden heard was the sound of her spoon hitting the bowl. Too soon, it was gone, and Eden stared mournfully at the bowl.

Then, she paced to the window and wondered if Xander was okay. When would he and Matt hit the asteroid? Was he afraid?

"Tell me the truth," the girl demanded after they had both studied their empty bowls for some time. "Did you hurt her?"

"No!" Eden protested. She couldn't keep the panic from her voice. "I didn't even know her, not really. I mean, I think I saw her around here, but I never...spoke to her."

That was true. She had just talked to Xander *about* her, but not directly *to* her.

"Helena said that someone strangled her, like they were really angry and wanted to hurt her. But she's not one of the troublemakers around here, not like *some* people."

Eden didn't know who this girl might be referring to, but her mind immediately went to Derry. She wondered if he had been seen in the same area this morning, because based on what he had done at her Olympics, she wouldn't doubt that he was capable of committing such a crime.

"Do you think Roman will really just say we're guilty of it even if we didn't do anything?"

Eden knew that this girl hadn't arrived with her a few days ago, at least she didn't think she looked familiar. Maybe she knew more about Roman and what to expect.

The girl lifted one shoulder in a shrug. "I don't know," she said. "I mean, I know that the whole rations thing is pretty serious. What if...this whole thing was a setup? I mean, what if he just wants to start knocking people out until there are only enough people to help this place run? It wouldn't be the first time people have disappeared."

"Do you know what's behind the door where Emily was found?" Eden asked. It was the first time she had used Emily's name, and Eden saw by the girl's widened eyes that she had noticed.

Eden tried not to act like it was a big deal, but she hoped knowing the victim's name wouldn't be her undoing.

"I...it's locked. How would I know what's behind it?"

"Because, well, I don't know. I just got here. I don't know all the rules or how everything works."

"No, I've never gone into the room. I work in the kitchen."

"Well..." Eden didn't know if this would help her or hurt her, but she didn't need that girl trying to make her look guilty. Maybe if Eden trusted her with some information, then the girl would trust Eden in return. "I've been in there."

"What? But you said-"

"I just asked if you had. But I know someone who was eliminated years ago, and he got me in there." Eden didn't know if it mattered if she mentioned Matt's name now. He was gone. She took a moment to consider that, the fact that Matt wasn't going to just walk through the doorway. Xander either.

"What is it?" The curiosity was plain on her face.

"People," Eden responded. She tried to remember the correct terminology for it, but she couldn't quite. "It was...I can't remember exactly. They're alive, but I think it must be the people who have disappeared. I keep hearing others say that their friends or siblings have disappeared, and in that room, they're there. It's like they're sleeping, like a long sleep."

"They're not dead?" the girl spoke the word reverently.

"No, I don't think so. I mean, I'm not the most sciency person," Eden cringed at her words. Science had been her best shot at a medal, but she still didn't think of herself as strong in that area. "They didn't look dead."

The girl made some sort of noise between a huff and a grunt as she leaned back in her chair and stared at Eden with disbelief. "You're not just making this up?"

"No, I swear."

"But, why would they do that? Just put people there? I mean, I've never heard of that."

"Supposedly, it's because there's not enough space for everyone."

"Because *you* were arriving."

"Yeah, something like that."

The girl studied Eden for another minute, and Eden eventually dropped her eyes, unable to make eye contact any longer. "Why did you tell me that?"

"Because it makes me wonder if we can trust the people in charge," Eden said. "I mean, if they didn't tell you guys and ask for volunteers... they must have just snatched people and put them there. Like kidnapping. It feels like a violation of their rights."

"I agree. That's not fair. I'm kind of a loner, but I know lots of people who've disappeared over the past couple of weeks. I tried not to ask questions. I was scared that if I started asking questions or making trouble, that the same thing might happen to me. But now, I guess it doesn't matter. I should have just walked away and pretended I didn't see her."

The girl winced. Eden felt like she had gotten to know her well enough over the past couple of hours, but she still didn't know her name.

"What's your name?" she asked.

"Briella," the girl said.

"Eden."

Eden started to offer her hand in a handshake, but that felt too awkward, so she pulled her hand back. "So... what do we do now?"

Briella shrugged. "I guess we just wait. We can't really do anything until Roman comes back."

Eden stacked both of their bowls and set them by the door, but the task took her too little time. At least they had been fed. That indicated that Roman wasn't quite ready to just chuck them out the nearest door and let them die while floating around in outer space.

There was no way to tell how much time had passed, but Eden knew it was a long time. She and Briella didn't have a lot to talk about after the initial questions about their own sets of Olympics had been covered. Eden just wanted to leave the room, even though she wasn't sure where she would go when she did.

Xander wasn't there anymore.

Even though Eden knew it in her head, the reality of it hadn't quite set in. She knew she would feel it when she looked for him that evening, presuming that she was set free from this prison chamber.

Finally, the door opened again, and Eden didn't care who it was or what questions might be asked as long as she got the opportunity to do *something*.

Roman looked ticked. She didn't know him well enough to read his face specifically, but the twitching eyebrow was pretty hard to ignore.

"You can go," he said, pointing to Briella. Then, he turned to Eden. "I'll talk with you alone."

"I'm ... you believe me?" Briella asked, taking a couple of steps to the door and waiting as though she thought Roman might stop her.

"Go," Roman urged.

Briella disappeared into the hallway without looking at Eden, and Eden's stomach sank. She couldn't be trapped in this room alone. She would literally go crazy, and this must mean that Roman thought it was her. How could she prove him wrong?

Roman shut the door and took one of the chairs, moving it to the other side of the table so that he was facing her.

"You and Xander are close," he said.

"Wh...yes," Eden admitted, taking her seat in the other chair. She wasn't sure what this had to do with anything. Would Roman "let her off the hook" because of Xander's sacrifice? Just thinking about it made Eden's throat hurt.

"How close?" Roman asked.

"Well, we're kind of... boyfriend, girlfriend," Eden responded. It felt weird to tell people that. Why was she embarrassed about such stupid things? "I mean, well, that's what we've been." She didn't want to talk about Xander in the past tense, but she knew what was coming.

"Why didn't you go with him on his mission to the asteroid?" Roman asked.

The questions were taking such a strange turn. What was Roman doing? Eden couldn't catch his line of questioning or what he might be planning, so she just answered him as honestly as she could. "Well, only two people were needed, and Xander volunteered with Matt. It would be stupid for me to go too. I mean, part of me thought about it, but I just couldn't."

"Because you didn't want to die," Roman confirmed. His face had changed from angry to serious.

"Yeah, that's about it," Eden confirmed.

"So you had no idea what they were planning to do?" There was something dangerous in Roman's voice, something that scared Eden.

"I don't... what do you mean? Xander told me they were going."

"Going where?"

"On the ship." Eden choked out the words. Her emotions rose within her, and she wanted to cry. "They were going to give themselves up for us. Why are you asking me this? I don't want to talk about it."

"I'm trying to figure out why you wouldn't go with them if you're as close to Xander as you say."

"I-" Eden stopped herself. She didn't think there was a point in explaining again that dying together wasn't as romantic as it had seemed when she had read about it in *Romeo and Juliet*. She had already gone through that once when she and Xander boarded the boat after their Olympics.

"You what?" Roman asked.

"What they did was good. I don't get why you're trying to be so negative about them."

"Because they're not headed toward the asteroid anymore," Roman announced.

Cold fear seemed to take the feeling away from Eden's feet. "They're... what?"

"They've turned the ship away from the asteroid. There's no way they're going to hit it, and by the looks of it, they're on their way to Earth to save their own butts." Roman pounded the table with his fist.

Eden swallowed down the excitement she had felt at first. Xander wasn't going to die! But then, she followed Roman's line of reasoning and understood why he was so upset. That meant that *they* were.

"Can't you just... build another ship?" she suggested, her mind frantically searching for solutions.

"No, we put the only thrusters we had on that one. I trusted Matt. I shouldn't have." Roman shook his head and rubbed at his eyes for a minute.

Fear for her own life took over the joy she had felt at first. What had Xander done?

Chapter 20

Xander understood that the building of this ship hadn't been designed to either last very long or to be an enjoyable ride, but a toilet would have been a nice addition. After he had drunk the whole bottle of water to quench his thirst, he started wondering what they were meant to do in this situation.

"Just recycle the water," Matt suggested when Xander glanced mournfully at the water bottles after another spin around the tiny space.

"In the water bottles?" Xander asked.

Matt shrugged. "Why not? We might not have a fancy filtration system here, but I've heard that you can actually drink your own urine. I mean, it came out of you, right?"

"Yeah, but it comes out of you because it's getting rid of things you don't need."

"Well, in this case you might need them again," Matt said. He stared at the computer screen, though he had stopped punching buttons. After a few hours of messing with the thing, he must have found the trajectory he liked best.

Xander floated away from the water bottles once more, but he couldn't deny that he had to do something. Earth was a lot closer now, but still not close enough. Grabbing the empty water bottle as it floated past him, Xander promised himself that it didn't matter how thirsty he got, he would *never* drink the contents of this bottle.

"How much longer until we're there?" Xander asked.

"This thing is saying ten hours," Matt responded. "Once we break through the atmosphere, though, gravity will take us down pretty quickly. I'm planning to land in water since you know, I don't have any landing gear."

Xander hadn't thought all the way to the landing yet. He had only thought about the fact that they had given up on everyone behind them. Eden was at the forefront of his mind, though his thoughts were periodically interrupted with his mother. It hadn't been *that* long since he had talked to his mother. She had to be okay...still alive.

How would she feel when she saw both of her sons?

"We need a plan," Xander said. "What part of the ocean are we going to land in? I mean, I can swim, but not for days."

"I'm trying to go for one of the rivers that cuts into the edge of Greenland. If I can get near Sisimiut, then good."

Xander rubbed his head, feeling significantly better now that he had used the bottle. "Yes, but how accurately are you able to aim it?"

"Right now, I'm going toward Earth. It's not like I can map out Earth's surface. We're too far away. When we're closer, about to enter the atmosphere, I think I can change the trajectory some."

"But you might not be able to," Xander responded, his thoughts catching on Matt's use of the word "think."

"Maybe. I mean, it's not like this ship was built to enter Earth's atmosphere. It was built to be in use for less than twenty-four hours."

Xander's stomach rumbled, but he didn't care about his hunger right now. Matt's plan was terrible, and it was all about himself. Matt hated living on the space station, so he had dragged Xander along, leaving everyone else to die. Now, he just wanted to find a nice place to live, hide out from the officials, and survive somehow without a job or a way to get one since they hadn't been inducted into society as adults. Great plan.

But the more Xander thought about it, the more he knew someone who could help them. "Hey, I've got an idea. You know the big research center on the edge of Sisimiut?"

"Yeah," Matt responded, studying Xander.

"We need to head there. Someone I know, he just won a medal this year," Xander glossed over the fact that Colt hadn't technically won anything. He was smart enough to have won something, and he had plans for fixing the declining living situation. Maybe he was shooting high, but maybe he wasn't. Colt had impressed Xander often with his knowledge and manipulation of numbers.

"And?"

"And maybe he could help us."

"With what? Getting food and a place to stay?"

Xander shook his head. His older brother was still only thinking about himself. Had he always been this selfish or was it something that had developed in the years since his elimination? "Maybe he can do something to stop the asteroid from hitting the space station. And maybe if he knew that people were up there, I don't know...we could spread the word about what's *really* happening to the eliminated."

Matt shook his head too. "No one will care. In fact, some people will probably think that it's a waste of resources- you know, people who spend all of their money on training their kids and have never had a family member eliminated. Or they'll think it's a good thing that at least they aren't just killed straight away, which is what most people assume."

"Look, I'm not just going to hide out in Greenland and let everyone up there die. I mean, we volunteered to help them. We have to at least try...even if we're going at it a different way than we said we would."

"We?"

Xander gritted his teeth and stared out the window again. It didn't look like they were getting any closer to their home planet. It was hard not to feel like they were just suspended in space, being fooled into thinking they were going anywhere.

"Yes! You signed me up for this and changed the plan without my input. Now, I'm changing your plan. We're not just going to look out for ourselves." Xander hoped that Matt would see what he meant, the importance of helping everyone on the space station, but at the same time, he feared that Matt was no longer the older brother he had known.

"Fine, we'll see what we can do, but I'm pretty sure the research center will have high security. We don't have weapons."

"We'll worry about that when we get there." At least Matt was starting to agree to the plan.

The ship shuddered, and Xander grabbed the edge of the window as he realized that his body suddenly felt slightly heavier. "Why did it do that?" he asked.

Matt was staring at the screen, and Xander stepped over to join him, determined to understand everything as it popped up. The red alert wasn't easy to miss, and Xander read the text easily, its meaning sinking into him.

"Fuel levels low?" he asked.

"I didn't think about that," Matt responded. "I guess they only gave us enough to get us to the asteroid."

"So we should be hitting the asteroid about now?" Xander asked. He checked the time on the corner of the screen, but it couldn't be right. According to that clock, it said they had been traveling for fourteen hours.

Matt shrugged. "I guess. I don't know what we're going to do if we run out of fuel."

"If?" Xander thrust a hand at the window. "Look at that thing! Earth isn't even close. We *will* run out of fuel if we're getting the warning already."

Matt pressed something, and the space within the ship snapped into darkness.

"What are you doing?"

"I'm trying to conserve as much energy as possible," Matt said.

The dull glimmer of stars floated in from the window, and Xander could see Matt clicking on things on the screen. "How much time do we have?" he asked.

He wondered what would happen when the engines shut off. Would they just float in the same spot forever? Would something push them toward the sun...or a star? They would probably starve to death before they burned up. Xander shook his head. This death was going to be a lot more painful than the one he had signed up for, and they wouldn't even be helping anyone this way.

He peered out the window again, too anxious to stay still.

Earth *did* seem a little closer. Maybe it was...or maybe he was just hopeful.

"How much time do we have left?" Xander asked.

Matt didn't answer him, and Xander kept his mouth shut so that his brother could do his work. He wasn't sure how much Matt had learned in the last three years, but Xander hoped that some important bit of knowledge had stuck with him, something that would make their fuel last until they reached Earth.

Finally, Matt sat back. "We have about an hour of fuel left, maybe two. The thrusters use it so quickly."

"Then?"

"Then, I guess...we'll see what happens."

Xander pushed away from the window, his shoulder bumping against one of the walls of their tiny prison. A few hours left, and then after that, who knew?

Chapter 21

The next morning, Eden clutched her empty bowl and stared up at the front of the room where Roman was standing on the table. Everyone watched him, taking in what he had just said. Roman had sworn Eden to secrecy about the whole asteroid thing before letting her out of the room.

Everyone around Eden thought that Xander and Matt had been successful, everyone who didn't work in the bridge anyway. But Eden knew the truth, and it made her want to scream or cry or both every time she thought about it.

Roman had a few guys in there working on another solution for the asteroid, but Eden wasn't hopeful that it would be successful. They had less than a week now until the asteroid would hit them. She wondered when it would be so close that people would see it out the windows. Roman wouldn't be able to lie to them anymore then.

"I have been honest about our rations problem, and I'm sure you have all felt the change. Now is the time for us to discuss solutions. We don't have enough for everyone, and the longer we put off fixing the problem, then the less everyone will have to eat."

Eden felt hungry even though she had just finished her breakfast, and she knew that she had another painful five hours until she would get the chance to eat again. The thought of more of that mush made her feel nauseous, but she couldn't turn up her nose at it.

Someone shouted out, "Kill the ones who just arrived!"

Eden whipped her head around as she tried to locate the voice, but it was impossible in a room full of people who were all looking around as though they had no idea where the voice had come from.

"*That's* not going to happen," Roman responded, moving his hands in a quiet down motion. "I'm looking for real solutions. Has no one thought this through?"

A hand raised at the back of the room, and everyone turned to look at the thin male. "We could...have another Olympics," he suggested.

The idea pierced through Eden.

A couple of people agreed right away. "Yeah, I mean, we didn't win before, but with all the real winners taken out, maybe we could."

Eden wasn't sure who "we" meant, but she didn't want to go through that again- that being the stress of the Olympics and the knowledge that she wasn't good enough. Sure, the best of the best had already won real medals on Earth, but that still didn't mean she had a chance of winning here.

"How many people do we need to get rid of?" someone asked.

"There are 592 people on this station right now," Roman announced. "It was only built to hold and support three hundred."

Eden didn't have to be a genius to know that meant that half the people in the place would be thrown out if they weren't "good enough." She wondered if the number Roman had just quoted included the bodies that were being held "asleep."

"I don't want to do that," someone else said. Eden nodded her head in agreement.

"That's just because you know you would lose," someone else shot back.

Everyone started talking at once, but Eden felt lost without having Xander here beside her.

"It's the only fair way."

"How else could we get rid of people?"

"We can't just make the garden grow things faster."

"We're all going to die if we don't do something."

Eden studied Roman at the front of the room who was turning his head back and forth to listen to the different arguments.

Roman finally held up his hands again and waited until everyone noticed that he was ready to talk. "This is why it's important to have a discussion," he said. Eden didn't like the patronizing tone in his voice like he was a kindergarten teacher.

"I think that an Olympics is a viable option, but I would like to hear others as well. Who else has an idea for a way to make this station able to support the current population?"

"Blow up the next ship of the eliminated before they get on here," someone else suggested. He started laughing, but not very many people found his joke funny. Too many of them had recently arrived themselves.

"Any other realistic and immediately helpful solutions?" Roman asked, clearly showing that he wasn't impressed with the last suggestion.

Eden cautiously raised her hand and immediately felt the attention of hundreds of pairs of eyes on her. "Would it be possible to build onto the station and make it bigger? I mean, we have the materials taken from the ships that arrive each year."

Roman studied her, and Eden didn't detect any friendliness in his eyes. Despite the distance between them, she could feel the cold annoyance clearly on his face. "We used a lot of those materials to build the ship that we aimed at the asteroid."

Eden noted that he didn't say anything untrue, but he also didn't make it clear that said ship hadn't hit the asteroid. Eden swallowed and lowered her hand, looking at the ground.

"What about another garden?" someone suggested. "I know there's not extra space, but there's got to be somewhere else. We have lots of seeds. Couldn't we just plant more food?"

Eden remembered the delicious slice of red tomato she had had with her dinner the night before, and her stomach longed for more.

"We can work on doing that," Roman said. "But that still wouldn't provide enough. We would need to triple production, and that's not going to happen."

The sick feeling in the pit of Eden's stomach refused to go away.

"I believe it's time we take a vote," Roman said when no one else produced a viable solution.

"Not everyone is here," someone protested. "Everyone in the bridge needs to vote too."

"They'll be given a chance," Roman responded patronizingly. "Unfortunately, we can't pull everyone from their morning shifts and expect this place to still run. I'm going to ask everyone to close their eyes, and we'll raise our hands."

Eden bent her head down and stared at the ground. She tried to remember all of the solutions that had been offered, but her mind was having trouble focusing. The only one she still remembered was the suggestion of another Olympics. She couldn't let that happen. She couldn't. Even though she had actually won a medal in science, everyone here had practical experience. Who would even make these tests? How did she know if they would be fair? It seemed the worst solution all around.

"You can only vote for one option," Roman said. "The option with the most votes will be what we do moving forward. Raise your hand if you think we should expand our garden efforts," Roman said.

Eden slipped her hand up. She couldn't remember all of the options, but she would be willing to work her butt off forcing plants to grow rather than have another Olympics.

"Put your hands down. Now raise your hand if you want to conduct our own Olympics." Eden heard people raising their hands, and she wanted to scream at them that they weren't being smart. How could they sign up for their own deaths?

"Raise your hand if you think we should cut the population by culling the newest members."

Eden's eyes widened as she continued to stare at the ground. Had that solution even been discussed? No way would any of the new arrivals vote for it. Besides, it seemed heartless just to kill them without even giving them a chance.

"You can open your eyes now," Roman said.

Everyone looked around, and Eden tried to read Roman's expression. "It seems that the answer is obvious even without the votes of those on the bridge. We will conduct our own Olympics. Arrive in the dining hall tomorrow at noon, no matter what your shift is, and I'll explain the rules."

Eden couldn't move. They wouldn't...not again. It wasn't possible. Everyone started to leave the room, going about their lives. Some of them didn't seem bothered at all by this announcement, but she wasn't okay with it.

She knew that she was supposed to return to the medical center, but after what had happened the day before, Eden worried about what might happen today. What if they accused her of killing someone else? As far as she knew, no one had been identified as the person responsible for Emily's death, and Eden continued to look over her shoulder when she was walking down the hallways.

She couldn't resist her duty, though, so she walked down the hallway to the medical center, hoping that there wouldn't be anything crazy like the day before.

When she opened the door, she saw that Helena was already there along with two of the three others who were assigned to that shift. Eden looked at each one of them in turn, wondering what had suddenly made them want to be responsible.

"Put on your scrubs," Helena said, pointing to the hook with a white jacket as well as the stack of clean masks. "We're doing another vasectomy today."

Eden slowly pulled on her sanitary equipment. It was like nothing had changed, like they hadn't skipped out on their shifts for a few days. Still, Eden was grateful that she wouldn't be the only one here in case of an emergency.

Once Eden had properly equipped herself, she sidled up to Helena to get more information. "What happened to everyone the last few days?" she asked. Helena was the most approachable, rather than the guys that never said anything to her.

Helena shrugged, but Eden thought she detected a little bit of remorse in her voice. "You know...if death is that close to coming, then what's the point? But now that they've solved the problem of the asteroid, I guess we need to get back to work."

"But you know what they voted about this morning, right?" Eden couldn't remember seeing Helena there, but the room had been crowded.

"Yeah, who knows? There's a reason we had to close our eyes when Roman counted the votes."

"So we wouldn't know what people voted for." Eden shrugged her shoulders. They had done similar things in class growing up. It wasn't like Roman had done something completely crazy.

"Sure, yeah, but the reason is because Roman had already decided what he wanted to do. He just wanted people to *think* they had had a voice in the matter."

Eden's eyebrows rose. "You mean that he was planning on doing an Olympics all along?"

"He probably planted someone in the audience to suggest it. I mean, come on, who would suggest it after what we all went through?"

"I thought it was someone who just missed by a couple of places, someone who thought they had a real chance."

"Most of the people who have been here for years are out of shape. They haven't trained. There's no place to really train, but I bet you that the workout room is going to have a waiting list now. People are going to take this seriously."

Eden gripped the edge of the counter.

Helena pointed to the drawer. "Get out one of the needles and clean it please."

Eden followed Helena's instructions, but she couldn't get rid of the haunting feeling hanging over her. "People can't really want that, can they?"

Helena shrugged. "All I know is that Roman wants to cut out half the population. You can bet that it will be the half of the population that doesn't believe in him, so what we're saying right now...it needs to stay between the two of us."

Eden nodded. "I won't say anything." But secretly, she wondered who really liked Roman, because everyone she had met seemed to have a problem with his leadership.

After their shift finished, Eden's first thought was Xander. She couldn't just walk down the hall and hang out with him, though. She wondered why he had abandoned the mission. It must have been Matt's fault. Maybe Xander hadn't known what Matt was going to do. Eden had to believe the best of him.

"Where are you headed?" Helena asked.

"I guess I'll get some lunch, then..." Eden didn't have an answer. Her mind flitted to the two rooms that could be called "entertainment" rooms-the workout room and the game room. Neither one of them was where she wanted to be. Before her mind could come up with an appropriate solution, Helena offered an olive branch. "You could study with me. If we're going to go through the Olympics again, I need to review."

Eden's stomach flipped. "I should probably do that too, but how will we study?"

"There are a couple shelves of books. I'll show you where. They're mostly boring reference books, but if everyone else gets the same idea as us, they'll be gone soon."

Even though Eden knew studying was important, she was more worried about her stomach at the moment. "Okay, after we eat," she agreed.

After a pathetically small lunch, Eden followed Helena up the stairs to the second floor and down a side hallway. She wondered how much they would cut back their food rations and how that would affect her Olympic performance when Helena stopped directly in front of her.

Eden stepped on the back of Helena's shoes without realizing and backed up. "Sorry, I was just thinking..." she said, but the words left her throat when she saw why Helena had stopped.

Just out of sight of the main hallway, a person lay on the floor.

Eden looked over her shoulder to see if anyone was watching them. Even though she knew it was wrong, she couldn't be wrapped up in this again. Her brain was jumping far ahead of her. They would really think she did it now.

Helena was already getting over her shock, though. She bent down and felt for a pulse. Eden stopped where the side hallway met the main hallway. A couple of people walked past without even glancing at her.

"Is he..." Eden asked, trying to get Helena's attention. When Helena looked up, she nodded, confirming what Eden had thought at first. Helena's pasty face matched the face of the still body.

"What should we do?" Eden asked, trying not to panic. "We need to report this, but what if they think we're responsible?"

Helena shook her head, and Eden didn't know why she wasn't speaking. Was she trying to say they shouldn't report it or that no one would think they were responsible? Helena continued to touch the person's face and throat, holding her fingers under the boy's nose as though feeling for breath before checking his wrist again.

But Eden needed to *do* something. "We have to report it," she repeated. Even though she didn't like Roman, she had to shift the situation out of their hands and put it in someone else's.

"Yes," Helena finally spoke. "But I don't want to leave him alone. Can you go to the bridge? Find someone who can take care of this?"

Eden saw Helena's mouth trembling, and she realized then that Helena knew this victim. This wasn't just a stranger. "Okay, I'll bring someone right away," she said, trying to stay calm even though she wanted to scream.

Eden hurried toward the staircase and to the bridge as quickly as she could. She dodged around people who were casually strolling down the hallway, then pounded on the door when she reached it.

"What?" someone shouted from inside.

"There's been a... a body. We found a body!"

Someone who was walking down the hallway turned and stared at Eden. "What did you just say?" he asked.

"A body," Eden repeated. "We found someone. He was hurt."

The door to the bridge opened, and someone Eden didn't recognize stared at her. "Where? I'll page Roman."

"Uh, second floor, down one of the side hallways. I don't know exactly. I can show you."

The guy shook his head and shut the door in Eden's face. Eden hoped he was going to do what he said. She hurried back to the staircase to check on Helena, and the guy from outside the bridge followed her.

"Someone's dead?" he asked.

Eden nodded as she gripped the railing and hurried back to the second floor.

"Who? What happened?"

"We don't know."

"Wasn't there somebody found dead yesterday?" he asked.

Eden swallowed. "Yes." She didn't want to talk about the part she had played in that one either. When she reached Helena, the older girl hadn't moved. She was still bent over the body checking it for signs of life as her long braids obscured the boy's face. If Eden didn't know better, she might think the person was sleeping. He looked peaceful, except for the ugly bruises around his throat.

"Is someone coming?" Helena finally asked.

"Yes, someone's coming," Eden assured her. She wasn't very good at comforting other people, but she stepped forward and put a hand on Helena's shoulder hoping that it would do something to make her feel a little bit better.

Even though Eden didn't like herself for thinking it, she was just hoping that no one would accuse them of causing this. They had been in the dining hall, but would anyone remember that? If there really weren't enough rations for everyone, then why would anyone stick up for Eden and Helena to keep them from being shoved out of the station?

Roman appeared behind the group of four- three living and one dead- a few minutes later. "Step away from the body," he growled. Another dark-haired male stood behind him watching the scene. Eden had seen him a couple of times, but he was definitely quiet, letting Roman take the reins in every situation.

"He's dead!" Roman shouted, throwing up his hands in exasperation. "How did this happen?" He swore as he stood up, glaring at the body like the person's death was a personal affront to him.

"Well, he's got to be taken out of here," he said. "We can put him in the lock for a few hours, then we'll need to put him out."

"Are you just going to throw him into space?" Helena asked, finally on her feet again. She was doing an excellent job of holding herself together, depending on how well she had known this person.

"We can't just keep him here. It would serve no purpose, and realistically, his body will start to decompose."

Helena's face crumpled, and Eden stepped forward, seeing that her friend was really struggling with this. Roman beat her to it, though. In the first display of humanity that Eden had seen from him, he laid a hand on Helena's shoulder. "I know it seems callus, but not doing it won't change his situation."

"I understand," Helena muttered.

Roman looked at the guy who had followed Eden. "You can help Percy take care of the body."

"Aren't you going to tell anyone?" Eden asked Roman, sounding bold despite the way she normally hid behind herself.

Roman turned his eyes on her. "What are you doing here...again?"

"I was with Helena trying to get a book." By this time, the two guys had shouldered the body. They carried him gently away, following Roman down the hallway as he muttered about catching the culprit.

Helena stood there, looking at the patch of floor where the body had been lying. "I'm sorry," Eden told her, but her words sound so light, frivolous. She knew they couldn't do anything to make Helena feel better.

"I think I'm just going to go to bed for a little while," Helena decided. "I just... I don't feel up to studying at the moment."

"Okay, yeah," Eden tried to encourage her. "I can walk you to your room." They walked quietly down the hallway until Helena stopped at one of the doors. She didn't say anything to Eden, just nodded to her before pushing the door open and disappearing inside.

Eden sighed and looked down the hallway at her own door. Who had killed these two people and why? What if they came after her next?

Chapter 22

The engine suddenly cut off. Xander was no expert in machinery, but the sudden quiet told him more than Matt could.

"It's done, isn't it?" he asked.

Matt just nodded, looking at the now-blank screen.

"No power at all?" Xander touched one of the buttons, but nothing happened. The space was completely dark except for a pale, eerie light coming through the window. Xander waited for the ship to slow down, for it to grind to a halt and just begin floating aimlessly.

He didn't feel the distinct thrust forward he would feel if someone pressed the brakes in a bus, though. Maybe it was slowing down so gradually that he wasn't able to feel it.

Xander stared out the window. They had gotten close enough to Earth that he could make out the distinct shape of North America to the left. It looked destroyed, not a green mass of land but a wasteland. Greenland's familiar triangular shape was directly in front of them, still small but distinguishable.

It felt like he was looking at a map in school, except this was no map.

"Can you think of anything we can do?" Xander asked.

"No, man. We're dead. I mean, I have no way of controlling this thing anymore." Matt pulled out some clothing that Xander had seen earlier and wondered about. "I guess I brought these for nothing."

"What are those?" Xander asked as one of the suits drifted open, and he saw it wasn't normal clothing.

"Doesn't matter," Matt said, tossing it on the ground where it slowly floated up toward the ceiling.

Xander pushed away from the window. He had already examined the whole ship, and he knew he wouldn't find anything new now. Still, he tried to look at each object with an open, creative mind, even examining the strangely silky clothing that Matt had thrown into the open cabin to float around leisurely.

None of the objects would be able to create power, but maybe there was something that could work as some sort of propeller. Xander bent under the computer screen, trying to see if there was anything underneath that could prove useful. The thing had been put together crudely, and the wires hung exposed underneath. Xander fingered them, but they barely even felt warm anymore. Anyway, he didn't know what he could do with them even if he managed to take them all apart.

He followed each wire from its base to the computer, wondering why there were so many. Maybe...

"How crazy do you think we'll get before we die?" Matt asked. His head and shoulders completely obscured the window, cutting out what little light Xander had been using. He slammed his fist against the bottom of the computer setup, but the lack of gravity meant that his fist barely made a tiny smacking noise.

Angry that he couldn't even punch something, he yelled. "This is *your* fault, Matt! Why did you do this? We're going to die, and everyone else is too! At least the other way would have been a quick death."

"Really? You're picking out which type of death you would prefer now? Hey, we have no idea how quick this will be. Maybe I'll surprise you and make yours really quick." Matt lunged at Xander, but what was meant to be a quick movement slowed immediately.

Because Xander was lying on his back under the computer, holding one of the metal poles for support, he couldn't really do anything but roll further into the cords. Matt floated away, laughing like it was a big game, but Xander's anger flared higher.

"You think this is funny?" he asked, emerging from under the desk and trying to turn right way up as his feet started to float above his head. Matt had no advantages over Xander, and Xander had all of the training on his side. Matt's speed wouldn't help him in a tiny ship that impeded all movement.

"You need to take responsibility for all of those people up there. Hundreds of people are going to die because of *you*!" Xander's hands curled into fists without him really commanding them.

Matt must have realized how angry Xander was, and he made the first move, pushing off the wall directly at Xander.

Xander ducked and turned in a complete circle, his fists in front of his face now. A small part of his mind told him he was being stupid, but a much larger part told him that Matt needed to be taught a lesson. Xander threw two punches in quick succession, landing one in Matt's stomach and the other just grazing his shoulder. Neither one of them felt like they had hit hard enough. Stupid gravity.

Matt lunged at Xander again, grabbing him around the middle, and they both spun in a rapid circle in the air. Xander's mind went into strategy mode, and he pushed off the wall closest to his feet, angling them toward the computer. Matt smacked his head hard against it. Gravity or no gravity, he had to feel something.

While Matt reached up to feel his head, Xander punched Matt in the face once, then twice. He stopped himself before the third punch as Matt tried to protect his face with his arms. The anger seemed to flow slowly out of Xander as he realized what he was doing and who this was. He took a few deep breaths, then pushed away from him, bumping gently against the far wall. He still watched Matt warily in case he decided to make another move toward him.

Xander wiped his hands on his pants, and Matt touched his face, trying to figure out what was hurting him.

"Here, uh, you can have my shirt for that," Xander said, peeling off his shirt and handing it to Matt to soak up the blood that was falling out of his nose in large bubbles. "Sorry, I don't know what got into me."

Matt swatted the shirt through the air, catching blood bubbles as they floated, then held it under his nose. After a minute, Matt smiled. "Death got into you," he said. "Man, you're stronger than you used to be."

"It's been three years since we've seen each other."

"Still..." Matt pulled back the shirt to evaluate the blood on it. "Who knew? You should have won a medal."

They seemed to remember at the same time that Xander had. Neither one of them said anything because it didn't matter anyway.

Xander sat against the wall, tying himself in so he wouldn't make himself dizzy with more uncontrollable floating and spinning. His brother might be laughing now, but Xander still didn't feel completely safe around him. Not that it really mattered if he died now or in a few hours or in a few days. Xander had no chances left. His luck had run out.

After sitting on the floor for what felt like a long time, Xander had run through all of the options in his head. He didn't want to die like this. He couldn't just wait for his body to break down or them to run out of oxygen. He would go crazy before then.

Matt had been staring out the window, and the lack of purpose was getting to Xander's head. "Matt," he said. "I can't just wait for death."

"Want me to make it come faster?" Matt asked, a little smile on the corner of his lips. "I've always thought it would be cool to try out cannibalism."

"No," Xander told him with an angry look. "You're not being helpful."

"At least I'm consistent." Matt turned back to the window, and Xander felt an unexplainable rage within him. He had to keep it down, though. He couldn't go crazy at the end. He wouldn't let himself.

"Xander, come look out the window," Matt said.

Xander rolled his eyes, but there was something in Matt's tone that said he wasn't joking around anymore. Xander untied the rope around his feet and pushed off the wall. Was it his imagination or did his body feel heavier? He hadn't eaten in quite a few hours, and every movement required a lot of effort.

Matt leaned back against the wall so that Xander could squeeze past him in the narrow space. When he looked out the window, all he saw was Earth. That was exactly what he had seen when he had last looked out the window, but something in his brain told him it seemed closer.

Xander frowned. That wasn't possible. He tilted his head and tried to look at it from a different angle, but the small window didn't allow for a lot of maneuvering.

"We're closer, right?" Matt asked once Xander had had a chance to get a good view out of the window.

"Yes," Xander replied slowly. "But I guess the ship just had a little momentum from when the engines were still on." He stared at Earth. They definitely weren't moving closer anymore. "It doesn't matter how close we are to Earth when we die; we still didn't reach it."

"No, but..." Matt squeezed back around Xander so that his frame filled the window again. "I mean, it *does* matter if we're still moving."

Xander stood as still as he could in the center of the ship, stretching out his arms on either side like he was trying to keep his balance on a tightrope. He closed his eyes and willed his body to feel some movement, something that would indicate they hadn't ground to a halt, but he just slowly floated upward until he bumped his head on the ceiling.

"We're not moving," he concluded. "Your mind is just playing tricks on you. We haven't eaten in hours, and we know we're going to die, even if it takes a couple of days." Xander shook his head. He wished he knew what to expect. He didn't think he had the courage to end things now, but he wasn't looking forward to the hours of contemplation that lay ahead. He plopped down on the floor again and stared across at the two water bottles that had long ago been emptied and refilled with a different kind of liquid.

Xander's throat felt parched, but he wasn't desperate enough to drink it. No way. He would never sink that low. What would be the point of putting off his death? Or maybe that would speed it up?

Another long while passed with neither of them speaking. Xander rested his head against his knees and closed his eyes, thinking over moments with Eden and things she had said, wondering what she thought of him now. Would she know that he had fought for hitting the asteroid like they were supposed to? Or did she believe whatever narrative Roman had told them? She was too trusting sometimes.

Xander's thoughts turned to his mother and father, but mostly his mother and how her cancer was progressing. Xander wondered if anyone looking up into the sky could see a metal contraption hovering there. At some point, he must have fallen asleep.

When he woke up, his neck hurt, and Xander took his time cracking it slowly. Matt was sitting on the other side of the ship, and he looked like he was sleeping as well.

Xander yawned and stretched, his stomach immediately demanding attention. They hadn't been given any food to take with them. Obviously, the crew on board the space station hadn't wanted to waste rations on two people who were going to die anyway, but Xander had to look. He remembered the packages of dried fruit that he had found in the medical center.

Even though he knew it was impossible, he began looking under and behind everything, his stomach driving him to do crazy things. His rustling must have woken Matt because Matt looked up and studied Xander closely. He had dark circles under his eyes, and he looked like he hadn't bathed in a long time. Well, neither had Xander. They had to have been on this thing for at least a full day by now, maybe longer. Time seemed to stretch in front of them infinitely without a clock.

No food. That much was clear, and Xander's arms already felt tired from all the pushing and moving that his searching had demanded. He took a deep breath and approached the window, intending to entertain himself with some deep thoughts while he stared at Earth.

"Matt!" he called as soon as he got a good look out the window.

Matt unfolded himself slowly and pushed off the wall, his body zooming forward. Xander waited. He didn't say anything, because he needed Matt to tell him he wasn't crazy. Matt stared out the window motionlessly before slowly turning his head to Xander.

"We're still moving," Matt concluded.

Xander nodded enthusiastically, energy suddenly flooding his veins. "I'm not sure how it's happening, but we're still moving. How can we move through space without engines running?"

"I don't know," Matt said. "I have no idea how it's working, but we're definitely closer. Last time, I could cover up the Earth by holding my thumb like this. Now, it takes my whole hand to cover it up. We must have entered Earth's atmosphere."

Xander moved suddenly, bumping his head on the ceiling as he pumped his fist into the air. He winced. "Okay, we're still moving," he said, accepting the new situation. He looked back at the window. Earth was definitely closer, and by the size of it now, Xander must have slept a long time. He stopped the crazy celebration and tried to be practical.

"How long do you think it will take us to reach Earth now?" Xander asked.

Matt turned to the computer, then shook his head. "I don't know. Before when I looked, it said thirty hours."

"Thirty hours since you turned it toward Earth?"

"Yes."

"How long do you think it's been?"

"More than half," Matt estimated with a shrug.

Xander nodded. He thought that was accurate. "I would agree with more than half. Okay, so we just need to survive another fifteen hours or so. We can do that."

"If the spaceship keeps on the same trajectory, we're going to land in the ocean," Matt told him. "We're going to have to swim. The hardest part will be getting out of the ship…" He reached for the silky clothing that he had discarded earlier. "We'll need these. When we enter the atmosphere, we'll have to jump out of the ship. We have to time it right so we don't burn up."

Xander stared at him in shock for a few minutes. "Burn up?"

Matt smiled teasingly. "I mean, you can if you want, but I won't." He fingered the material. "They may not have figured out how to stop global warming, but at least they found out how to create a material that protects against high levels of heat. It won't work for very long, but… it should keep us safe."

Xander swallowed and looked at the thin material nervously. Trusting that material with his life… he wasn't sure he could do that. He turned his mind to other questions. "You said you were aiming for water near the land, right?" Xander asked.

"Right…but it was also hard to be very accurate when we were so far away, and I've never aimed something like this before. No telling what's driving it now."

Xander focused on the positive. "We're getting there. It's a possibility. That's better than before."

"I'm just hoping what I estimated was correct," Matt said, his eyes shut tight as he recited information. "Global warming has changed Earth's atmosphere, so we should be able to breathe at… was it 200,000 miles up? I can't remember the number. These suits have oxygen packets, but those only last up to five minutes. It's not a long term solution, but it should get us low enough, especially if you take in oxygen and hold it for a minute. Don't try to breathe quickly."

Matt continued giving instructions. "We'll have to leave the ship at just the right moment. I'll let you know when. Oh, God. I hope these work. But if the pressurization..." Matt started muttering something else, but Xander just peered out the window again.

He knew he was checking too soon to see a difference in their position; he should wait at least an hour between times looking out the window if he wanted to see a real difference.

Xander had never had to pass time like this before. It seemed painful as he waited for the hours to pass. He counted sixty seconds out, marking the minutes with his fingers. Then, he marked sets of ten minutes with his toes until he had reached an hour. It proved at least mildly entertaining since he had nothing else to do.

Once he reached an hour or what he thought was an hour, Xander pushed hard against the wall so he could reach the window, not wanting to wait another second to see their progress.

"We're a *lot* closer now!" Xander exclaimed with the excitement of a little kid seeing the ocean for the first time. "I think we might get there in a few more hours."

Matt evaluated their position and agreed with him. "Maybe five or six hours," he said.

Xander sat back down in his same position and began to pass the time with his counting again. It was boring, but it worked. He allowed himself to check their progress after each hour, each time scared that he might note they hadn't moved forward at all. He hardly noticed the pain in his stomach now.

One hour.

Two hours.

Three hours.

Four hours.

Each time as Xander moved toward the window, his body felt heavier. Now, the Earth wouldn't fit fully in his view anymore. "We're getting close," he said. They were definitely headed for the ocean, and he could see the edge of Greenland not too far away. He hoped that he would be able to find the energy to swim all the way from wherever they landed.

"We're going to make it!" Matt said behind Xander. They hugged each other in excitement, and Xander thought of how Eden would always do a little dance leap when she was happy about something. He missed her a lot, but he cared more about staying alive at that moment.

Xander couldn't pull himself away from the window as they grew closer and closer. "We're going to make it," he announced again even though it wasn't a new revelation to either of them.

"We should go ahead and put these on," Matt said, handing him the cool fabric. Xander frowned at the one-piece suit, then began pulling it over his legs first. As he pulled it over his legs and bare chest, he instantly felt an icy sensation like he had stuck his hand in a cool glass of water.

"Are you sure about this?" he asked as he got to the hood.

Matt had already pulled his hood over his head. Just a thin piece of see-through fabric flapped above his head, ready to cover his face. "Do it," he commanded. "When we hit Earth's atmosphere, we're going to have gravity pulling on us too. We'll start falling faster. Really fast. We need to be ready to get out of here as soon as the ship starts getting hot." Matt ran his fingers along the edge of the hatch they had used to enter the ship so long ago.

Xander nodded. He wasn't going to drown in this thing after all he had been through. "Okay, the latch looks simple. We just push this up, then push, right?"

Matt nodded. "That's what it looks like. I should have paid more attention when they put us in here."

Suddenly, Xander felt something pulling him against the window, and he knew it was the strength of gravity. He let it pull on him until he was smashed against the window.

He felt it warm against his skin like a freshly brewed mug of coffee.

"It's hot now!" Matt yelled, leaning the exposed skin of his face close to the metal. The ship seemed to be falling at hundreds of miles per hour, but Xander wasn't fascinated by the mechanics of it anymore. He could barely pull himself back from the window, and pushing against the walls seared his hands.

"We have to get out of here now then!" Matt yelled, fiddling with the latch. "It's going to burn up! I thought we had more time! Cover your face with the mask and breathe slowly!"

Xander bent forward and forced himself to take a step up the slanted floor, bracing himself against one of the walls with his leg. He felt a strange warmth, but nothing hot enough to worry about.

"We can't just jump," he said as Matt finally flung the latch open.

But Matt had already rolled down the last piece of fabric and sealed it around his face. He nodded to Xander, then he disappeared as soon as he had pulled his body out of the hatch.

The air crept into his lungs, but he still felt like he was choking. He sealed the face mask shut and maneuvered the oxygen bag into place, feeling immediate relief as the front of the ship started to smoke.

Freaking out that he didn't have a parachute or anything to slow his fall, Xander took one more step across the ship's floor, fighting the gravity that wanted to fling him against the wall. How had Matt just jumped out of the ship? Realistic concerns played through his head, then the window behind Xander burst into tiny pieces, and he saw a tiny flame erupt on the front of the ship. The tiny flame quickly became bigger, eating at the metal around the nose of the ship.

He didn't have time to play around with practicality anymore. He had to go. Xander pulled himself up, once again feeling a warm sensation when his gloved hands touched the ship's metal. There was no time for standing on top of the falling ship and contemplating if he should jump or not.

As soon as he was out of the ship, the wind whipped him away from it. His hands frantically flapped like a confused ostrich before his descent began in earnest.

He screamed for a good thirty seconds before he realized that he had to conserve oxygen, and that he hadn't died yet.

The dry oxygen burned through his lungs. Xander was plummeting toward the water fast. He didn't know how long it would take him to hit it, but he had to turn himself around or he would hit it face first.

He reached for the front of his suit and felt the oxygen bag. It was half-deflated. He had a couple more minutes before he had to test the air's level of oxygen. Trying to conserve it, he took slow, deep breaths, almost forgetting how fast he was falling for a moment.

Xander struggled in the air to turn until he was falling feet first. He looked around and saw Matt below him, just a short distance from the surface of the water. Next, Xander located which piece of land would be nearest. He would have to swim, and far, but he wasn't going to give up now. He could see the research center not too far away, and he had time for a quick smile as he fell.

Suddenly, his lungs burned, and Xander fumbled with the latch on his suit's mask. It opened, and he sucked in the air around him. Oxygen, real oxygen.

Xander's feet plunged into the cool water, and the water covered his head less than a second later.

Chapter 23

There wasn't enough room for everyone to sit in the dining hall, so they all stood, craning their necks to see Roman in his familiar position on the table. Eden wondered if anyone else thought about how gross it was that the bottom of his shoes were on the table that was used for serving them food.

"I wanted to explain the rules to everyone at the same time," Roman said, but Eden had to guess at some of his words. Lots of people were still talking, and she shifted back and forth on her feet as the nerves hit. Helena was standing a couple of people away, and there was still a sad downward turn to her lips.

Roman whistled, but it still wasn't loud enough. A couple of other people started yelling at the rest to be quiet, and it broke into a madhouse. Eden crossed her arms. Who did Roman's friends think they were trying to run anything? They clearly couldn't do it.

After five minutes of loud chaos, the group finally settled down.

"Okay," Roman said, crossing his arms and looking confident above them. "We need to go over the rules for our official Olympics." He said it with a smile like he was proud of them or something. Eden turned over what Helena had suggested, that Roman had already decided this was what he wanted and that he hadn't taken a real vote.

"There are going to be four competitions, and they've been tailored specifically to fit with life here. Some of the competitions in the Olympics on Earth aren't useful here. The competitions will be- controls, gardening, medical, and physical."

Eden frowned. She didn't know much about any of those subjects, though she had been learning something about medicine in the last week.

"We'll hold one competition a day, and there will be seventy-five winners of each competition."

Eden did some quick math. He was still planning to cut the population by half. Looking around, Eden tried to judge her competition by how confident they looked. Only a small number of people worked in medical- five to eight each shift, so she was pretty sure that there wouldn't be a lot of people able to beat her. Still... she needed to start paying attention.

"We'll go in the order I just called. Controls- or the brains- will be to-morrow. Gardening, the day after that, etc. Got it?"

"How are you going to have a gardening competition?" someone shouted out. "Make people grow plants quickly? That's not something you can do in a day."

Roman looked annoyed by the question, but he answered it anyway. "Since *someone* doesn't seem to understand how the competition works, I'll explain." He paused dramatically. "You'll find out what you're required to do when you have arrived at each competition. If you can't figure out where the competitions will be held, then you're not smart enough to compete. *If* you don't win in any of the four competitions, then you'll be taken to the hatch and..." Roman made a motion with his hands that looked like he was throwing someone out of the station.

A sudden picture of nearly three hundred bodies being pushed into the atmosphere to float around the station as they decomposed made Eden grab her stomach. This was sick, disgusting. She couldn't...

A couple of people protested. "Are *you* going to compete?" someone asked Roman.

"Who's going to decide the winners?"

"Who's making up the rules?"

All very good questions, but Eden was fairly sure she already knew the answers, and they all pointed back to Roman.

He held up his hands for silence again. "I have no problem competing," he explained which surprised Eden, "but we *do* need someone to judge. I have selected myself and two other vital members to the organization of this station. The competitions are pretty simple as far as who wins or doesn't win, but we'll be there to make sure that things are timed and judged correctly. We are keeping it as fair as possible."

A few people started grumbling, and Eden looked at Helena. Helena brushed the hair out of her eyes, then started shouldering her way out of the crowd. She clearly had somewhere to be, but Eden wasn't sure where that could be. What else was there to do besides soak in the news that it was all starting over again?

Eden decided to follow Helena. Maybe she would make good on her offer to study with her. As Eden tried to sneak through the crowd, though, someone stepped backward into her.

There was nothing she could use to brace herself, and she tumbled to the ground. "Ow," she complained as she hit at least one other person on her way down. A couple of other people landed on the ground as well, and Eden flinched.

"Sorry, sorry," she apologized repeatedly.

Someone bent down to offer her a hand up, and Eden took the hand without thinking. As she was crouched, halfway to her feet again, she realized who it was- Derry. Eden yanked her hand out of his so hard that she elbowed someone behind her.

That person yelped and shoved her back so that she went sprawling frontways onto the ground. Eden sucked at the air around her, but the oxygen seemed to have disappeared. Her lungs burned as she tried to remember how to work them.

Finally, oxygen burrowed into her lungs, and she could breathe again.

As she tried to get up and see what had happened exactly, someone shoved her back to the ground. "You should just stay there," a voice said threateningly. Eden couldn't see her attacker, but she lay motionless on the ground, scared.

She could hear people on the other side of the room disagreeing about something, but no one seemed to notice her still sprawled on the floor. Eden rolled onto her side, surveying the people around her. A couple of them were looking at her with strange expressions, but no one said anything as she climbed to her feet. Eden examined her arms and discovered that one of her elbows had a long, red mark down it from where she had slid her arm against the carpet.

"Who..." she started to ask, but none of the people around her would make eye contact.

Eden couldn't find Helena, but she thought she might know where she had gone- either the bookshelf that Eden still hadn't seen because they had been distracted or her bedroom. Eden finished squeezing her way out of the large room and walked down the hallway which was eerily empty. She should go to the second floor and find Helena.

Just as Eden was opening the door to the stairway, she heard her name in a guy's voice. "Eden!"

Eden turned around and saw Derry walking quickly toward her. She froze for a second. There was nothing she could do- move, speak…

Then, she remembered who this was, and she flung the door to the stairs open, taking them two at a time.

She had just reached the top of them, more out of breath than she should have been, when Derry opened the door at the bottom. "Eden," he said again. "Why are you running away from me?"

Eden paused with her hand on the second floor door. She slowly edged the door open. She couldn't be afraid of him. That was dumb. He had just tried to help her. However, even with her rational thoughts, Eden knew she could never think of Derry as a nice person.

"I'm in a hurry to catch up with my friend," she explained. The door was now completely open.

"The friend you were following in the dining hall?"

Maybe he had just made a lucky guess or maybe he had been watching her. Eden shivered. She didn't like the feeling that Derry had been tracking her movements. "Yeah," she answered.

Then, she ducked through the doorway and let the door to the stairs close behind her. She decided to try to find Helena's room, worried about what might happen if she ducked down one of the side hallways again. However, when she was halfway down the hallway, peering in the empty bedrooms along the way, she heard the door to the stairs thump open. Derry had arrived on the second floor. He had every right to be there- his room was somewhere along its length- but at the same time, Eden knew he was following her.

She whirled around, hoping she was close to Helena's room. "What do you want?" she asked. Her voice sounded harsh, maybe even brave, and Eden was glad that Derry wouldn't be able to tell how nervous he made her.

"I was just trying to talk to you," Derry said. "I know you're in a hurry, but maybe if you have a minute…"

"What do you want to talk about?" Eden put her hands on her hips and watched him carefully. He wasn't that much taller than her, and he was pretty lanky. Still, she remembered watching him through her half-drugged eyelids as he had wrestled with Xander. Xander was one of the best, but Derry had still managed to stick him with a knife. Derry wasn't carrying any weapons now, though. At least, she hoped he didn't have one.

"I just," Derry shrugged like it was no big deal, "I thought it would be nice to get to know each other. You know, as real people."

"Why should I get to know you? Last Olympics, you tried to kill me."

"Okay, that's too far. I wasn't going to kill anyone."

"You think that drugging me so I couldn't compete fairly wasn't the same as signing me up for elimination?"

Derry cocked his head to the side. "I've never thought of it like that before. I guess…okay, you have a point. Look, let's call a truce."

Eden didn't like that he was making her either openly declare war on him or agree to be his friend. Neither option was one she liked. "Fine," she agreed, just because she didn't want Derry as her enemy. "We can call a truce, but I still need to check on my friend. She wasn't looking…very well."

Derry nodded. "Sure, yeah, go check on Helena."

Eden's stomach froze. How did Derry know her friend's name? He probably knew Eden's because he had selected who to kidnap at the prior Olympics, but Helena's? Eden didn't like the creepy-crawly feeling she got around him, so she hurried to Helena's room with the hope for a feeling of safety once she reached it.

Chapter 24

Xander sputtered as his head emerged from the water. Air. Oxygen. Breathing. Those were the only things that occupied his mind as he kicked his legs, trying to remain in place as his body remembered how to take oxygen to his brain.

Xander took a long breath, then let it out. Then, he used his arms to spin around in a circle.

"Matt!" Xander called out.

He didn't see his brother's dark head, but he did see the ship about to hit the water, and Xander didn't want to be close to it when it landed. The whole thing was on fire now, and it looked like some sort of speeding bullet as it made its way toward him.

Xander struck out in the direction of some distant mountains, determined to get out of the way of the fiery object.

He heard the splash behind him, and a few moments later, waves washed over him. Xander held his breath and didn't try to fight them. He just had to keep swimming forward. He knew logically how to deal with the situation, but that didn't stop the panic within him.

What if Matt had been exactly where the ship landed?

Even though he was moving, his body was freezing. He felt like he had plunged into icy, arctic waters, even though he had swam in this very ocean before without feeling like it was cold.

The water seemed suddenly alive with sea life. Something brushed his leg, and Xander hoped it was just a fish.

Even though he knew his muscles had to be warming up as he swam, he still felt like his whole body was freezing over. Remembering the suit, Xander fumbled with stupidly cold fingers to take it off. As he peeled off the layer of protection, the warm water instantly soothed him.

Who cared about the suit now? It had served its purpose. He finished kicking it off in the water and realized that he had lost one of his shoes in the process. It didn't matter. He had to keep swimming.

Finally, he couldn't move forward any longer. He had to take a break. As Xander approached a foreboding brown shape in the water, he realized that it was a piece of driftwood, not an animal like he had feared. He grabbed onto it as he gasped for air. Once he could breathe again, he evaluated the land in front of him. He had gotten closer, but he still probably had a couple of hours of swimming in front of him. His one shoe felt heavy now. He wavered between trying to save it and letting it go. It was hard to think past swimming anymore.

"Matt!" Xander called once he had caught his breath again. He whirled around and searched the waves behind and beside him. The water lapped up and slapped him in the face, and Xander wiped at his eyes. He didn't hear anything, and Xander wondered if Matt hadn't survived.

They had jumped out of a burning spaceship without parachutes. Their likelihood of survival was low anyway, but still...Xander didn't want to do this alone.

He turned back so that he was facing the land. His arms had had a chance to rest now. He needed to get back to swimming.

Xander pushed himself forward, counting his strokes in sets of twenty. He could do this. He could get closer. Xander looked up a few times and saw that the land was closer but still too far away.

He put his head down and continued. Finally, the rocks that edged the coast of Greenland seemed within reaching distance. He would have to be careful or the waves might slam him up against them. Xander swam sideways as he searched for a spot where he would be able to climb the rocks.

There. That spot looked safe enough. "You can do it," Xander told himself, wasting breath on the words because he so needed their encouragement.

He didn't put his face in the water now. He had to watch the water at all times. The water seemed to propel him forward, and Xander's hands scrambled across the slimy rocks once he reached them. The water pressed him into the rocks, scraping his chest, but Xander kept from hitting his head. Then, as the water receded, he pulled himself up onto the ledge.

It wasn't enough. He needed to get higher. So after only three or four deep breaths, Xander stood, his legs wobbling underneath him. He climbed the short rock wall above him until he was on the main ledge.

He looked out over the world to see if he recognized where he was. Yes, he was on the very edge of Sisimiut. Matt might not have known what he was doing, but he had managed to get them back to Greenland.

Xander looked around as he plopped onto the rocks, the water splashing up several feet below him. His arms trembled, and all Xander wanted to do was close his eyes and sleep. But he couldn't. He had to find Matt.

Standing, he slowly made his way around the bay, his eyes alternatively searching the water and the rock ledge.

"Matt!" he called again before looking over his shoulder. There were some houses, but they were a good distance away from the ocean. He didn't think anyone would hear him clearly enough to know what he was saying. Besides, it didn't matter.

There!

Xander spotted Matt swimming toward shore, but he was a good half mile away from him. Xander waved his arms above his head until he was sure Matt had seen him, then he plopped down. Matt had it now, and Xander needed the rest.

The sun burned into his skin. He didn't realize how much he had missed the sun until he had lived in the shadow of the moon for a week. He closed his eyes and let it dry the salty water droplets off his skin.

Right now, he couldn't think about a plan or what they would do. He just wanted to enjoy being alive, something he hadn't been so sure about over the past few hours.

"Hey," Matt said as he stumbled over and collapsed beside Xander. He too had gotten rid of his suit. "We both made it." He leaned over and coughed up some salty water.

"Yeah," Xander responded, eyeing his older brother through one squinted eye. "But you look like a whale ate you then spit you back up."

"That might have been nice. Wouldn't have had to swim all that way."

At least nearly dying hadn't taken away his brother's sense of humor. Xander didn't feel the need for conversation right then, so he closed his eyes again and let the sun continue to dry him. He wasn't sure how much time passed, but when he heard Matt stirring on the rocks beside him, Xander knew that it was time to get moving. They hadn't come here to sunbathe.

"Are you ready to move?" he asked.

"You said you have some braniac friend," Matt reminded him. "Where is he?"

Xander recalled the details of the adulting ceremony and Colt's penchant for science. "I think he's at the research center, but I'm not sure of that."

"You're not sure? We're going to what...break into the research center and maybe be arrested for something you're not sure about?"

Xander nodded. He stood up, his legs still aching from the long swim. He looked down at himself. He had one shoe and his shorts. His shirt had been lost sometime while he was escaping the space capsule. His hair hadn't seen a comb in a while, and he knew he was starting to sprout some facial hair. He looked a mess.

"Yes, that's what we're going to do, because there's nothing else we can do. A bicycle would be a lot of help right now."

Xander surveyed the coast. Even though he and Eden had never come this far down the road, he knew where they were. Exploring every part of his world by bike meant that he knew all of the back roads, exactly where everything was. It would come in handy now.

"Don't you think we should go see Mom first?" Matt suggested. "Just in case something happens, and your idea doesn't pan out."

Matt's suggestion was tempting, but Xander shook his head. "You're the one who made us come here. We have less than a week, probably only five days now, to figure out a way to stop that asteroid. If we can do that, well, at least we will have done what we said even if we did it a different way."

Matt ran a hand through his hair. "And what if we can't find him? Or we're arrested? Then what was the point of going through all that?"

Xander couldn't stand the reluctance. "Hey! *You* wanted to come here. We're here! Now, let's do something about the people up there. I'm *not* just going to mosey around visiting family while they die." Xander clenched his jaw as he thought of Eden.

Matt finally gave a slow nod of approval. "Fine. We'll give this one shot. If we mess it up or we can't get in or we can't find this guy, I'm not going to wander around looking for smart people who take pity on us. I'm going to start my life over here."

Xander wasn't sure what sort of life Matt thought he could start in a place where he wasn't supposed to exist, but he didn't want to waste time arguing that point now. He nodded in the direction of the research center- a large building on the edge of Sisimiut. He had never visited it personally, but everyone knew that the best scientific minds each year were moved there, no matter where they had originated.

"I guess we should start walking there," Xander said aloud. "We can figure out a plan along the way." He glanced at Matt's feet. He still had both of his shoes, though they were waterlogged and looked heavy.

Xander had to pick his way carefully over the rocks. Some of them were large and smooth, but there were just enough pointed rocks to keep him on his toes. Finally, they had reached the end of the rocky coast and walking was easier. Xander slid off his one shoe and carried it, flinging little droplets of water with each swing of his arm. Good thing the road was fairly smooth.

"What does this guy look like and why do you think he'll help you?" Matt asked.

"He's kind of small. I mean, you can tell just by looking at him that he's not competing in any of the physical competitions." Xander realized he was still talking about the Olympics like they were approaching, not like they had already passed. He had to get over that thought process. "He has round glasses, blonde hair, pointed nose."

Matt nodded at each descriptor. "Sounds like a hit with the ladies," he said.

Xander rolled his eyes. "Your derogatory comments are going to do nothing to help any of us. If you're going to be like that, then keep your mouth shut when we find him."

Matt held his hands up. "Freedom of speech isn't a thing anymore?"

"Not when you're insulting the only person who might help us. Anyway, his name is Colt, and we sat beside each other on the plane to the Olympics. I got to know him more during my time there."

"So, a friend," Matt concluded.

Xander just shrugged. Who cared what title he had as long as he was able to help them? "We're going to explain the situation to him. He'll probably be surprised to see us because he knows that I was eliminated."

"But wouldn't someone in the research center know that we were up there? Wouldn't they be watching us?" Matt asked. "I mean, obviously not with cameras at the station, but maybe just checking on us through a telescope every once in a while?"

"I don't know, and honestly, it doesn't matter at this point." Xander shut down the conversation and looked up to check their progress. They still had a few hours of walking ahead of them.

When they finally started nearing the research center, Xander wondered if they should be more inconspicuous. They hadn't passed any cars along the road, but most of the people who worked in the research center lived in the housing units surrounding it. There wasn't the need for a lot of traffic along the road.

"Have a plan yet?" Matt asked Xander when they were less than a mile from the place. Xander studied the distance from where they were to the building. He had never seen it up close. It looked like it was three stories tall, but some of the windows stretched across multiple stories. He couldn't tell much about entrances and exits from that distance.

"Yeah," Xander said. His hair and shorts had already dried, though his shoe was hanging on stubbornly to a semblance of dampness. "I'm going in, and I'm going to ask for Colt."

Matt studied Xander, and he could tell that his older brother didn't think he was serious.

"Look," Xander explained, hoping that he was right. "When I first arrived at the space station thing, they couldn't find my name on the list of eliminated. That means that when the info was sent up there, they had me still marked as an official adult down here."

Matt nodded his head slowly, following his logic.

Xander continued, "That probably hasn't changed in the last week; I see no reason why they would be rushing to change it. So, if they ask me who I am, I'm still on their list."

"Okay...so you're saying you could get lucky."

"Maybe, but I don't even know if anyone would be guarding the door. I mean, it's probably not like people try to break into the research center every day."

"So what am I supposed to do while you skip in there and introduce yourself as an adult?"

"I guess you can wait outside." Xander shrugged. "I don't know. I'm not planning to get into a physical fight, and..."

Matt pointed at Xander. "Man, you look like you've already been in a couple. You've got a bruised eye, and you're missing half your clothing."

Xander looked down at himself, and some of his confidence faded. He looked like exactly what he was- a refugee from the space station.

"Okay," he responded. "So what do I do? Just steal some clothes from the first person I come across?"

Matt shrugged. "I didn't say I had an answer to it, just that you can't look like a normal adult, because no normal adult would walk around like that."

"I can at least have a decent pair of shoes," Xander said, motioning to the ones Matt was wearing. They had stopped their squeaking after about an hour of walking.

"Man, I'm not giving you my shoes. If you don't come back, I'm left with your measly one."

"Hey, two shoes will help me look more adultlike. I can just claim...I don't know, I was mugged on the way here. They took my bike."

"And your shirt? Because it was that wonderful."

Xander smiled just a little. "Yes, exactly. Now hand me your shoes."

Matt grumbled, but he slowly unlaced his shoes and handed them over to Xander. Xander joyfully traded him his one shoe and put on Matt's. They were a size too big on him and kind of flopped a little when he took a step, but for a short distance, it would be fine.

"Okay, look, there are some rocks. Just stay there until I come back out."

"And if you don't come back out?"

"Then...go find Mom. Tell her what happened." Xander set his mouth in a straight line and marched up to the door, swerving around six or seven bikes that were parked out front. He hoped that no one would stop him, but more than that, he hoped Colt was inside.

Chapter 25

Eden wanted to watch the first competition of the second Olympics, but she wasn't going to participate in it. She knew nothing about the controls or electronics or anything else other than how to turn on and off a computer and navigate the internet, not that there was internet here.

A lot of people had gathered outside the bridge, and Roman was opening the door and letting them in one by one. No one was able to observe the test, and Eden wasn't sure how they were making sure it was fair. But after everything she had learned about the way this place was run, she wasn't sure that "fair" was the most important standard on Roman's list.

Eden sat silently with her back against the wall, clearly staying out of the line of those who wished to compete. She watched the others' faces as they came out of the room and tried to guess who would win medals. It was a bit like her own competition as she wondered how many she would guess correctly.

A few people came out of the room with their heads hanging or their shoulders hunched. She could tell they hadn't done well. After a while, watching their faces started to get boring, but Eden didn't know what else she could do. Lives hung in the balance here, and even though she knew this would mean death, she couldn't look away.

At some point, someone came out of the room with an angry face. The guy's every step seemed to shake the whole hall. "They *lied* to us!" he stormed.

A couple of people in line turned to watch him go, but they weren't about to give up their chance at the test. Eden stood and followed him down the side hallway to the main hallway, keeping a little distance between the two of them. She wanted to know, *had* to know what was going on.

"Um, excuse me," Eden piped up, hating how babyish her voice sounded.

The guy turned around, and Eden could see that both of his hands were curled into fists.

"You want to know how they lied?" the guy asked. "That asteroid they told us about, the one that was being destroyed? Yeah, well, it's still coming toward us!"

Eden opened her mouth, trying to think of something to say. When Roman had told her about Xander and Matt leaving their planned course, she hadn't thought at first about what it meant for all of them. She had just been worried about where they had gone and if they would die. But now, the fear returned in full force.

"Here they are making us compete like we're going to run out of food, when there's an asteroid that's going to hit us in six days! They tried to hide it from me too. I switched camera views, and they scrambled to cover it up. Too late! We're all going to die."

Eden still couldn't think of anything to say, but the guy was turning away from her already. Someone came down the hallway toward them and asked him to repeat what he had just said. Eden knew that it would be all over the station in a matter of hours. She didn't feel like going back to watch what little she could see of the competition now. She just wanted to know that Xander was okay.

Feeling restless, Eden started wandering the halls of the space station, even though her stomach told her that she should conserve her energy. If she sat down and thought about Xander, she might start crying. But if she was moving, it was like her body couldn't find the energy to make tears too.

Eden turned down the hallway where the little library was, and she stopped just as she was crossing the threshold between the main hallway and the side hallway. This was where she and Helena had found the second body. It didn't matter. She knew it didn't matter, and it wasn't like the body was still there. Reluctantly, Eden forced herself to move forward to conquer her unfounded fears.

She turned the corner and saw...nothing. There were two shelves of books, though some of them were missing now, but no body. Eden breathed a sigh of relief and went over to look at the books. The ones that had been left behind were fiction titles. All of the nonfiction had been gleaned as study materials most likely.

Eden selected a title from the shelf and pulled it out to read the back cover. It had been a while since she had read "for fun," but maybe a book would distract her from the end of her world.

When she heard a sound, she turned around and found Derry watching her. Eden jumped, dropping the book. She bent down to pick it up automatically, then quickly straightened.

"You're into books?" Derry asked, strolling up to the bookshelf like he visited every day. He didn't seem to read Eden's body language as she took a big step backward so that they wouldn't be within arm's length. She clutched the book to her chest like some sort of shield.

Derry turned to look at her when she didn't answer. She wanted to yell at him or respond "smartly," but none of her smart, sassy comebacks ever came to mind when she was staring someone down, especially someone who threatened her as much as Derry did.

Finally, Derry took his eyes off of her and selected a book from the shelf. He held it in front of him, and Eden took a step sideways so that she could be closer to the main hallway.

"Did you know that guy died here?" Derry asked.

Eden's heart hammered in her chest. "Yeah, I found him," she told him.

Derry's eyebrows rose. "You *found* him? You mean, you just walked down here and saw he wasn't moving? What did he look like?" The fascination in Derry's eyes as he stared her down bothered Eden.

"He was...clearly not alive anymore. It's not something I'd like to talk about." She nodded to Derry like a civilized woman, then bolted out of the hallway. She was halfway down the main one when she realized that she had passed the door to her room already.

She ducked back and through the doorway, taking a few deep breaths once she was inside. She reached for the lock, then realized that there wasn't one. None of the bedrooms had locks, and suddenly, the feeling that Derry was watching her...always keeping his eyes on her... crept up her neck and made her spine tingle.

Chapter 26

The sun shining on the glass front doors made it impossible for Xander to see anything as he strode, shirtless, up to the building. He hesitated as he reached for the handle, but he knew that he couldn't allow himself to give into doubt.

The handle, hot from the sun, almost burned his hand, and Xander winced as he pulled the door open and took a couple of steps inside, blinking as his eyes adjusted to the relative dimness. He was in a small lobby area, but there was no receptionist or guard or anything like that. He could feel the difference in the air quality though, and closed his eyes as the air-conditioning washed away some of the heat from outside.

The fact that all of the world's best scientists lived and worked here and there was nothing guarding their projects bothered Xander just a little. A set of stairs to his left curved upward, but Xander had no idea where Colt might be working.

The stairs called to him, though, so Xander went on instinct, not wanting to stand in the lobby for too long. He had noticed a camera behind the front desk, and he knew that if someone was actively watching the cameras, they were already wondering who he was and what he was doing there. They might even be looking him up on the database of adults.

At the top of the stairs, Xander saw a bland hallway stretching out to either side of him. Doors were spaced methodically down the hall with little plaques to number them. None of the plaques happened to tell him what was *behind* the doors, though, or who worked in each room.

It would probably be a good idea to walk around first and see if he recognized anyone. Even if he didn't see Colt, he might see someone else from his Olympics. Maybe they would help him, even if they didn't know why he was there or what had happened to him. He had to bank on the fact that they would just remember seeing him win a medal in wrestling, not the fact that his face hadn't crossed the stage at the adulting ceremony.

"You aren't supposed to be up here," someone called from the other end of the hall.

Xander turned and tried to keep his body language relaxed as the person approached him. Xander had never been one to stereotype, but most of the brainiacs who worked here would probably be easy to beat if things happened to turn into a physical fight.

"Sorry," Xander responded. "I was looking for my friend Colt. He said he works here now, since he became an adult." Xander infused confidence into his words even though he wasn't wearing a shirt. What if Colt hadn't begun working at the research center yet? Wouldn't he have to train first? Then again, Colt had also had some radical ideas. Maybe he wasn't in a typical position at all.

"Colt Gerbert? Oh yeah, he just started here." The guy smiled, and Xander instantly felt more at ease, like this wouldn't be so hard after all. "But we're not supposed to have social visits while we're working. Didn't he tell you that? Where do you work?" The guy gave Xander an up and down, clearly confused by his lack of proper clothing.

Xander blinked. "Oh, I'm just...training to be an official."

The guy stared pointedly at Xander's unclothed chest. He didn't have to ask the question, and after admitting that he was training to be an official, Xander thought that telling a story about how someone had stolen his bicycle on the road might paint him as a hypocrite.

"Oh, it's a weird kind of training," Xander said as though he had just noticed he wasn't fully dressed. "They make us survive the elements with no food, water, that sort of thing. It's supposed to teach us resistance." He shrugged and turned the attention off himself. "So, where can I find Colt?"

The guy pointed behind Xander. "He works in Lab #8, but we're not supposed to have visitors."

"I won't get him in trouble," Xander promised. "Thanks for the help. What was your name?"

"Preston," the boy responded.

"Well, nice to meet you, Preston." Xander raised a hand in a goodbye wave and checked the plaques until he found Lab #8. He could feel Preston watching him as he twisted the door handle.

Even though the door clearly *could* lock, no one had locked it for some reason. Xander peeked his head in and was relieved when he saw Colt immediately.

"Hey!" he said, greeting Colt.

Colt carefully lifted his head from what he was doing- it looked like he was building some sort of machine- and stared at Xander. Then, his eyes grew wide.

"You're...you're...how are you here?" Colt glanced at the door behind Xander, then back at him. Meanwhile, Xander took in the lab around him. The room was small, just larger than the dorm room he had occupied at the hotel of the Olympics. Colt was the only person in it, and Xander was glad that they had some privacy to talk. He shut the door firmly behind himself.

"I thought you were eliminated!" Colt exclaimed, carefully placing the wires he had been connecting on the table and taking a step toward Xander to look at him more closely.

Xander and Colt had never been best friends, but Xander had felt a healthy respect for the smarter boy. Seeing him now made Xander feel a little closer to home.

"I was," Xander responded. "But apparently, elimination doesn't mean death."

Colt stared at Xander open-mouthed, and Xander started giving him as much information as he could as quickly as he could. "They took us to a boat and drugged us. When we woke up, we were on a space station. People have been sent there the last seven years of eliminations, but not everyone, just some of the eliminated."

"They've already created a successful colony in space?" Colt asked. He didn't sound like he thought Xander was lying, but more like a kid who had been left out of a secret.

"I don't know if I would call it successful." Xander touched his stomach when he thought of the disgusting slop they had been fed. "But people are living up there."

"So… so… how did you get down here? I mean, were *you* sent up there or just the others?"

"I was up there, and so was everyone else in our group. I even found my older brother. He was eliminated three years ago."

Colt's eyes shone. "Did you see a girl? She has blonde hair like mine, really long, and she's super smart."

Xander shrugged. "I don't know. There were a lot of girls. I might have, but I'd have to see a picture to know."

Colt nodded, and he moved to a wallet on a small table by the door. He pulled out a picture, and Xander swallowed. He knew *exactly* who it was.

"Emily," he said, looking at Colt for confirmation.

Colt nodded. "Yeah, her name is Emily. She's alive?"

Xander nodded. "Yes, she's alive. I actually worked with her for a few days."

"Doing what?"

Now that Xander saw the picture of Emily next to Colt, he knew that they must be related- siblings or cousins- but Colt was getting too caught up in the details. They had a bigger problem here. "We worked in the kitchen together. She was the only one in there who was nice to me."

Colt smiled confidently like that was exactly what he would have expected from Emily. "Does she-"

"Colt, I'll tell you everything I know about Emily later, but I need your help first."

"What's wrong?" Colt asked, his face shifting from dreamy remembrance to focus.

"There's an asteroid headed right toward the space station. They have no way to move the space station out of its orbit. The asteroid is going to hit the place and kill everyone in a few days."

Xander had lost track of time while they were traveling in the ship, but he estimated they had fewer than five.

The panic was clear on Colt's face. "Everyone up there knows about it?" he asked. "And they sent you here to get help?"

Xander weighed his options of explaining the truth. He finally nodded. "I thought of you first because I know you have so many ideas of how to build things, how to solve problems. Maybe you don't know what to do, but someone else here could help? Maybe if people here knew what really happened to the eliminated, they would want to do something about it."

Colt nodded. "There has to be something we can do, but I'll need calculations. I need to know the angle of the asteroid's movement and its speed. Do you know the space station's orbit?"

Xander shook his head. "I don't even know if anyone up *there* knows where we are exactly. I know it took us at least a full day to get back here, and we almost died when our ship burst into flames as we got closer to Earth."

"The re-entry." Colt nodded knowingly. "I'm surprised that heating suppressants weren't supplied to prevent that from happening."

"Maybe it would have if it had been built by professionals, but some guy who didn't win a medal put it together in two days." Xander threw up his hands and shrugged his shoulders. Then, he realized that he was staring at someone who hadn't won a medal. Colt was only standing there in the lab because Xander had offered up his medal. If he hadn't, then Colt's inability to focus while taking a test would have meant that he would be up on the space station at that moment. Though...he might be someone good to have around in situations like asteroid collisions.

After a moment of awkward silence, Colt moved to a computer. "Let me run some numbers, and I'll get my friend to let me use the telescope. We'll have to wait until tonight, though, to see much."

"What time is it?" Xander asked, trying to orient himself with a clock. He didn't realize how often he made his decisions about what to eat or do based on the hour the clock showed.

"It's 2:34," Colt responded, pulling up a simulation program on the computer. Xander stood behind his shoulder and watched as Colt put in some sample numbers.

"I can't actually do anything until we know where the space station and asteroid are and at what point they will collide, but this can help give us an idea of what kind of machine we'll need." Xander remained quiet as he watched Colby's fingers fly across the keyboard much more deftly than Matt's hand.

Xander stood up straight, suddenly remembering his brother waiting outside. How long would Matt wait before he got impatient and left?

"When does everyone here finish working?" Xander asked.

"Most of us finish at four, but there is an evening/night shift for those who are researching space as a possibility for colonization. I just don't understand how no one has said anything to me about the existing space station." Colt frowned and studied the computer screen for a moment before making a few adjustments. "I've talked about my ideas for making a sustainable space station or an environment on Mars, and everyone says we're not ready for that yet."

"Maybe it's because we're some sort of experiment," Xander explained. "And it's failing."

"What do you mean by 'failing?'"

"I mean that we don't have enough food. Even if the asteroid weren't coming for us, something would have to be done. They've tried to put some bodies in stasis, but I don't know how well it's working."

Colt turned away from the computer and openly stared at Xander. "I wish I could go up there," he said.

Xander shook his head. "You *don't* want to be up there. We may have rations down here like up there, but you still feel hungry after you eat up there." He kept his mouth shut about the sludge that they were forced to eat. Even though it was disgusting, he couldn't just focus on the negatives. Besides, he was distracting Colt from his work.

"So... Emily," Colt reminded him. "Tell me how she's doing. Is she okay up there? You said she works in the kitchen. She never liked cooking before. I'm surprised she's doing that."

Xander shrugged. "We didn't really get much choice. I was assigned my position, so I assume she was too. Anyway, she seems pretty good at it." It didn't take a lot of talent to make sludge, but Xander needed to encourage Colt in any way possible to get him to save the station. Now that Colt had a clear reason for helping though, Xander was sure he would follow through.

Xander's stomach grumbled loudly, protesting its lack of food.

"Are you hungry?" Colt asked as though it weren't obvious. "You can have the rest of my lunch."

Xander wasn't going to wait to be asked again. He dove on the bag that was by the door and almost ripped it getting to the contents. There was half a sandwich left and a tiny mandarin orange. He knew he should save half of it for Matt. It was only fair, but his hands were shaking as he ripped the sandwich in half. He set half of it on the table and turned his back to it as he tried to make the three bites' worth last longer.

"No, really, eat it all," Colt said, waving to it.

"I should give some of it to Matt," Xander explained. "He's...he made this journey too. I'm sure he's hungry." Even though Xander had eaten the whole piece, his stomach felt just as empty as before.

"Oh," Colt made the sound, but Xander could tell he was already tuning him out. Xander wasn't offended; he wanted Colt focused on the task he had been given. So, Xander grabbed up the remaining part of Colt's lunch.

"I'll take it out to him right now, okay? I'll be back."

"Just...stay out of sight when everyone leaves at four," Colt replied. "I'll come find you when we can access the telescope."

Xander nodded. It's not like there was great security there, but he also didn't want a couple hundred people to walk past him and wonder who the shirtless guy was.

Once he was outside, it was easy to find Matt crouched behind a large rock, one of many that scattered Greenland's landscape. "Food," Xander said, holding out his offering.

Matt's eyes widened, and he snatched it out of Xander's hand quickly. Xander looked away while Matt fed himself. Xander could still smell the ham and bread, and he had to fight some sort of primal urge to snatch it back from him. Obviously, finding more food needed to be at the top of their list now that they had located Colt.

"What did you do? Raid the fridge or something?" Matt asked when his mouth was clear again.

"No," Xander shook his head, allowing himself to look back at his brother now that the food had been eaten. "Those were Colt's leftovers."

"So you found him. That was...easy."

"Don't sound disappointed. Yes, it was easy. There doesn't seem to be a lot of security here, though Colt said we need to stay out of sight an hour from now when everyone gets off."

Matt nodded. He looked toward some of the researcher housing that was a short distance away. "So the houses are empty right now?" he asked.

Xander followed his older brother's gaze. "Maybe, but if they have families, they won't be."

"Let's take a chance."

Xander knew that it was wrong, that they shouldn't go raid houses, but his stomach was dictating his moves now. "Okay, let's go, but we need to be careful. As of right now, I don't think my presence has alerted anyone. But if we get caught…"

"I know," Matt responded, already moving in the direction of the houses.

Xander hurried to catch up with him. "And we should only take a little bit from each house," he added as he wondered how easy it might be to find a shirt.

"Thank you, Xander, for your expert thievery advice." The sarcasm was clear, so Xander shut his mouth even as more warnings ran through his head.

The houses were built right next to each other- townhouses- but far out of town. Xander could see that the main door was open on the first one, with only a thin pane of glass separating the inside from the outside.

"Someone must be home," he said.

"Let's split up," Matt suggested. Then, he darted away from Xander toward another row of the houses. Xander knew that someone could be watching them. They should assume that someone was looking, so he tried to play it casual, walking up the steps to each house and knocking on the door with one hand while trying the doorknob with another.

Locked. Locked. Locked.

Apparently, no one trusted anyone else. Everything was locked up. He reached the end of his second row without success. He was just trying to decide if he should try the back doors when he heard a shout.

"What are you doing here?"

Xander's first instinct was to run, but he forced his legs to stay in place. He couldn't run. It had to be close to the time when everyone got off work, and that would provide a lot of witnesses.

He lifted a hand and waved to the woman who was approaching him. When she got closer, Xander realized she wasn't as old as he first thought. In fact, she had probably just become an adult in the most recent ceremony. Her features looked vaguely familiar.

"Hasn't the main shift finished yet?" Xander asked, motioning to the research center. "I'm supposed to meet up with a friend, but she isn't home."

"Finishes at four," the girl said, studying him. "You look *so* familiar."

A half-truth was better than a complete lie. "I just became an adult in this last ceremony. You too, right? I think I kind of remember you."

"Yeah…" the woman answered slowly. "I don't know. You *do* seem familiar. Where do you work?"

Xander jerked a thumb over his shoulder as he pointed at the main city of Sisimiut. "Work down there. Doing some training to become an official now."

"Why are you dressed like…that?" the woman said, motioning her fingers in the direction of his shirtless torso.

Xander shrugged. "Why not? I *did* say my friend was a female."

The woman smiled, then laughed, and Xander was glad he hadn't completely lost his touch with people after being locked up in a tiny ship with Matt for so long. "Anyway," Xander said. "I guess I'll just sit here and wait until everyone finishes work. Thanks."

Xander picked a random porch and sat down, and the woman took her cue to leave. Xander waited about five minutes to make sure, but then, he heard the sound of talking and laughing, then footsteps. It seemed like four o'clock had arrived, and he needed to find a safe place to wait it out until it was nighttime and Colt could use the telescope.

Wishing he could know that Matt was okay, Xander slithered under someone's back porch and rested his chin on his hands as he lay on his stomach. He hoped darkness wouldn't take too long to come.

Chapter 27

The medal ceremony for the first competition was complete, and Eden felt sick inside as she watched Roman hand out tiny, silver badges that were supposed to be medals. Everyone's name was written down, but he also stressed that they shouldn't lose their new medals.

Eden hated the repetitiveness of it all. She had thought that once she had passed through the Olympics once, she wouldn't have to deal with it again. Yet here she was... facing the very real possibility that she could be pushed out of the hatch.

She didn't want to think about it anymore, so Eden decided to take a walk around the ship. There was still an hour until supper, and walking was the only thing she could do to keep herself busy. The workout room had recently been filled with aspiring individuals who were determined to win medals in the physical test. Eden knew better than to even try with that, especially with no separation between male and female competitors.

As she walked, she thought about the two bodies that had been found- one female and one male. The only thing that connected them was the fact that they had both died the same way- strangulation.

Helena had shown Eden the report, and Eden had seen the bruises on the guy's neck for herself.

Eden couldn't help wondering *who* had done it and *why*. She had her own suspect, of course, but she didn't know everyone on the space station. There might be other people who had grudges against those two.

Turning down a side hallway, Eden crept forward, almost sure that she would find another body. But no, of course not. She was just paranoid now. Eden reached the end of the hallway and swiveled around.

She forced herself into each side hallway she passed, because the station was already small enough. She couldn't be scared of part of it or that would make it feel even smaller.

The second floor was fairly empty as most people were looking for entertainment at the moment, not napping. Eden turned down the side hallway and heard a grunt. It was a tiny sound, but it alerted her. She froze right there in the entrance of the hallway.

Something hit the wall, at least that was what it sounded like, and Eden forced her feet forward. It was probably nothing. Nothing was happening, but she had to see for herself.

As she came around the bend, Eden couldn't force herself forward any longer. She saw everything in less than a second, but her eyes then hovered over each person as her brain tried to process it. Two girls, both of them were on their backs. Both of them weren't moving, and one of them was looking directly at Eden, her eyes glazed over.

Standing over them was Derry. His hands were trembling as he slowly turned to look at Eden. Eden didn't give Derry the chance to say anything or to come after her. She turned and ran, holding onto the corner where the two hallways met so that she could swing herself into the flow of things. She was next. She was next.

Derry knew that she had seen him over the bodies, and he was coming to get her. Eden knocked on one of the doors along the way, eager to get backup, her knuckles aching from how hard she pounded. No one answered, but Eden couldn't risk standing in the hallway anymore. She pushed the door open and ducked inside.

She breathed heavily as she fumbled at the handle for a lock. There was no lock. She knew that.

"Eden?" Helena asked.

"Oh, you're here!" Eden said, her breath shaky, glad for a friendly face.

"What happened?" Helena stood from her bunk bed, placing the book she had been studying to the side.

"I...I think I found out who killed those two people. I saw him with two others, and they already looked dead to me."

Helena's face visibly paled. "Okay," she said, trying to sound confident. But Eden could hear the tremble in Helena's voice.

"He saw me," Eden said. "He knows I saw, and he's going to come after me next. I don't have the kind of skills to fight someone off. I'm not strong!"

"Okay, sit down," Helena said, trading places with Eden. She leaned so that her back was against the door, effectively forming a blockade for anyone who wanted to enter the room. Eden sank onto Helena's bed, trying to remember how to breathe normally.

"Tell me exactly what you saw."

"I went down that hallway, the one with the books. I heard a noise, like someone was in pain. Then, I saw two girls on the floor. They looked dead, but I didn't see who they were. Derry was leaning over one of them."

"Who's Derry?"

"He came with my group last week," Eden explained. "He tried to hurt me back at the Olympics so I wouldn't be able to win a medal. And now, he's hurting other people. He's probably trying to up his chances to win a medal in these Olympics."

"But we found that first body before we even knew about the Olympics, remember?"

Eden nodded. "Well, I don't know why he did it, but he did it. But if I go out there, he's going to come after me."

She was sure that Derry was waiting on the other side of the door. Helena shook her head. "We stick to the main hallways, and we get to the bridge. If Roman isn't there, we find someone who can go get him. We'll tell him what you saw. He's good about dealing with stuff like that."

Shakily, Eden nodded. "Okay, can we go right now?" she asked.

Helena agreed. "Let's go now."

Eden stood up and followed Helena out of her room. When they reached the hallway, Eden looked up and down its length. She didn't spot Derry among the few people there, and she breathed a sigh of relief. She had been overreacting. Maybe Derry hadn't really seen her clearly. She had turned and run before taking the time to study his face.

"Let's go," she said, and Helena led the way to the bridge, setting a confident pace. Eden strode quickly to keep up with her. When they reached the door, she felt like she might actually survive the night. Helena knocked loudly, and someone opened the door a minute later.

"We need to speak with Roman right now," Helena said. "It's about two more deaths."

The guy looked surprised and worried. "He's not here, but come inside. I'll get someone to find him."

Helena and Eden waited inside the control room, and Eden's eyes instantly went to the cameras. She tried to look like she wasn't watching them, but she couldn't help searching for the asteroid. She almost didn't expect to see it. They would be hiding it, right? Because who would want everyone to know that Xander and Matt had abandoned their mission?

Guilt settled in Eden's stomach even though she knew it wasn't her fault.

There it was on the top right camera view. A brownish, reddish thing. It didn't look very menacing, but Eden knew that was only because of the distance. When it got closer, she wouldn't think that anymore.

"Are you feeling okay?" Helena asked Eden, and Eden jumped. She had been caught watching the screens, but Helena didn't seem interested in them. She had bought the story that the asteroid had been taken care of, just like most other people here.

"Fine," Eden responded.

"Okay, what's going on?" Roman asked as soon as he entered the room. He saw Eden, and Eden thought he frowned, even if it was only for a second. Maybe he didn't like her because of her association with Xander, but she had to make him understand what had happened.

"I...two more dead bodies...and someone was there."

"Please speak clearly," Roman said, folding his arms and closing his eyes like he was searching for a shred of patience.

Eden took a deep breath. "I know who's responsible for the deaths, the stranglings."

Roman's eyes popped open, and he peered at her. "Okay, let's all three talk about this in a private room."

Roman led Eden to the room where she had been imprisoned after the first death, and she didn't like the feeling of entrapment that settled over her. However, this time, Roman's manner was less accusing and more curious. "Go ahead. Tell me exactly what you saw."

Eden recounted the scene as best as she could. Roman listened intently, his eyes on Eden the whole time.

"Do you have any more proof that he committed this crime?" Roman asked.

Eden shook her head. "I didn't actually *see* him do it, but he was there. He looked, maybe, angry?"

Roman pressed his lips together and shook his head.

"That's not all," Helena said. "You told me that he did something similar at the Olympics."

"Really?" Roman looked interested now. "Tell me about that."

Eden explained how Derry had kidnapped her and other girls and drugged them so that they couldn't really do anything. "If Xander hadn't found me, I don't know what would have happened. Xander was even stabbed in the back trying to get me out of there," Eden concluded.

"Well, that seems like enough proof to bring him in and talk to him," Roman said.

"You're just going to...talk to him?" Eden asked.

"We'll start with talking," Roman said. "I don't want you in here while I'm asking questions, but you can listen outside the door if you want."

Eden's stomach did a strange dance as she realized that this was actually happening now. Helena tapped Eden's shoulder, and Eden stood.

Roman had already exited the room. "What's going to happen to him?" Eden asked in a whisper.

Helena shrugged. "Hopefully justice."

"But he's not going to admit that he did it," Eden protested. "He's kind of, I don't know, good at wiggling out of things." She thought about how he had been caught back at the hotel on Earth, but then was *still* allowed to come to this space station instead of whatever happened to the other group of eliminated.

Helena shrugged. "Come on."

They waited a short ways down the hallway, and Eden heard Roman and Derry coming. It sounded like more than two sets of footsteps, though, and Eden peered out from where they waited long enough to see that Roman had two friends with him.

"I didn't do it!" Derry protested. "I swear! I'll swear on my mother! Whatever you want!"

The door closed behind the group, and Eden crept up closer. It was easy to hear the conversation through the doorway, but Eden wasn't sure if that was because Derry was speaking so loudly or because there was no sort of soundproofing happening. Her stomach complained about their rations, and Eden wondered if it could be heard through the doorway.

"I just want you to tell me what happened," Roman said. His voice was clear and steady.

"I was just going down the hallway, and I saw two people laying on the ground. So I went to check on them, and they weren't breathing."

Eden traded looks with Helena. That was a good story. It would explain him bending over the one girl. But she didn't believe it for one second.

"An observer says that they heard a noise from one of the girls on the ground. If you say they were already dead, why were they making noises?"

Eden nodded her agreement with Roman's question.

"Because..." Derry didn't have an answer for that right away. "I think I made some sort of noise when I found them. It surprised me, freaked me out."

Eden couldn't hear any words for a moment, and she wished she could see Derry's face. Was it turned up in that all-knowing grin or did he realize that he had really been caught?

"And I know who reported me," Derry went on. "It's Eden. She's never liked me, so she probably just made up some story about watching me strangle them."

"How do you know they were strangled to death if you didn't do it?"

"Because...the marks on their throats. I mean, it's kind of obvious."

Roman made some sort of disbelieving noise, and Eden nodded encouragingly at Helena. Maybe Roman would believe her after all, because if Derry wasn't locked up, Eden wouldn't feel safe walking the hallways anymore.

"Do you have any proof that you *didn't* do it?" Roman asked. "What were you doing directly before you found them?"

"I was in the game room for a while," Derry responded.

"You didn't go to the medal ceremony."

"No, I knew I wasn't going to win one."

"Huh," another scoff of disbelief from Roman. "Are you planning to compete in one of the competitions?"

"Yeah, physical. Look, I didn't do it, and you don't have proof I did. You have to believe me."

"What about the people you attacked back at your Olympics?"

"That doesn't...that was different."

"How?"

"I was doing it for my girlfriend. She stood no chance of winning a medal, so I was helping her out. And I would never have killed the people. In fact, all of them were fine afterward. It was just a game, nothing serious."

Eden heard movement in the room, and she backed up from the door. Roman exited the room and crossed his arms as he stared at Eden. "He denies it," Roman announced.

Eden was fairly sure that Derry could hear them through the door. "You can't let him go," she said. "Please, it will happen again if you let him go."

"I need to think about it," Roman decided. "You should go to dinner. It's almost time."

Both Eden and Helena took the order and headed to the dining hall. Eden glanced over her shoulder, but Roman didn't let Derry out of the room, at least not while Eden was watching. Still, she felt sure about what she had seen.

Chapter 28

Once it started getting dark, Xander and Matt could move around more freely. It was harder for people to recognize them without the sunlight, and everyone was relaxing, having fun, calling to each other.

"Let's find Colt," Xander said, leading the way to the research center.

He pulled at the handle just as he had earlier, but it was locked now.

"What?" Xander almost shouted, trying the handle again. "I opened it earlier."

"They must lock up the building at night. They don't want someone sneaking in and stealing the technology."

"Apparently, we're only allowed to sneak in during the day." Xander paced away from the door, then back. "Colt said that there's a night shift. They have to get in and out somehow."

"Must have keys." Matt didn't seem at all bothered by this turn of events, but Xander felt the panic rising. They had to do something *now*. He didn't know how long Colt would need to fix the problem, but if they didn't hurry up, then they would run out of time.

"How are we going to get in there?" Xander asked. He paced back and forth out of the motion-sensored light that had flashed upon his approach.

"Maybe he doesn't need us," Matt responded. "I mean, we told him about the problem. He's the brain. We should just wait until he says something. Don't you think?"

"It's not like we have much of a choice." Xander could see another door on the other side of the research center. He wanted to try it, but he also knew that most likely, it would be locked as well.

He and Matt waited in the darkness, watching the researcher housing from a distance as everyone enjoyed their evening. It seemed so...peaceful.

There was none of the worry and stress of living on the space station with not enough rations and close quarters. Xander had almost forgotten that there was another kind of life as his empty stomach constantly drew him back to the reality of the moment..

"I want to see Mom," Matt announced after the housing area started to get quieter. Xander didn't know what time it was...or even what day it was, but people must be getting ready for the next day of work, going to bed, or just hanging out watching television. That seemed like such a luxury. Xander hadn't realized how much he missed staring at a screen for an hour and forgetting about his life.

The front door opened, and Xander hopped to his feet. The light in front of the building reflected off Colt's glasses, and Xander rushed forward, almost feeling like he could hug the guy.

"Colt!" he said.

"We need to hurry," Colt said, handing Xander a shirt. "I got this for you," he said. Xander pulled the shirt over his head as he followed Colt inside the building, Matt right behind them.

Colt didn't talk as he led them to a room on the first floor. He had to use a key to get into the door, and he held it open for them as they passed into a room with walls that stretched up three stories high. The dome-shaped glass ceiling hung above them, and a telescope bigger than several people disappeared into the glass, appearing out the other side.

"Whoa!" he said, pausing to admire it. He blinked and realized that Colt had hurried on without them. He was at the base of the telescope, adjusting a few knobs. He held one of them steady as he peered into the eyepiece.

"I've located the space station," he announced, his voice echoing oddly in the large room, "and the asteroid threatening it. Do you want to take a look?"

Xander stepped forward and bent down, blinking a few times as his eye adjusted to the strange scene in front of him. The space station looked so small, so unimportant in the grand scheme of things, but he knew how many people were on there- one of them someone very important to him.

Stepping back, Xander turned to his new best friend. "So now that you know where they are, can you run the calculations?"

Colt nodded. "I've already done so. If we want to adjust the asteroid's course, we need to launch something, I'm thinking a missile, in the next twenty-four hours."

"Twenty-four hours?" Xander confirmed. "Are there missiles just sitting around waiting to be launched?"

Colt cleaned his glasses and adjusted them on his nose before answering. "To my knowledge, there are missiles located in northern Greenland. Of course, I can't calculate the exact angle of the launch until I know the coordinates of their starting position. However, I have estimates that prove it can effectively destroy the asteroid."

Matt stood up from peering into the telescope. "So you can save them?" he confirmed.

Colt didn't answer right away. "Well, I can't do it on my own. I don't have control over the missiles, and I'm not going to sneak around trying to figure out how to set one off."

Of course Colt wouldn't break the rules. Xander paced back and forth. He could hear voices coming from another part of the building, and he looked around for a place to hide. Colt waved away his worry. "They're just working on calculations for creating a colony on the moon."

"Who would be able to give you permission to launch the missiles?" Xander asked.

Colt shrugged. "I don't know. That's not my area of expertise. I can ask Greg. He's my coordinator, but I know it wouldn't be him. Someone above him, maybe several someones. And in order to get their permission, I would need to explain the problem of course."

Matt nodded. "You can show them what we just saw in the telescope. How many people do you think know about the space station?"

Colt scratched his head. "I would say roughly twelve percent of those working here at the research center, but that's just a guess. Certainly no one from the most recent years knows. My guess is it would only be those with level three security clearance, and then, not even many of them would know."

Xander cut in. Colt could talk for hours about percentages and likelihood, but Xander needed something to be done. "Can you call someone? Get their help? Tonight? If we only have twenty-four hours, we can't just wait for the right person to stumble in here."

"Right," Colt agreed. He pulled out his cell phone and began scrolling. Xander went to the telescope again and peered into it. The conversation that had been taking place in another part of the building now became closer.

"...the bubbling is consistent with some sort of astral descent. However, no foreign matter was detected."

"The amount of dead sea life can't be ignored. We need to send a team to investigate in the morning, as soon as it's light."

Matt exchanged looks with Xander. The voices sounded like they were coming closer, and even though Xander might be able to create an excuse for being there, Matt couldn't. Xander pointed to an area behind a group of tables that was big enough for them to hide. Just as they were settling silently into their spot, one of the voices greeted Colt.

"What are you doing here so late? I thought you were still on the day shift."

Something clattered across the floor. "I...uh, wanted to use the telescope to check some calculations for the prototype I'm building. Works best at night."

"We've discovered something you might be interested in," the other voice said. It was clearly a woman's. "Seems like something landed in the ocean today, something hot enough to kill over a thousand fish. They have been washing up on the rocks and drying out, but they're already dead by the time they hit land."

"Oh?" Colt didn't sound casual enough. He sounded like he was nervous, hiding something. "What was it?"

"We're not sure, but we're writing up a report right now and will send a team down to investigate tomorrow. Do you want to be part of the team?"

"Actually," Colt said. He cleared his throat. "Take a look in the telescope, will you?"

No one said anything for a minute, and Xander couldn't see what they were doing. "What...you found out about the space station?" the man's voice asked.

Well, clearly *he* already knew about it then.

"Yes, I was checking some calculations for the prototype I'm building, and..."

"You already told us that." The man's voice didn't sound as indulgent now, more irritated.

"Well, I discovered it, and if you look to the right of the space station, you'll see an asteroid heading directly toward it."

The woman gasped. "You're right! It's going to completely destroy it. How many people are on the station?"

"I don't know," Colt responded. "But something has to be done immediately if we stand a chance of knocking the asteroid off course."

"So you weren't here checking calculations at all. You were here looking at things you weren't supposed to be looking at." The man's voice had gone even lower and more serious.

Xander wavered. Should he step out of his hiding place? He couldn't let Colt get in trouble for something Xander had pulled him into. Besides, tomorrow, someone would discover the ship wreckage fragments in the water and know that someone had attempted to get back to Greenland. These people were smart and would connect the dots.

Turning softly, Xander motioned for Matt to leave the building. Then, he stood.

"Excuse me," he said. "I'm the one that told Colt about the problem." He came around the end of the desks, and he felt the disapproval of the two immediately change their focus from Colt to him.

Xander felt exposed and wished that he had been able to dress properly. Still, clothing hadn't been his first concern upon reaching this place.

"Who are you?" the woman asked, taking a step toward him. The moonlight shining through the glass reflected off Xander's face.

"I'm Xander Coxon," he said. Now was the time to tell what had happened to him. Maybe if everyone knew, then they would be willing to help. Everyone had to know someone who was eliminated, right?

"I was eliminated a week ago and sent to the space station that Colt just showed you. Upon arrival, we were alerted by the leader of the space station that an asteroid was going to hit us soon. It would destroy all of us, so...we built a tiny spaceship from things we had around. And, I came here in a desperate attempt to get some help." There was no need to go into the details of how he was supposed to sacrifice himself by hitting the asteroid.

"You're eliminated," the man said. He apparently hadn't heard the rest of what Xander had said.

"Yes, I was," Xander responded. "But now everyone is going to die."

"But..." the woman didn't seem to understand his story either. "You were eliminated. That's what is supposed to happen. I didn't know they were sending everyone to a space station. I thought..." She looked confused.

Okay, maybe Xander had overestimated the brains of the researchers.

"All I'm asking is that you do something to stop the asteroid from destroying the space station." Xander searched for something that would cause them to take up his side. "I'd be happy to return once the problem has been solved, but I thought that someone here might take pity on a few hundred people dying, especially when you have the resources to solve the problem."

The man pulled out his cellphone and started pressing buttons. Xander stood his ground. "Well?" he finally asked when neither of them responded. Colt stood to the side clutching his clipboard and looking terrified.

The woman suddenly turned on him. "Do you know him? Why did he come to you?"

"He, um, we met at the Olympics," Colt explained. "I think we should help him, help everyone on the space station."

"Officials are on their way," the man said, putting his phone back in his pocket. "You can't just come back here after you've been eliminated. Elimination wouldn't mean anything if we let people wiggle their way back into society. We have all *earned* our place here."

Anger grew within Xander, but he had to stay calm. He wouldn't help anything by getting mad. "I understand, and like I said, I'm happy to return to the space station." That was definitely a stretch. "But there won't be any space station to return to if we don't do something. If you don't help me."

"That's not our decision to make," the woman said, at least giving Xander hope that she was thinking about helping them.

"Well, can I talk to the person in charge of those decisions, whoever would have control over launching a missile?"

A couple of officials marched in, and Xander pushed down the urge to fight them off. They were just going to take him to a room and question him more, and Xander didn't mind talking. He wanted everyone to know his story. If he could tell people what *really* happened to the eliminated, they had to help him, right?

"Put your hands up!" one of the officials commanded, and Xander complied.

"Hands up!" he shouted again. Xander's hands were already up, but then, Xander realized that they weren't yelling at him. They were yelling at Colt. Colt's face trembled as he dropped the clipboard to the ground and shakily lifted his hands.

The officials roughly handcuffed both of them and led them out of the room.

"I'm sorry," Xander told Colt. "I didn't know they would react like that."

Colt didn't respond, and they were taken to different rooms. Xander might not have the chance to apologize again, but he still had a chance to save the people on the space station.

Chapter 29

Dinner was much more satisfying than lunch or breakfast. Eden was given a plate of real food, even if the tomatoes in her salad were tiny. Eden had never been a big fan of salad before, but now, her mouth watered as she looked at it. She saw her roommates across the dining hall, and Eden weaved her way through the groups of seated individuals to sit with them.

She hadn't taken the time to get to know them very well, but they seemed nice enough.

"Did you hear that there were two more dead bodies found?" Nicole asked as soon as Eden reached them.

Eden swallowed. It seemed she wouldn't be able to escape talk of the murders even here. She nodded. "Yes, and I saw the guy just finishing up the job."

"You saw it happen?" Jazzy asked. "Who was it?"

"Some guy named Derry," Eden replied. "I knew him before we came here, and he wasn't a nice guy."

"What did you see?"

But Eden didn't want to retell the details yet again. She just shrugged her shoulders as she took a bite of her salad. "I don't really want to talk about it if that's okay. Anyway, Roman knows about it now, so he'll take care of Derry."

"But did the guy confess or deny it?"

"Oh, he denied it. He wasn't going to admit to it. He's not that kind of guy," Eden replied, fully knowing that he never spoke honestly or felt guilty about anything.

"What do you think will happen to him?"

Even though Eden didn't want to talk about it, the other three girls seemed happy to discuss the situation as though they were thethe jury.

The dining hall started to get quiet, really quiet, and Eden knew something was happening even before she saw them. Rotating so that she could see the far doorway without spilling the food in her lap, Eden saw Roman marching into the dining hall. Directly behind him was Derry who had his hands restrained. Two more guys who were acting like bodyguards marched Derry forward.

For the first time since Eden had met him, Derry didn't have the self-assured, smug look he usually did. He looked worried.

"Today," Roman said, climbing up on the table as people rushed to clear away the unserved food, "another crime has been committed. Two people have died."

Those who hadn't heard the rumors started whispering furiously, but Eden just tried to watch Derry without looking like she was watching him.

Roman waited patiently at the front of the room, not trying to shush everyone as they conveyed their shock. Derry's jaw was set, and Eden saw the anger in his eyes as he finally brought his head up and stared defiantly out at those gathered.

"We have captured the person responsible," Roman finally announced when the room had grown quieter. "I have brought him here because I think this is too serious a decision for me to make on my own."

A few people started talking again, and this time, Roman didn't display as much patience. As he tried to motion for them to be quiet, Derry shouted out, "I didn't do it! I just saw them on the ground! He has no proof I did it!"

That hushed everyone up as they listened to Derry's shouted defense of himself.

"You'll get a chance to speak," Roman told him in an irritated voice. He turned back to everyone and spoke loudly over Derry as Derry continued to try to speak. Eventually, one of Roman's friends covered Derry's mouth and led him outside the room so that Roman could have his turn.

"As you can see, he is very opinionated." Roman smiled like he had said something funny, but Eden didn't think anything about this situation was humorous. "The fact is that four people have died of similar methods- strangulation. All of them have died down the side hallways that don't get as much traffic, and Derry has been around when three out of those four have taken place."

Eden frowned. She hadn't known that Derry was at the scene for one of the other murders.

"We now have a witness, who we won't make testify for sake of anonymity." Eden was grateful for that. "However, she saw him actually finishing the deed on one of the two bodies today. I will give Derry a chance to speak, but once he has had a chance, I want us as a group to vote on what the consequence should be."

"A life for a life!" someone called out from the back of the room.

Eden tried to see who it was, but it was impossible. Too many people were crammed into the room, and the sight of some of the medals that other people had already been given reminded her that there were still competitions coming up.

"Let's hear what he has to say first," Roman said congenially. He motioned to someone at the doorway, and they brought Derry inside again.

He started talking as soon as he was in the room. "I didn't do it. They're framing me! I swear I didn't do it!" He spoke earnestly, but Eden knew him. She *knew* what he was capable of doing. Her throat closed, though, and she couldn't say anything.

"He's the one who hurt those girls in the Olympics this year," someone else said. The crowd turned to look at the speaker, and Eden was glad it didn't have to be her. The speaker explained.

"It didn't happen to me, but someone I know was drugged and taken to his room. Who knows what would have happened if someone hadn't found them in time?"

Eden's mouth felt dry as she remembered that night.

"No mercy!" someone else called out.

"Kick him out!" someone else shouted.

Roman let the raucous shouting go on for a few minutes before he motioned for everyone to quiet down again. "Are we in agreement then that Derry should be eliminated from the space station? If you are in favor of this decision, raise your hand."

This time, there were no closed eyes. Eden didn't even have time to think through what was happening before the majority of the people in the room had raised their hands like a field of sunflowers springing up suddenly.

"Well, that's settled then." Roman looked smug as he crossed his arms. "I do think it's only humane, though, to give Derry an hour or two to reflect before we put him outside. Is anyone opposed to that?"

No one said anything. At least they were allowing him that small mercy. Instead of taking Derry out the way they had brought him, they paraded him through the room to the hallway where Eden had first entered the station- the long hallway with all the windows.

People stood aside and let him pass, but Eden's body reacted too slowly. She couldn't seem to make herself move.

"Eden!" Derry called, seeing her clearly in the open path that had been left for him. "Tell them! Tell them I didn't do it! You didn't see me do any-thing! I was checking for a pulse!"

Eden swallowed, trying to moisten her throat. He sounded so convinc-ing, but this was...Derry. Eden's eyes dropped to the ground, and she felt Der-ry brush past her, grabbing at her arm. Then, he was gone from the room.

Talk exploded as everyone began filtering out of the dining hall to the rest of the space station, but Eden was stuck in that one place.

"Eden?" a voice said nearby.

Eden's head snapped up, and she saw Helena looking at her with concern. "Are you okay?"

"Um...uh," she answered, real words stuck in her throat.

"He deserves it," Helena told Eden. "Don't feel bad. I see the guilt on your face."

"It's just that..." Why was Eden making excuses for him? "He sounded so convincing, and I keep going back in my memory trying to replay that mo-ment. I think they were already dead when I got there. I wasn't...I didn't see him killing them, just over them. What if someone had seen me bending over the first girl and had assumed I murdered her?"

"You don't think he did it?"

When Helena asked the question straight out like that, Eden had to ad-mit that she couldn't put away the suspicious feeling that Derry was com-pletely responsible for whatever had happened. But there was just enough doubt that she couldn't be 100% sure.

"I don't know," she finally said. "That's the problem. I don't know." She cleared her throat. "He made a joke the other day about someone dying. He didn't care about it."

Helena didn't say anything for a while. "Just because someone has done something bad doesn't mean that they are 100% bad. You feel sorry for him because he's still a person, still human. But we have to be honest with ourselves. There are only going to be three hundred people allowed to stay on here. Do we really want him to be one of them?"

The answer didn't require any thought. No, of course not. But Eden wasn't sure if it made her a bad person because her answer came so quickly. Just because she didn't like him didn't mean he was automatically guilty.

The room had mostly emptied out, and Eden glanced toward the doorway where Derry had gone. It led to the same hallway where she had last seen Xander, and in that moment, she missed him too much. All she wanted to do was ask him what she should do.

"I just want some time to think," Eden said, hoping Helena would take the hint.

"Okay, I'm going to be in my room studying for the medical test."

They parted ways, and Eden walked down the hallway. As soon as she stepped in front of the long row of windows, she pressed herself against the glass, wanting to see some sign of Xander. But she couldn't. He was gone, and she didn't know anything other than that he had decided not to save them.

Chapter 30

Xander paced the length of the room, rehearsing arguments in his head. Fairly certain that someone would come to ask him questions, he knew that he might only have a few minutes to tell them about the eliminated and convince them to help. If he could get enough people on his side, then they would at least let Colt go forward with the missile launch.

The clock on the wall made an annoying ticking sound, reminding Xander that he might not have as much time as he needed. Colt had said they would have to launch the missile by the next evening. Most people were probably asleep right now, and Xander wasn't sure if this sort of "research center break-in" would constitute a worthy cause for them to get out of their beds.

Colt had been placed in another room, and Xander wished he could talk with him. Maybe he could learn more about the other researchers, learn what would convince them.

The door clicked open, and a group of four people filed into the room. Xander only recognized one of them. They stood in a line against the wall, and the one Xander had seen before spoke to him.

"Please tell everyone what you were telling us earlier."

Xander took a deep breath and let the words out in a sudden flow. "I volunteered to be eliminated even though I won a medal in wrestling, because I couldn't let my girlfriend go through that alone. I wanted to hold her hand when whatever happened... happened. I didn't expect us to arrive at a space station, but when we did, I wanted to live more than anything else. My brother has been living there for three years."

All of their eyes remained trained on him, so Xander continued in the same even voice. "He works in the control room, and he told me, right after

I found out that I had a chance to live after all, that an asteroid was going to wipe out the whole place in a week more or less."

One of the researchers reacted, her mouth dropping open. Xander acknowledged her shock. "I was also bothered by this, and I offered to do what I could to help. Here I am, asking for your help. I'm not asking that you let us come back down to Earth. I know that would be too much, but I am asking that you allow Colt to help us by destroying the asteroid. I'm sure you all know someone up there, and even though you probably already thought they were dead, they aren't. They're alive."

"Is there a girl named Allison with curly, blonde hair?" one of the researchers asked.

Xander cleared his throat. He knew he had seen quite a few blondes, but he wasn't sure what classified as curly hair exactly. He certainly didn't know a girl by the name Allison. "I'm...not sure. There's a lot of people up there, and I was there for less than a week."

"What about a black boy named Martin? He has glasses?" another researcher asked.

Once again, Xander wasn't sure. He had seen a black boy with glasses, but that didn't mean it was Martin. "There's hundreds of us up there," Xander replied, wishing he had paid more attention to names and faces. He hadn't known how important it would be.

That didn't stop the others from asking about more names, but Xander couldn't answer any of them with certainty.

"Maybe if we can save the space station," Xander proposed, knowing that he had no authority to go through with this plan, "then we could set up some sort of communication line. I could tell you exactly who is on the space station."

One of the researchers clutched her stomach. "My Jordan might be alive," she whispered.

Another researcher stared at Xander stoically. "What proof do you have of what you're saying?"

"I can't provide the proof, but Colt can show you through the telescope-the asteroid and the space station."

"We've looked up your record," one of the researchers said, presenting him with a tablet. On it, Xander saw his own face staring up at him. "It doesn't say you were eliminated here."

Xander scrolled quickly through his own information. It was a public profile of himself, so it didn't have too many details about his life. However, the researcher was right. By all accounts, it looked like he was still living in Greenland.

"That's because...I won a medal. It seems like they never fixed it in the system when I gave my medal up because my girlfriend was eliminated."

The researcher wasn't buying his story. "I've seen that space station before. It's abandoned. It was a project to try to start a colony in a place that won't overheat, but it failed. That's why we're here today, still trying to come up with an alternative."

Xander didn't know how to respond to this researcher who was so sure that he was lying. "I'm not sure what else to show you." His eyes lit up. "I arrived by spaceship, something we built out of the few materials we had. It landed in the ocean just off the coast over there." Xander pointed in the general direction of the ocean. "There's got to be some sort of test you can do to prove where it came from. Oh," another idea suddenly hit him, "or you could meet my brother. He was supposedly eliminated three years ago, but he's still alive."

"We need to discuss this matter among ourselves," one of the researchers told him, "and with the others. We'll let you know if we have further questions."

Then, they filed back out of the room and left Xander by himself. He couldn't help it. He tried the handle just in case it had been left unlocked, but it hadn't. Of course it hadn't.

He had presented the information he had. The only thing he could do now was wait and hope that they would be sympathetic with his situation. Even if not everyone agreed, maybe some of them would be convinced enough that Colt would be able to get the supplies he needed.

Xander clasped and unclasped his hands into fists as he walked back and forth. Even though he hadn't slept in many, many hours- it was hard to know how much time had passed- he didn't feel sleepy now. He just needed someone to give him back the hope that had been kindled when he had seen Colt.

After half an hour, someone came and motioned for Xander to follow him. Xander didn't recognize this new person, but he clearly worked at the research center. There was something about his glasses and clothes that told Xander he was smart enough to be there.

"Where are we going?" Xander asked, not hesitating to follow the man.

"Big meeting," the guy explained. "This is important enough to wake people up apparently." There might have been a little bit of bitterness in his voice. Apparently, the man really was upset about being woken up so that other people didn't die. Poor him.

The new room was a lot bigger, and the walls were covered with drawings for different machines. The details contained in them made Xander's head spin as he tried to count the people in the room. Colt was shifting back and forth nervously at the front of it, and Xander took his place beside Colt. Colt smiled at Xander, but Xander could see the nerves behind his friend's smile. Colt was not the kind of person who would enjoy speaking in front of a roomful of people.

"We are going to take a vote," one of the researchers at the table announced. "But first, we all want to hear you explain exactly what is happening."

So, Xander once again gave his explanation of the space station and what he had learned upon arriving there. He tried to keep it short and focus on the most important aspect of it- the fact that people were going to die if they didn't act quickly. Then, Colt took the reins and explained the technical aspects of what helping them would look like- what would be required of the research center itself.

Once Colt had finished, Xander looked pleadingly at the researchers. He knew that some of them had been in bed, and he wished this had come at a better time. However, they were all here now.

"Let's vote," the researcher at the end of the table suggested. "Everyone in favor of helping these two and those on the space station, raise your hand."

"Hold on," someone said just as a couple of people began raising their hands. They quickly snatched them back down. "Aren't we going to discuss this first? We've heard their evidence, but I think it's important for us to consider all aspects of it."

"Glen, if you have something to say, go ahead."

"I'm just saying that if they're telling the truth, and the eliminated really are living up there, why don't we know about it? Besides, they've been eliminated. Isn't the point of elimination that we aren't wasting precious resources on them anymore? If they were worth saving, they would be down here- in Greenland, Alaska, or Russia- and contributing with jobs."

"I've got to cut in here," someone else said. "I understand what you're saying, but they're asking for one missile. We haven't used them in years. It's not really a big deal if we give the kid one and let them save these people. Besides, I'm sure some people you know have been eliminated, and you could be saving their lives."

"But the point of elimination is-"

"We know what the point of it is," the second person said, cutting into the first researcher's speech.

Xander shook his head, and his shoulders hunched forward. It was clear how this was going to go. They weren't going to come to any sort of decision soon. What if there was some way he could convince them to decide?

Looking at Colt, Xander leaned sideways and whispered. "What can we do to make them shut up and vote?"

Colt shook his head. "They always take a long time to make decisions," he replied.

Xander looked around the room, searching for something he could use to convince them- something that they wouldn't be able to ignore. He swallowed when he saw some supplies on a counter- supplies that he was sure were meant to build the machine depicted on the walls, but supplies they probably wouldn't want broken. He could always threaten them...

Xander zoned back into the conversation and realized that they were still debating the same thing. He tried to cut in politely. "I don't know if you realize this, but we need to hurry. The asteroid is moving toward the space station pretty quickly, and if we don't act soon, then it will be too late."

"It's moving at approximately twenty-three kilometers per second," Colt added to make Xander's point. Wow. That was fast.

The person at the head of the table nodded. "We need to vote now, Glen. There isn't time for any more debates. All in favor of using our resources to help save the space station, please raise your hand."

Eight hands went up. Xander's eyes flitted to those who hadn't raised their hands, counting them up immediately- six. Even as the head researcher told those opposed to raise their hands, it was already clear how the vote had gone.

"Well, it looks like you can proceed, Colt," the head researcher said.

Relief flooded Xander's body. He wouldn't need to do anything drastic.

"What do you need in order to be successful?" the head researcher asked.

Colt and the head researcher began discussing the mechanics of it all, and Xander took a step back to lean against the counter. His stomach rumbled, and Xander wondered if now that he wasn't officially under arrest, he was free to wander around again. Maybe he should tell Matt the good news, but Xander hadn't seen a hint of him since he suggested that he get out of there.

"Excuse me," Xander said, nudging Colt. "Is there a fridge around here somewhere? Or a cafeteria? Somewhere I can get something to eat?"

"Down the hallway to the left, then to the right."

Xander nodded and followed Colt's vague finger pointing to a host of snacks. There wasn't a cafeteria or anything fancy like that, but the fridge did look like a few people had left their food in there for a couple of days. Knowing that someone would probably be mad in the morning, Xander started heating up the food and shoving it into his mouth. It tasted *so* good after the crap he had eaten on the space station.

Xander's stomach protested, telling him to stop, but he couldn't seem to control his hands as they brought food to his mouth.

Finally, he thought he would vomit if he ate anything else, so he sadly replaced the rest of the leftovers in the fridge and decided to find Colt and see how his progress was going.

As Xander wandered the hallway, he heard something outside the front of the research center that he could only describe as movement. He wasn't in any hurry as it seemed like Colt didn't really need him to complete his task, so he decided to check it out.

Turning toward the doorway, Xander saw the familiar official uniform outside the front door. Two, then three of them passed by, hurrying to the side door.

From Xander's earlier examination of the research center, he knew that there were two doors- two entrances. Without thinking through what he was really doing, Xander stepped forward and slipped the lock into place on the door so that it couldn't be opened from the outside. It wasn't like the lock would keep someone out if they were *determined* to get inside, but it would stop them for a little bit.

Then, Xander jogged around the hallway on the first floor, trying to locate the other door. When he found it, a more secure metal door, he slipped that lock into place too. Just as it clicked, the door rattled.

He could hear voices outside. "Hey! It's locked!" someone shouted. "He promised it would be opened."

"We can't break in," someone else said. "This door was built to withstand attacks."

"The front ones are mostly glass. We'll go through those."

On that note, Xander hurried back down the hallway, more prepared now that he knew where he was going. He reached the entranceway and surveyed the group on the other side of the glass doors. It looked like there were at least eight or ten officials. Someone clearly had friends in high places and had sent these officials to stop the missile launch. The light illuminated the officials like ghosts as they tried to stare into the darkened lobby.

Xander was hidden from them, but only momentarily. It didn't take a genius to figure out that the glass wouldn't hold if they started trying to break it. He had to do something if he was going to keep them out of here. Xander looked around for anything he could use to threaten them, but the lobby was stark. He could take them one on one if it came to a physical fight, but he didn't think they would calmly walk through the doors one by one and allow him to take them on. No, he had to do something bigger, something to scare them out of even *trying* to break inside.

Chapter 31

Eden wasn't sure why she did it, but she couldn't help herself. She found the room where Derry was being held. For a long time, she didn't do anything about it other than pace outside the door and listen to his occasional shouts about his innocence.

Having no idea how long Roman would give him until he tossed him off the space station, Eden knew that if she was going to say something, it had to be now. The look of desperation on Derry's face continued to flash before her eyes.

Pausing outside his door, Eden took a couple of deep breaths. "Derry?" she said. Her voice sounded weak, and Eden tried to do something to strengthen it. She cleared her throat, but it seemed as though Derry had already heard her.

"You have to help me!" Derry started pleading through the door. "They're going to kill me, but I didn't do it. I swear! I will swear on anything—a Bible, my mom. I swear I didn't do it!"

Eden could hear Derry's ragged breathing on the other side of the door. "What proof do you have?" she asked. So far, it didn't seem like Derry had recognized her voice, and Eden was grateful for that. She much preferred to get information from him as a faceless voice than someone he knew.

"I shouldn't have to *have* proof that I didn't do it! They're supposed to have proof that I did! I swear I was just standing there looking at the bodies. I didn't even think they were really dead. I thought it was someone trying to trick me. It..."

Eden understood the disbelief that had passed through her when she had first seen a dead body too. It was hard to accept.

"Hey! Are you still there?" Derry shouted through the door.

"Here," Eden answered, glancing up and down the hallway. Other than the stars peeking through the long bank of windows, she was alone. And for the first time since she had met Derry, she didn't feel scared being so close to him. It probably helped that he was on the other side of the locked door, but still.

"Help me, please! I didn't do it! Just because I was stupid before doesn't mean I did this. I'll do anything, but I do *not* want to die!" The desperation was clear in his voice, and Eden felt a swirl of pity growing within her.

"I can't help you," she finally said. Because really, she couldn't. There was no use giving him false hope.

"You have to do something!" Derry pleaded. "Talk to Roman! Or talk to one of his friends! Convince people! It's not fair!"

Eden stood silently on the other side of the door, but even though he was starting to convince her of his innocence, she didn't think there was anything to be done. Besides, almost three hundred people were going to be eliminated after this fake copy of the Olympics had finished. Why shouldn't Derry be one of those people?

A guilty, dirty feeling in her stomach, Eden took first one step away from the doorway, then another.

This wasn't her problem, and she shouldn't feel badly that Derry would be thrown off the space station. He deserved it more than most people. She could hear Derry yelling through the door back there, but she hurried to get further away.

When Eden joined the rest of the population again, she realized that the second competition was underway. Even though she hadn't planned on competing in gardening, she knew that the medical competition would come up quickly, and she didn't feel prepared at all. Eden slid away from the people watching so that she could find Helena and study.

"Roman! Roman! Roman!" A group chanted as Eden entered the hallway. The chanting didn't sound like the kind of cheering people might do at a sporting event. Instead, it sounded angry.

Curiously, Eden followed the sound of the voices, wondering what else could possibly be going on.

"Roman! Roman! Roman!" the chanting continued. This time, the shouts were accompanied by the sound of something smashing.

Eden hesitated. Should she really go toward something that sounded violent? Worried, Eden decided that knowing what was going on was always a better option than not knowing. She reluctantly approached the noises, pausing when she reached a nondescript room near the medical center.

She didn't know what the door held, but by the chants, she would guess Roman was inside. The group wasn't saying anything other than his name, but all of them seemed pretty angry. Eden was searching for a familiar face when someone on the edge of the group grabbed her arm.

"Roman lied to us!" the person shouted directly in Eden's face to be heard over the chanting. "The asteroid is still going to hit us!"

Even though Eden already knew this information, the seriousness of it hit her when she realized how angry everyone was. "What...happened to the two people sent in the ship?" she asked.

The person shook his head. "I don't know. No one knows. Maybe they never really left, but we're all going to die in a few days, and Roman is making us carry on with these Olympics like idiots." The person joined back in the chanting, and Eden stood on the edge of the group, undecided.

"Go tell more people," the guy said, shooing her off. "Everyone should know!"

But Eden wasn't about to go spreading this news. Why ruin someone else's day? Still, the noise of the crowd seemed to draw attention quickly, and more and more people joined. Instead of being on the edge, Eden was soon in the center of it, even though her mouth still refused to cooperate.

"Are you sure he's in there?" a girl asked, rubbing at her throat. "He's not coming out."

"Then let's break in!" someone shouted. A couple of people threw themselves ineffectively against the door, thumping painfully into the strong material.

Eden tried to wiggle her way out of the crowd, but more and more bodies kept appearing. She didn't want to be a part of this.

Finally, after freeing herself from the crowd, she took a deep breath. Too much was happening, and Xander wasn't there to help her process what it all meant. She needed a place to think, and despite what Derry said about not being responsible for the strangulations, Eden felt safer going down the side hallways with Derry locked up.

Once she was on the second floor, Eden went down the hallway that held the books. There were a couple of chairs at the end of the hallway, and she might be able to just sit there and relax for a little bit.

But they were already occupied...by Roman.

"Did you know a bunch of people are looking for you on the first floor?" Eden asked. It seemed the most logical thing to do- let him know that he was needed.

Roman nodded. "Yeah, they're the reason that I'm here right now."

"Oh." Eden didn't move, either to take one of the other chairs or to back her way down the hallway. She studied Roman, the way he held his hands together in a tent in front of him and realized how much responsibility must rest on his shoulders. He didn't look *that* old. If he had been one of the first to arrive, that would put him at twenty-five. But if not, then he was even younger. Eden couldn't imagine making the decisions for everyone here.

"Apparently, they found out that the asteroid is still heading toward us."

"That's kind of a problem," Roman agreed with a nod.

"What are you going to do about it?"

Roman raised his eyes and stared directly at Eden. "This time, I'm not going to do anything. I'm going to let everyone else handle it. I tried doing something, really tried, and..." Roman shrugged. "So, I'm done trying."

Their leader was giving up?

Eden swallowed. This was the part where she was supposed to inspire him and remind him why he had been chosen or had selected himself for leadership. He would feel inspired and know just what to do to save the space station, but Eden didn't have the words for this person she barely knew.

"Well, just thought you should know," she finally concluded.

"Yeah, thanks," Roman said, still avoiding eye contact.

Eden turned to go, feeling like Roman was staring right through her until she rounded the corner of the hallway. Frowning, Eden wondered why Roman was hiding out if he was such a great leader, but then again, everyone deserved a rest every once in a while, even leaders.

Chapter 32

The officials still hadn't forced their way into the building when Xander returned. He breathed heavily, holding his weapons of choice- gasoline and a lighter as well as a floor lamp. Since guns, along with anything else that was specifically designed for injuring others, had been outlawed around the time Xander was born, he had no experience with them and was glad that he hadn't found any.

Before he took a stand, he had to see where Colt was and what progress had been made. Xander set the weapons quietly in the shadows just outside the lobby, then ran down the hallway to the main room. He wasn't sure if he was exactly supposed to be free or not, so he tried not to flaunt his appearance in front of the scientists as he wove his way across the room to Colt.

"Hey," Xander said quietly just by Colt's shoulder. "How's the progress?"

"I've almost finished with the calculations now that I have the missile's complete information and measurements."

"So what does that mean?"

"It means that we can put in the calculations to the missile, and it will be able to hit the asteroid." Colt turned away from the computer for a minute. "Emily will be safe."

Xander pounded Colt's shoulder with his open hand, harder than he meant, and Colt stiffened. "But aren't the missiles stored somewhere else?"

"We can input data from here," Colt explained. "No one has to actually go out there for the launch."

Grinning wildly, Xander stepped away from Colt, and one of the men who had been in the official meeting grabbed his arm.

"What are you doing?" he asked in a rough voice.

Xander glanced over the man's shoulder to the door that led to the lobby. "There are some officials here," he told him. "They look like they're going to break in."

The scientist rolled his eyes and motioned for Xander to get out of his way. "Stop making up stories."

"I'm not making it up!" Xander almost yelled. "Come see."

"I'm busy," the scientist said, clearly not caring that the officials might storm in there. Huffing, Xander hurried back through the building to the lobby area, not quite entering it.

The glass doors did nothing to keep the sound out, so Xander could hear the officials talking clearly. He listened, trying to quiet his breathing.

"Glen said we should just come in," one of them said. "He would be in the research room."

"Well, we can't just come in if the doors are locked," someone else responded.

"The side door is too."

"Do you think he wanted us to break in?"

"No, I don't think so. We're not here on official orders, just his."

"Maybe we shouldn't go in at all." Xander continued to listen to the conversation. The name, Glen, was familiar. Was that the scientist he had just tried to convince of the officials' appearances? His lack of sleep was muddling his thoughts.

"What if he's tied up somewhere and can't open the doors? He said that someone who was eliminated came here and started telling stories. What if he's been threatened for trying to get rid of the eliminated guy?"

"We don't just work for Glen."

"But he's our friend, and we've always helped him before."

"Doesn't mean we have to now."

Xander's breathing had returned to normal by now, and he rolled his shoulders back. Whatever the officials might be about to do, they didn't seem as threatening as they had when they first appeared. He would take them on so Colt could finish what he had started.

"We are going in," one of the officials said, stepping up to the glass doors. He pressed his face against them, shielding his eyes from the light so that he could see into the dark interior more clearly. "No one is in there. We'll have to break the glass, but we're allowed to respond to calls for help. We'll call it that if someone asks. We're going in."

Xander stepped forward so that the man could see him. The man stumbled back immediately at Xander's appearance from the shadows.

"Someone's in there!" he exclaimed.

"You will back off," Xander threatened. "Or I'll set this whole building on fire." Xander shook the can of gasoline at them to make his intention clear.

Even though not everyone could see him because of the light surrounding them, his voice was loud enough. The officials started talking amongst themselves.

"Now we have a real threat and a reason to enter. We need to go in now."

"No way! I'm not risking myself against some maniac."

"He's going to burn down the building! The research center is the most important building we've got."

Without more discussion, one of the officials stepped forward and threw a rock at the glass door. His movements were so quick that Xander almost got a faceful of rock. He moved just in time.

The glass shattered, tinkling onto the floor as the rock continued its flight through the lobby and punched a hole in the wall. Xander's heart raced as he realized that threatening them might have been the wrong thing to do. He had to prove that he was serious.

Xander popped the top off the gas can and started sloshing it on the ground by the doors, his heart racing. Would it even catch fire? The floors weren't made of wood. Could this type of laminate or tile even burn?

A hand reached through the hole, gripping for the handle, and Xander sloshed some of the liquid on the hand. The man drew his hand back, and Xander continued with the sloshing, wondering how quickly the fire would spread and if he would be able to get away in time.

"Hey!" one of the officials shouted. "He doesn't even have gasoline!"

Xander paused, the gas can half-full in his arms. He raised his nose and sniffed the air, and his stomach sank. The guy was right. He didn't smell that acrid smell of gasoline. It smelled like…water. Xander ran his finger along the edge of the hole and brought it to his nose, sniffing hard. Nope. It was water. He threw the can on the ground, and the water began to leak out more quickly.

He was stupid! What kind of threat would they think he was when he was pouring water all over the place he was supposedly going to set on fire?

One of the officials laughed and reached his hand through the broken door. Xander only had one weapon now, so he grabbed the lamp in his fist and hoped it would be enough. He glanced over his shoulder, but he had no way to monitor Colt's progress.

The hand found the lock and turned it, and the broken door burst open. The official ran inside, but his confident sneer quickly changed to surprise as he slid across the floor, stopping himself from a full-on faceplant by using his hands in the glass shards to break his fall.

Xander smiled as the official yelped and cradled his cut hands. Maybe Xander's can of water would be useful after all.

The second official to enter the building was much more cautious. He studied Xander and the pole in his hands as he entered. Xander was relieved to see that none of the officials carried guns. Even though they had been out-lawed, Xander hadn't known if some officials might still possess concealed weapons like the ones at the Olympics had carried. This official embodied what Xander had hoped to become when he won his medal, so whoever he was, he would have had the same training as Xander, just more practice. And Xander had a lamp.

"There are ten of us," the official announced. "I suggest you back up."

Xander shook his head. He wasn't going to get distracted with talk. Once the official had sloshed through the puddle of water in front of the doorway, he crunched over the glass, never taking his eyes off Xander. Another official squeezed through the open doorway, then another, and another. None of them attacked Xander, and Xander wasn't ready to make the first move. But if he didn't move now, then he would be fighting them all at the same time.

The first official was picking glass shards out of his hands and seemed like he would be useless. One against nine. How could he work things to his favor?

Xander took a step backward. If he could get them to the hallway where it was narrower, then they couldn't come at him from all sides.

"Are you the person who was eliminated?" one of the officials asked. He crossed his arms and didn't look like he thought hand-to-hand combat was going to start anytime soon.

"It's more complicated than that," Xander responded. His eyes swept the group of officials, all of them inside now. The lobby seemed a lot smaller with so many bodies in it.

"Tell us then," one of the other officials requested.

"This isn't storytime," Xander responded. "You just broke into the research center, and I'm pretty sure..." Xander wasn't sure who to call on to back up his statement. "The scientists won't be happy about that."

"We were called here to take care of you," one of the officials said. He stepped forward and narrowed his eyes, and Xander could tell he was the kind of guy who had a temper. Xander took another step backward.

One more step, and he would be in the hallway. This hallway didn't lead toward the largest room of the research center, or if it did, then he wasn't aware of it. He was betting on the officials not knowing their way around this building, but maybe he was wrong to think that.

Oh well, it was too late now, because he couldn't change his mind and take the other hallway.

"Was my name used?" Xander asked.

"Doesn't matter. You're not supposed to be in here, and we can't let a threat like you go wandering around the building."

The official leaped at Xander, and his muscles reacted a moment later, throwing up the lamp as protection. He hit something, though he couldn't quite tell what, and he jerked the lamp post back toward himself again. The official didn't look injured, and as he came at Xander again, he seemed ready to dodge the lamp.

Xander countered with the lamp post, trying to hit him in a way that would knock him out, but the man ducked again. Then, the official grabbed the lamp and ripped it out of Xander's hands.

It clattered to the floor in the hallway. Xander would now be facing the man head on. He crouched into a ready position, wishing that he hadn't wasted the last week in the space station not conditioning.

The official dove at Xander, but he knew the move and dodged out of the way.

Breathing in and out steadily and keeping his eyes on the official, Xander waited for the next move. The official was quick, darting for him again. He grabbed Xander around the middle, and Xander stumbled backward.

Gravity pulled him toward the ground, but Xander turned so that he fell on the official rather than the floor. His fall cushioned, Xander quickly wrestled the man's hands to the ground, holding them in place. In a normal wrestling match, this would be where the whistle was blown as Xander held him in place.

But this wasn't normal. And just as Xander waited for the whistle, another official attacked him from behind, pulling him off the first one.

Xander stumbled backward and hit the wall, but not hard. The first official started getting off the floor while the second one shouted commands. "Spread out! Stop what's happening! We've got this one!"

Even though Xander didn't want the rest of the officials to infiltrate the building, he knew that taking on all of them was impossible. The other officials streamed down the other hallway. Xander had to warn the others. He had to warn Colt that they were coming. If only Matt were here to back him up!

Taking a deep breath, Xander screamed. The scream ripped through his throat and tore through the building, leaving him feeling empty. One of the officials leaped at him, pushing him to the floor as Xander struggled to regain his breath. His arms moved automatically, all of his training coming back.

His fist pummeled into the side of the official's head, and the official keeled over. Xander stared at him, waiting for him to move, but he didn't. No way would he just... give up. What if Xander had seriously hurt him?

"Hey, are you okay?" Xander asked, aware of the other official to his left. He leaned over and shook the fallen official's shoulder. "Man, get up. You okay?"

The guy didn't respond, and Xander started looking around for a medic or someone who could help him, but the other official jumped on Xander, saying something unintelligible.

Xander couldn't worry about the other guy right now. He had to deal with this threat, so he twisted his body away from the official's headbutt. Turning, he took the official head-on, shoving him against the wall.

They both toppled to the ground, and Xander struggled to stay on top. He pinned the official's arms, and even though the official kicked his legs and tried to unseat Xander, Xander knew that he was in control. The official wouldn't be able to move. Now was the time to talk.

"Why are you here?" he asked.

The official ignored his question for a solid minute before he finally realized that Xander wasn't going to give up his position. He had fairly tackled the official and overpowered him.

"We got a call. Someone is using research center resources to save people who should be dead anyway."

"The researchers voted to give all of the people on the space station another chance. Why should *you* decide they don't deserve it?" Xander hissed the words out as he tried to listen to what was happening in the rest of the research center.

Grunts, then a metallic sound like a door slamming loudly against the wall.

Xander looked back under him at the official who had ceased struggling. Xander's muscles remained taut, waiting for him to start fighting back again at any second. Neither one of them said anything for a solid minute as Xander tried to figure out what to do. He needed to get to where the rest of the fight was taking place, but he couldn't leave this official alone.

"I'm sure you know someone who was eliminated. Don't you want them to have a chance to live longer, even if life on the space station is nothing compared to here?"

The official didn't answer. For the first time, Xander looked into the guy's eyes, and he saw genuine emotion. Maybe it was fear or worry, but the official was human. Xander hung onto that, because he didn't think the official could fake the emotion coming out of his eyes.

"Please help me give them a chance. I'm not asking for food or help or a bigger space station or...or anything. I just want to destroy the asteroid that's going to hit them in a few days. They shouldn't have to die like that."

The official still didn't say anything, but Xander didn't feel the resistance in his arms anymore. Xander leaped off of him in one smooth move, leaving the official on the floor. The official slowly climbed to his feet and eyed Xander.

"You were up there?" the official asked, nodding toward the ceiling of the research center.

"Yes, I was up there." The thing that Xander remembered most was the horrible food, and his stomach turned over thinking about it.

Xander took a step backwards, and the official didn't move to follow him. Xander didn't want someone attacking him from behind, but he had to get into the main research room and see what was happening. After another step backward, Xander turned and sprinted down the hallway.

He reached the door to the large room with the telescope and saw that the door handle had been smashed. It was easy to open, and Xander flung it against the wall as he passed through.

Chaos reigned inside the room, and Xander turned his head from person to person, trying to figure out what to do first. One official held Colt securely in a chair and was tying his wrists together.

Other officials were arresting members of the board, but only certain members. None of these people were trained to fight, and they were putting up little or no resistance.

Xander quickly counted up how many he was facing. The eight officials who had split off from the first two were here, and there was no one to back Xander up. Unfortunately, his loud entrance meant that seven of the eight officials were looking directly at him.

"It's the wrestler!" one of them shouted. A couple of the officials broke away from their tasks and rushed toward him. Xander took a few steps away from the doorway so that he had open space around him.

Two of the officials reached Xander at the same time. They looked at each other, like they didn't know what was supposed to happen next. Good. Being an official in a relatively peaceful place must mean that they hadn't had to engage in physical combat very often since their training.

Xander dove at one, knocked him off his feet, and turned to the other. Even though the first one was getting to his feet already, Xander couldn't waste time focusing on only him.

Just as Xander was tackling this second official, the first one hit him from behind, right in the spot where he had been stabbed at the Olympics.

Xander fell over, curling into himself as pain radiated throughout his body. His limbs seemed useless as he tried to move them.

"We've got him," one of the officials announced.

The pain slowly subsided, peeling away from the edges of his vision as an official stood over Xander. He couldn't just lie there! Xander put a hand on the floor to push himself up, his body still not ready to move at its regular speed.

A foot stepped on his hand, not hard enough to crush his fingers but hard enough to let him know that he should stop trying to move.

"Stop!" someone shouted. It distracted the official long enough for Xander to slip his hand out from under the official's foot and get to his knees. The pull in his back slowed him down, but Xander took in the scene again.

All of the officials were still up and ready to fight, and he was the only person capable of doing it, but who …

Xander saw that the one official from the hallway was standing in the doorway, drawing his companions' attention. "We don't have to listen to Glen. I think we should help the people on the space station. Doesn't everyone deserve to live?"

Xander slowly finished climbing to his feet.

"It's not our job to decide that. It's our job to enforce what has already been decided," one of the officials argued.

Another official agreed with him as Xander made his way to Colt. He would untie everyone, but Colt was the brain behind this thing. Just as Colt's ties came loose, someone noticed what Xander was doing.

"Stop him!" an official shouted, and suddenly, Xander was facing three officials at once. He was outnumbered, always outnumbered, but that wasn't going to stop him from trying.

Two of the officials rushed Xander at the same time, and he had to focus on one. He stepped out of the way, swiveling to the one on the right. As Xander wrapped his arms around the middle of the official's body and brought him to the ground, the other official jumped on Xander.

Xander ignored the punch to his left arm as he pinned the other official. Just as he was about to punch him, he realized that it was a woman. That shouldn't change anything, but he couldn't...he couldn't just punch her.

In that moment, another official used his hesitation to drag Xander off the female official, pushing him to the ground. Xander struggled, but he was pinned down once again. His morale started to fade as he realized that he really stood no chance against so many.

His arms pinned behind his body, Xander conceded his defeat. However, when he looked up, he realized that Colt wasn't there anymore. Xander craned his neck, trying to spot his genius friend, but he wasn't there. Everything inside Xander hoped that Colt was doing what needed to be done to send the missile into the asteroid. But maybe...Colt had wanted to get out of this. He hadn't asked to be dragged into a battle that night.

Even though his hands were being tied behind him, Xander still searched the room, evaluating the people inside it from all angles as he looked for some ray of hope.

"He said that if they didn't launch the missile tonight, then we're safe from a potential war," one of the officials told another.

Safe? Xander couldn't believe that the officials were trying to make this a matter of safety. "Sure, you might be safe, but everyone up there will *die*," Xander couldn't help himself. The sarcasm was heavy in his voice. Three of the officials turned to look at him, studying him closely as though trying to see what kind of expert he might be on the subject of the space station.

Xander thought about Eden up in the space station. Surely by now she knew that they hadn't hit the asteroid. Would everyone know? Or would Roman keep it a secret?

The officials continued to talk amongst themselves, and Xander tried to figure out who the leader was. And above the officials? That would be the government- the ones who made the decisions about everything. Did they know what was happening? For some reason, Xander didn't think they would be very sympathetic toward his situation if they did.

"He said that they would have to launch the missile before tomorrow at 8 p.m. and even that might be too late."

Xander listened closely to the important information.

"So what are we going to do when everyone arrives for their shift in the morning?"

"It's already morning. Almost three a.m.," one of the officials informed the others.

"Real morning, when the sun is up," the other one joked back.

These were real people, and Xander had to be able to do something to convince them that the people up on the space station deserved saving. "Have any of you had someone close to you eliminated recently?" Xander asked. "Maybe I know them or saw them up there."

A couple of the officials looked interested in what he was saying, but none of them responded to him.

Desperate, Xander kept talking. "What about a dark-haired girl with glasses, a little shorter than me? Her name started with an M."

No, no takers for that one.

"I bunked with Vincent. He's been up there two years. Connor- just eliminated last week. And Parker. He was eliminated last year- real white kid who was smart enough to work in the bridge."

One of the officials wouldn't stop staring at him now, and Xander knew he had caught his attention. "Yeah, Parker said that he almost won a medal in endurance, believe it or not."

The official walked straight over to him, and Xander tried to think of something else that he could remember about Parker. "He's a quiet kid," Xander added.

When the official reached him, he leaned down and looked directly in Xander's face. "I suggest you shut up," he said. "If you don't, I'll punch you so that you *will*."

Oh, maybe his little plan hadn't been working after all.

Xander shut his mouth but stared back directly at the official to show that he wasn't giving in yet. He was just giving his brain a chance to think.

Suddenly, he heard footsteps, lots of them, and Xander whipped his head around to the doorway he had come through half an hour before. Everyone else looked in that direction too, and Xander had never been so relieved to see Matt's scraggly beard before.

Behind him were other familiar faces, people that Xander hadn't seen in years but he recognized as Matt's friends. Some of them clutched pathetic weapons, things that weren't meant to be used as weapons, but that looked like salvation nonetheless.

"Matt!" Xander shouted.

Even though his back was still hurting, he wasn't going to be left out of this fight. Matt said something to his friends, and they spread out. The officials were quickly realizing that these guys meant business, and they looked around for something to use as a weapon against the intruders.

Matt was behind Xander immediately, fumbling to untie his hands. "Anyone else who can fight?" Matt asked.

"None of the researchers, and these officials are well-trained."

Hands free, Xander leaped to his feet and faced the official coming toward him, losing sight of his brother. He grit his teeth and dove toward the official, taking the offensive move rather than defensive.

The official fell easily, and Xander held him in place, looking around for something. He didn't want to hurt him, not seriously, but he had to get him out of the fight. Forcing the official to his feet, Xander shoved him into the chair he had just been occupying and tied the official's writhing hands.

Then, Xander moved in front of him, feeling like he was playing a game of capture the flag. The tied-up official was now the flag, and Xander was determined to guard him so that he couldn't re-enter the fight.

Each of Matt's friends was engaging an official in a fight, and some of them were doing better than others. Glancing at the tied-up official, Xander moved forward and grabbed an official from behind as he attacked one of Matt's friends, whirling him around and to the ground.

"Got him!" Xander shouted to the other guy so that he would help one of his friends. The official rolled Xander onto his back, but Xander never stopped moving, not giving the official a chance to really pin him down.

He slid out from under the official, then kicked his leg out from under him. "I don't want to hurt you," Xander said, trying to sound threatening as his back radiated pain.

The official slowed for a moment, and Xander kicked his other leg, right behind his knee. The official tumbled forward groaning, and Xander leaped to his feet, looking around for who might be the next threat.

A few of the officials had been exchanged for the board members in the chairs, and there were only four still fighting. Xander jumped into another fight, assisting Matt in putting the official face-down on the ground. With a knee in the official's back, Xander breathed heavily.

"Give me something to tie him up!" Xander shouted, and someone tossed him one of the ropes that had been used on a board member. Like he was fighting a snake, Xander struggled to grasp the official's hands and tie them together.

Breathing heavily, he stood.

"We're done," Matt said, gasping for breath as well.

The floor and chairs were littered with tied-up officials.

Xander laughed. "We took on a bunch of trained officials. Who knew that was possible?"

"Especially with these guys," Matt joked, bumping shoulders with one of his friends.

Xander approached someone who was lying on the ground and clearly not wearing an official's uniform.

"Hey, you okay?" he asked.

The guy gripped his side, and Xander saw blood. "Oh, not okay then," Xander said. How had a knife entered the fight? Weapons of any kind weren't permitted in Greenland, but knives were considered a kitchen implement.

"Anyone here know medical stuff?" Xander asked, looking around at Matt's other friends. They all shook their heads.

"We can take him to my friend," one of them said. "Jay will know how to fix him up."

Xander didn't have time to worry about who this friend was or how medically savvy he really was. He needed to find Colt and make sure that things were progressing.

"You're a brave guy," one of the board members said, clapping Xander on the shoulder as he ran out the door.

There, in the room where he had originally found Colt, his spectacled friend was bending over a sheet of paper.

"Are you ready?" Xander shouted. "Can we shoot it?" He didn't want to take the chance that another wave of officials might come to the rescue of their friends. Besides that, they hadn't been exactly quiet, and some of the scientists might have been awakened.

"Ready," Colt said with a nod. "I just wanted to check the calculations on paper one more time."

Chapter 33

Eden chose not to attend the official launching of Derry from the ship. She couldn't hear him pleading with her again. Instead, she decided to find a quiet corner and prepare for the medical portion of the Olympics. She had fewer than twenty-four hours, and she didn't feel prepared at all. At least Helena was going to meet her and help her study.

"What are you doing studying?" someone asked as he walked by her in one of the side hallways. "The Olympics are off."

"What?" Eden's head snapped up, and the book fluttered closed.

"The asteroid is going to kill us. I'm not spending my last few days participating in a dumb competition, and everyone else agrees."

Eden didn't know if "everyone else" was really an accurate description. What if this one person had just decided that? She needed to study and be ready. She ducked her head back into the book and waited until the person passed. She kept hearing footsteps, which was distracting her from doing any sort of studying. She snapped her book closed and decided to find a quieter place. As she rounded the corner, she found Roman staring at her.

She tried to leap back, but because she was so close to the wall, she only succeeded in bumping her head.

"Ow!" she said, reaching up to rub the sore spot. "What-" she said, trying to think of a friendly way to start a conversation. That was when she realized what was behind Roman...or who.

"She-" Eden pointed at the body, the female who was no longer able to move. "You-"

Then, she saw the murderous look in Roman's eyes, and she tried to scream. She couldn't think of how to fight him or anything practical. She froze until Roman's hands were around her neck.

As he squeezed the oxygen out of her, she stared helplessly into his eyes and flailed her legs, hoping to kick him. Even though her legs thumped against his body, he didn't seem to react.

Spots entered the corners of her vision, and she gargled as she desperately tried to suck oxygen in.

"Ah!" someone shouted from behind Roman. The grip on Eden's throat released, and she tried to remember how to breathe. Even though the pressure was no longer there and oxygen could freely enter her lungs again, she gripped at her throat, trying to pull away a pair of hands that weren't there anymore.

"He did it!" Eden tried to say as she crawled to her feet. Helena was kicking at Roman as he approached Helena with his hands outstretched. His hands gripped her throat, and Eden struggled to scream. She needed help. They all needed help.

It came out of her throat like a gargled gasp instead of a scream. She had to move, to attack Roman. Then, Eden saw a chair further down the hallway. Finding her footing, she grabbed the chair by the back and thumped it down on Roman's head.

He crumpled to the ground immediately, and Helena touched her throat. Roman didn't move, but he groaned. Eden's shoulder slumped forward. Good. She hadn't killed him.

"What happened?" Helena asked.

"He... attacked me." Eden studied the girl who was lying on the ground. "Is she ..."

Helena bent down and touched the fallen girl's throat. She shook her head. "He must have hurt her already."

"But I thought Derry..." Eden said, trying to wrap her mind around what had happened.

Roman groaned and started climbing to his feet. Even though he moved shakily, fear coursed through Eden.

"We have to tie him up," she said.

Neither of them had anything. As Roman rose to his feet, the cold, calculating stare had disappeared. He approached them with fury on his face. Eden ran down the hallway. She had to get away from him.

"Helena!" she called back. Hearing Helena's footsteps behind her, Eden slowed only a little as she turned the corner and kept running. She had to get somewhere with other people. Roman wouldn't attack her if the whole space station's population was watching, would he?

The garden. The greenhouse. The competition.

Eden pounded up the stairs, and there was a crowd of people in the third floor hallway. She breathed heavily as she tried to tell them what had happened.

"Roman tried to kill me!" she shouted, then felt immediately embarrassed when everyone turned to look at her. "He... he's the one behind the strangulations," she explained. She touched her throat, but only faint red lines showed where bruises would appear later.

Helena appeared behind Eden, and Eden looked behind Helena, waiting for Roman to appear and show who he truly was.

Some of the people looked back at the competition, but others continued to stare at Eden, waiting for something else.

A couple of people immediately defended Roman.

"Roman wouldn't hurt anyone," someone said.

"Stop making up lies. You're the one who said Derry did it."

How did they know that? Roman had said he wouldn't reveal her identity, but... Roman had just attacked her.

"I promise I'm not lying!" Eden shouted, near tears.

Helena nodded next to her. "Roman did it," she insisted.

A couple of people continued to shout back at them, calling them liars, saying they just wanted the attention. Eden touched her throat again. She could still feel Roman's hands around it.

"Listen!" Helena said, waving her hands to get more attention. She whipped her braids over her shoulder. "Roman is dangerous! He's the one responsible for-"

"Shut up! You're distracting the ones who are competing!"

Eden saw one of Roman's close friends start walking toward them, and she elbowed Helena. Helena's face set into a challenging look, but Eden just wanted to run and hide. "He's not going to listen to us," Eden whispered. "We should get out of here."

When Eden saw another one of Roman's friends heading toward them, she turned and ran, going directly to her room and not worrying about Helena back on the crowded floor. They wouldn't hurt her in front of everyone. Eden shoved the frame of the bunk bed up to the door so no one could get in, and she was glad that none of her roommates were present.

Hoping that she was safe there, Eden curled into a ball on her bed and let her mind wander. It didn't wander too far from Xander though, and she hoped he was okay, even though she knew that was impossible. There was no way he could still be alive in the tiny spaceship after so much time.

Suddenly, the alarm on the wall blared, and Eden jumped up, smacking her head for the second time that day. It wasn't a meal time or the morning alarm. What was going on?

Eden shoved the frame aside, crept to her door, and cracked it open. People up and down the hallway were doing the same thing. Other people were running down the hallway to the stairs on either side.

"What's going on?" someone asked.

"Something's happening in the bridge!" a passing person shouted at her.

Eden couldn't help it. Her curiosity pulled her out of her room and to the stairs, even as the stairs crowded with other curious people. She had to know what was happening. Was this it? Was this the end?

She glanced over her shoulder to see if Roman was watching her. He wasn't though, and she didn't spot any of his friends.

The whole space station was going to explode.

She looked around, waiting for the place to burst into flames or fall apart or... something. Heading for the window at the end of the hallway where the bridge was located, Eden was able to squeeze between a couple of people. She saw something that looked like it was on fire in the distance. At least it wasn't going to smash into them at any second. Unless...

It seemed to be getting bigger as she stared at it.

Eden frowned. What was happening? Had the asteroid sped up or...

"It exploded!" someone shouted. The news passed down the hallway.

Xander had done his job? Eden's heart leaped in excitement, knowing that the asteroid wasn't going to hurt them. They would have a chance to live. Then, her heart slowly sank as she realized that meant that Xander was gone. Truly gone now.

Eden lowered her head and let the sadness consume her.

"It broke into a bunch of pieces."

"The asteroid is gone."

"We're going to live."

People were shouting, some excited, some overwhelmed. Others started talking about the Olympics and what that meant for them.

Eden pushed her way through the crowd again. The asteroid, the biggest threat to her life, was gone, but that also meant that the person she was closest to was really gone. She didn't understand how it was possible, but somehow, Xander had managed to pull it off. They were safe...but were they really with a leader like Roman?

Epilogue

Xander sat in front of the board. Some of them were missing, and Xander thought he knew why. Deciding on something as a board meant that they had to abide by that decision, and *some* of them had called the officials behind the others' backs.

Now that the missile had successfully decimated the asteroid, the board had one more situation that required their attention- Xander.

Xander had already explained his story at great length, including that he had won a medal but given it up to be with Eden. Now, they were ready to give him their decision.

"Xander Coxon," one of the board members said, drilling him with a stare. "Some of us think that you're a hero, risking your life more than once, not only for this girl but for others as well. Some say that you gave up your medal, so you obviously don't care about living here in Greenland.

"However, I think that you have earned our respect. We don't have sole decision-making power, so we had to run any decision by the higher-ups. Now that we've had a chance to discuss things with them, we've decided that you deserve to make your own decision. If you wish, we will send you back to the space station to be with this girl who seems to be the reasoning behind all of your decisions. On the other hand, if you wish to stay here in Greenland, there is a space for you among the officials. You've certainly proved you're worthy."

Xander swallowed hard. He had been wondering if they were going to execute him. He hadn't thought he would be faced with a decision like this. He looked down at his lap.

"Can I... think about it?" he asked.

"You have twenty-four hours to decide," the head board member told him.

Xander nodded and excused himself from the room, the weight of the decision heavy on his shoulders.

WAR BREAKS OUT ON EARTH as Xander is faced with the choice of a good life in his old community or being sent back to space where he will be with Eden but lose his chance to have a normal life.

Eden, who has no idea that Xander is still alive, struggles to make it through the space station's version of the Olympics and attempt at population elimination. Luckily, she makes a new friend who helps her forget some of her lingering sadness from missing Xander.

How many people will have to die in order for the two of them to find safe places to live? And will they ever see each other again?

About the Author

Laurel Solorzano has enjoyed writing since she was in middle school, exchanging manuscripts for years with her best friend. After traveling the globe for a time, Laurel set her goal to become a published author. As she works teaching English and Spanish, she writes stories in her free time. Laurel currently lives in Raleigh, North Carolina with her husband, Yader.

Read more at https://www.laurelsolorzano.com.